Together Again in Tenerife

Ian Wilfred

Together Again in Tenerife
Copyright © 2024 by Ian Wilfred

ISBN: 9798873977888

Cover Design: Avalon Graphics
Editing: Laura McCallen
Proofreading: Maureen Vincent-Northam
Formatting: Rebecca Emin

For Ron

Acknowledgements

There are a few people I'd like to thank for getting *Together Again in Tenerife* out into the world.

The fabulous Rebecca Emin at Gingersnap Books for organising everything for me and who also produced both kindle and paperback books. Laura McCallen for all the time and effort she spent editing the book, Maureen Vincent-Northam for proofreading, and the very talented Cathy Helms at Avalon Graphics for producing the terrific cover.

Finally for my late mum who is always with me in everything I do.

Chapter 1

'Debs, where are you? It's time for me to leave for the airport and I need to give you your instructions for the three days I'm away.'

There were two things Debbie Gonzalez hated about that sentence: one, Steven calling her 'Debs' and two, his thinking that he needed to tell her what to do while he was away with his mates playing golf in Portugal.

'Please tell me you aren't going to work like that, Debs. I've spent five hundred pounds on your hair extensions so you should use them. You know how important it is to give the right impressions to our clients. After all, you're the face of "Nails Designed By Stephone". Speaking of faces, you need more makeup. I've left that new lipstick on your dressing table for you to wear today and the minute you get to the design studio Jenny's going to do your new nails to match the lipstick. And another thing, make sure you post photos of the nails and the lips on social media. Just because I'm away for three days, it doesn't mean you can let our standards drop.'

'Steven, you went through all of this last night at least half a dozen times. I'm not a child. I'm a twenty-five-year-old woman.'

'It's not Steven, it's *Stephone*. If you can't remember to call me by my correct name, how will everyone else? Come on, Debs, up your game.'

'I'm Debbie, not Debs. Now, is that everything? Because I need to get ready for work.'

It wasn't everything.

He went on to explain that he had picked out outfits for her to wear to work for the couple of days he was away, and told her she wasn't to eat any junk food, adding that he would be checking what she was eating on the cameras of an evening. Debbie stood listening quietly and just when she thought he had finally finished, he handed her a piece of paper with the names of the five blokes he was going off to Portugal to play golf with. Next to the names were their social media accounts and he made it clear that she had to like and share once they posted something, but it was important to make sure that if he was in any of the photos, he looked good. She also had to be sure to include the hashtag of the men's different businesses with every post.

'Right, I'm off. Remember, Debs, while I'm away you're the face of the business. Don't let me down. Aren't you going to say something?' he asked when she remained silent.

'Have a good holiday,' she ventured.

'It's not a holiday, it's about promoting the business,' he said haughtily.

With that he was out the front door.

Debbie felt numb, though that was no different than usual these days. The only bright spot to look forward to over the next few days was the fact that she wouldn't have to listen to his ceaseless demands ... unless he caught her doing something on the cameras he didn't agree with, of course. That wasn't an issue though – her first stop when she parked her car in town would be a bakery. There were no cameras in the staff room of the salon, so he'd never know she'd bought cakes. The idea made her smile and she immediately decided that she would also stop somewhere on the way home from work to buy a big meat pie. She'd have to park somewhere to eat it though, as he'd be able to check up on her at home.

****

'Morning, Jenny, sorry I'm late. Seeing as *he's* away, I've brought treats! But we'll need to be discreet and not let the other staff see as no doubt someone would love to tell him I was eating the wrong food while he was away.'

Jenny laughed and took the bag of treats off her as Debbie unlocked the door and switched the alarm system off. They had a good hour before the other staff arrived, which was plenty of time for a cake or two in addition to getting Debbie's nails done as instructed.

'By the way, Debbie, Stephone has given me a list of the photos he wants me to take for the social media accounts, and the times he wants them to go live, but apart from that we can relax and enjoy not having him breathing down our necks. Come on, give me a smile. You need to make the most of this time and bring back the old Debbie; the one I used to have so much fun with, the laid back girl who was always out to have a good time, the Debbie I knew before she met Steven – oh, sorry, I mean *Stephone*. Remember all the good times we had in Tenerife when I came to visit you while you were working there? You worked hard and we certainly played hard!' she said with a laugh. 'Those times seem a million years ago now. When you met Steven and fell in love with him your life changed, almost as if someone flicked a switch. The old Debbie disappeared and, to be honest, she's never come back... I'm sorry, I've said too much. I'll shut up now.'

'Don't be sorry, Jenny. I forget most of the time that he's changed his name, and as for the old Debbie being gone... It has nothing to do with meeting Steven – I just grew up. This is who I am now.'

Jenny didn't reply, she just concentrated on doing the nails, and Debbie felt uncomfortable. She knew there was so much more Jenny likely wanted to say – things that she had been hinting at for the last two years – but the two friends had been over it all so many times, there was little point in diving into it again.

By the time Jenny had finished Debbie's manicure the other staff had arrived. No treats had been eaten in the end and the excitement Debbie had felt buying them had gone. Still, she didn't want them to go to waste so she told the staff they were a treat for them while Steven was away.

****

As instructed, Debbie posted the photos Steven had requested of the nails and lipstick on the salon's social media pages throughout the day. She also liked and shared all the pics of Steven and his golfing buddies on the plane and arriving at the golf resort.

Looking at the appointment book she saw that there was just one more client due to arrive before they closed – Rebecca, another old friend from Debbie's school days, who was having her nails done by Jenny. As she sat looking through the appointments for the following day, Debbie thought back to her conversation with Jenny earlier that day. She felt bad about how it had ended and the fact that they had hardly looked at each other all day, let alone talked further. As the other staff started to leave, she thanked them and told them to have a lovely evening.

Rebecca wasn't due for another ten minutes and Debbie thought she should try to break the silence with Jenny. They had been friends for so many years and she hated that they weren't talking, but Jenny needed to understand that she had moved on with her life. The happy-go-lucky Debbie was gone, replaced by a strong businesswoman.

She was just plucking up the courage to say Jenny's name when suddenly it was too late – there was Rebecca heading towards the door.

'Hi, Rebecca, I love your coat. It's very cheery,' she said brightly as her friend stepped inside.

'Thank you! I thought since summer is on the way it was time for a little bit of bright colour. Now to get the nails summery like as well! Hi, Jenny, how are you both? And isn't someone missing?'

'Yes, Steven – I mean Stephone – is away in Portugal playing golf with his mates for a few days. Can I get you a coffee while Jenny starts on your nails?'

'Forget the coffee, Debbie, and come to that, forget the nails. Let's go out tonight! While the cat's away the mice can play and all that. Where do you both fancy going? A nice cocktail bar? Or a restaurant? Oh it's going to be just like the old times, just the three of us! Who knows, we could even end up in a club, dancing the night away,' she said with an excited shimmy.

'Sorry, Rebecca, not for me. I'll go and make the coffee though – sounds like you might need the energy! – and Jenny can get going on your nails.'

Debbie went into the kitchen and as she waited for the kettle to boil she could feel herself welling up with unexpected emotion. Here were two of her best friends, women she had shared everything with, and she was snubbing them. But more than that, it made her wonder – what *had* happened to her? How had she ended up here? She caught a look at herself in the mirror and took in the perfect hair and the thick, over the top makeup. Yes, it looked polished, but one only had to look a bit closer to see that her eyes were dead. Where had the spark gone? Where was that pretty young woman she used to see in the mirror every day? The one who smiled and

5

embraced life? This wasn't her, this glossy, over the top persona Steven had created. She felt sad but quickly pulled herself together. She made the coffees and headed back out into the salon. She knew her friends would pounce if they sensed her emotional turmoil, so she had to put on a smile and give the impression that her life was perfect and she was loving every minute of it.

Jenny had started on Rebecca's nails – thank goodness, as it meant there would likely be no more talk of going out – but as Debbie put the three coffees down on the table, she could see her hand shaking and her legs suddenly felt like jelly. Who was she kidding? There was no putting on a brave face for her two friends; they could see right through her.

'Are you ok, Debbie? Do you want to talk about it?' Jenny asked gently.

That was it, the tears started and then the sobbing and ... oh my goodness, she couldn't stop. She hadn't even realised how much she'd kept bottled up inside her for all this time.

'Go on, Debbie, let it all out. We have all the time in the world and we're both here for you, aren't we, Rebecca?'

'Absolutely.'

Debbie took herself off to the bathroom to wipe her face, her heart still racing. She had let her guard down and she would never be able to put on that act again with her two friends. But what would happen next? It was clear that they could see she was unhappy, but how could they help? She was in a situation she couldn't get out of. Her flat had been sold to buy the salon and her savings pot that she had worked so hard for was quickly running out. Actually, Steven's trip to Portugal had probably properly emptied it. She was back to square one, a renter with no savings – how had she let it go so

6

wrong?

'Are you ok, Debbie?' Rebecca asked gently as she rejoined them in the salon. 'We want to help in any way we can. You really don't need to be living like this; your life could be so much better – so much happier.'

'The thing is, I don't have any means of changing things. I've sunk everything into this business and into my relationship with Steven. I can't walk away. What would I do? Where would I go? I've made my choice and I have to stick with it.'

'No, Debbie, you haven't chosen this life – Steven has. From the day you met him you gave up thinking for yourself and I know it's probably hard to admit but he controls everything, doesn't he?'

Debbie nodded sadly, too ashamed to speak.

'You could go to your mum's or your sister's, couldn't you?' Jenny suggested.

'Yes, my mum would welcome me with open arms, but that would feel like such a step backwards after having owned my own flat. And I know that my sister would just be a replacement for Steven. She would organise me just like she did when we were younger. Because she's two years older than me she's always thought she could tell me what to do. And going to her would mean enduring her talking incessantly about her perfect life with Alexander. They have it all – a great business and a fabulous relationship. No, thank you. I have to stick it out and make this work with Steven.

'Thank you both for having my back but I think I need to be alone. Jenny, would you be a dear and lock up when you've finished Rebecca's nails? I promise I'll be ok,' she added, seeing the concern still written across their faces. 'Please don't worry about me. Good night.'

****

7

Once back home she had a shower to get rid of the perfect image she had to maintain in public. Feeling more like herself, she popped a ready meal into the microwave and poured a glass of wine. She knew she'd get a phone call from Steven at some point, making sure she had done everything on the to-do list he'd left for her, and in the meantime, she decided she would look at a few estate agents' sites. The dream of buying a house with the money the nail salon was making was the only thing that kept her going – the light at the end of the tunnel – and there were so many little properties that would suit her perfectly. She started to feel better and reminded herself that her life wasn't that bad after all.

****

Three hours later there had still been no call from Stephen. She was ready for bed but thought she'd better do one final check of all the social media accounts for the lads with Steven, as the last thing she needed was him waking her in the night because she hadn't shared some post.

She opened Instagram and could not believe what she was seeing. She immediately called Steven.

'Steven, what have you gone and done behind my back? How could you?'

'Debs, darling, what's wrong? Why are you upset?'

'Why do you *think* I'm upset? You promised me that once we were making money we would buy a house and now that will never happen because you've put down a deposit on a golf villa in Portugal!'

'Why are you so upset? We're perfectly fine living in our rental and this villa will be good for the business image and a great investment. Besides, I got a deal as the five of us have shared the purchase. We can talk about it more when I'm back but for now I have to go. The lads are waiting for me; we're off out to celebrate our exciting new venture!'

Debbie stared at her phone in disbelief. Had he honestly just hung up on her after what he'd done?

If he thought they would talk when he was back he was kidding himself. Because she was done. This was the push she'd needed.

She stood up and moved to the closet to grab her suitcase. By the time he returned, she would be gone for good.

Chapter 2

It wasn't what Sarah Gonzales was going to say to her mum that worried her, but rather the thought that once the call had been made, her life would forever change. There would be no going back.

'Hello, Gina speaking?'

'Hi, Mum, it's Sarah.'

'Hello, Sarah! It's lovely to hear from you. Is everything alright?'

'Yes and no. I'm phoning to let you know that I'm on my way to see you. Would it be ok for me to stay for a little while?'

'Of course, darling! You know you don't need to ask though; your room is always ready for you. Will Alexander be coming as well?'

'No, just me. I'm headed out now so I'll see you in four or five hours. And ... thank you.'

Sitting ready to drive off, Sarah paused before putting the key in the ignition. She still found it hard to believe that she had made the decision to leave Alexander. She knew the hard part was over but also that this was only the beginning.

But what else could she do? He had cheated on her and though he had promised it was a one-time thing and it would never happen again, she knew herself well enough to know that she would never be able to forgive him – not today, not next week, not even in a year's time. No, when it came to her relationship Sarah saw things in black and white. Their life together was over.

The journey to the midlands would take around five hours and Sarah knew exactly where her planned stops would be. That was just who she was – everything in her life was planned and organised down to the minute. It had always been like that. She was the kind of person who liked to cross T's and dot I's.

She had found out about Alexander cheating on her two days ago and she had used the time since to get organised and plan. She'd packed carefully, contacted the landlord, spoken to a solicitor and her accountant, and been to the bank to open private accounts separate from her and Alexander's business accounts and transfer the funds she'd need. Standing appointments had been cancelled for now and everything had been methodically ticked off her to-do list.

Her next stop was the Cactus service station, where she planned to buy a cheese sandwich, a packet of plain crisps and a coffee, all to take away. Her life might have fallen apart in one area, but that wouldn't stop her from being organised and in control everywhere else.

Pulling into the service station Sarah checked the time, pleased to see that she was doing well. After a quick nip to the toilet and a stop to get her meal deal, she would be back on the motorway within twenty minutes.

Walking back out of the shop she paused to let a family come through the doorway and her eyes clocked a big stand of greeting cards. Without even thinking she walked over to take a look at the back of the cards to see what company had produced them, making a mental note to remember the brand name and mention it to Alexander. But no ... what was she doing? All of a sudden her heart was racing and she could feel the tears coming. She made a quick exit back to the car.

Right, pull yourself together, Sarah. You were just caught off guard. Alexander isn't in your life anymore and neither is the card business you ran with him. It's his business now, not yours, and so you don't need to be looking for new ranges, artists, or suppliers. Now come on. Eat your sandwich, drink the coffee and get back on the motorway.

****

Two hours later she was nearly there, and nearly ready to tell her mum the truth. What had she to lie about? She had done nothing wrong. *He* was the one who had cheated on her with a client.

Finally pulling into the drive at her mum's house she was caught for a moment by the absence of her dad's car. Even after five years the sight felt wrong. Oh, how she missed him.

Before she could get lost in the grief that surged each time she was reminded of her beloved dad, there was her mum on the doorstep with a huge smile.

She needed that smile more than ever today.

'Hello, darling, how was your journey?' her mum called as she stepped out of the car. 'It's so lovely to see you. Do you need a hand with your bags?'

'No, Mum, I'll leave it and unpack after I've had a cup of tea, if that's ok.'

'Of course it is. Now, come in and tell me all your news. How's Alexander? Busy as usual, I expect, out on the road selling the greeting cards.'

Gina went off into the kitchen to make the tea and Sarah nipped to the bathroom. Looking in the mirror she told herself she was fine and that she just needed to be honest and explain everything to her mum. Then she could unpack the car and focus on organising her bedroom.

Come on, Sarah, be clear and to the point. You can do it.

****

'Oh, Sarah, I'm so sorry. I really don't know what to say,' her mum said once the truth was out there. 'Are you sure you can't forgive him? No, of course you can't. Don't listen to me. I hope you know you can stay here as long as you like. This is your home and always will be. Now, I think we could both do with some food. What would you like to eat?'

'I'm ok for the moment actually. I think I'll unpack the car, sort out my room, and get organised first. Would that be ok with you?'

'Of course, darling,' her mum said, pulling her into a hug.

As she got up from the sofa Sarah could see tears in her mum's eyes. She knew her mum worried for her but also that she wouldn't want Sarah to be with someone she couldn't trust. And that was the heart of the matter – she couldn't trust Alexander anymore. Picking up her car keys she headed out to get everything. It was time to organise her new life.

****

It was nearly seven-thirty by the time she finished and sat down to dinner with her mum.

'This is lovely, Mum. I've missed your cooking.'

'Thank you, darling, it's nice to prepare a meal for two. It's been five years since your dad died and I still can't get used to cooking for just one. Some days I cook too much and then get upset with myself over the wasted food.'

'Try not to be too hard on yourself, Mum. We all miss him and it's an easy mistake to make. Speaking of meals, where did you go to eat when Debbie and Steven came to stay for your birthday?'

Sarah was surprised to see her mum a little flummoxed by the question. Why didn't she want to talk about the visit? Had there been an argument when they came to stay? Keen not to upset her mum further, she didn't pursue the conversation. Instead, she chatted about the neighbours and their family who lived in Tenerife.

'I'm afraid things aren't good in Tenerife, Sarah. Your Aunt Iballa isn't well and she's struggling with her hip and legs. Walking is a big problem and running the bakery in Kalanchoe with your Uncle Ancor has become increasingly difficult. It looks like she might have to go to Gran Canaria for an operation soon.'

'But surely cousin Ergual could take over from Iballa while she's off?'

'From what I understand, Ergual is rarely there. But you know what he's like. He's always been work shy because your aunt and uncle have spoiled him since he was a little boy, and apparently working in a bakery is "beneath" him. Iballa and Ancor have lovely Ruben who has worked for them for many years and is more than capable of doing all the baking, but he lacks confidence when it comes to the customer service side of things. Also, apparently Ergual and Ruben don't get on. They haven't spoken to one another for years, ever since there was a big falling out when they were teenagers.'

'I remember Ruben from when we were children there on holiday. He was always too shy to join in and didn't say a lot.'

'Your dad always said he would be perfect running the bakery and that he just needed his confidence built up – and, of course, your uncle not interfering. I sometimes wonder if that's the problem with Ergual as well. Perhaps if your uncle encouraged him a little more and gave him room to put his stamp on things, rather than dismissing him all the time, he might get involved. Anyway, I hope that Iballa and Ancor can find a solution so that Iballa can get the care she needs. Shall I make us a nice cup of tea? You go into the lounge and get settled. There's … something I need to tell you, and to be honest I don't really know where to start.'

Sarah started to panic. Was something wrong with her mum? Was she ill? She tried to settle her panic as she carried the plates to the kitchen and her mum put the kettle on. When she went back into the lounge she sat on the edge of the sofa, ready to give her mum her full attention.

'There you go, darling,' Gina said as she handed Sarah a steaming mug of tea.

'Mum, what is it? Are you not well?'

'Oh no, Sarah, it's nothing like that. I just … I need to explain to you about the weekend Debbie and Stephone came to stay – yes, Stephone. He's changed his name from Steven.'

'Legally? Why? I thought that he was just using that as the name of the nail bar to sound a bit fancier.'

'Yes, legally, and he gets quite upset if you accidentally call him Steven. Now, it's best I just tell you what happened and not what I think about it, that way you can come to your own conclusions. When they came to visit they stayed at a hotel rather than here at the house, and they arranged for a taxi to pick me up and take me there. Stephone came to meet me in reception – it was so posh and upmarket – and after a quick hello he led me through to a lounge where Debbie was waiting.'

Gina stopped talking.

'Yes, Mum, and…?'

'Sorry, darling. it's just … I didn't recognise her. No, that's not true, I would always recognise my daughter, I just mean that she wasn't the Debbie I know. She looked like she had just walked off a chic magazine cover; her hair was perfect, the makeup was immaculate and the clothes lovely. She was wearing a bright red tailored suit and don't get me wrong, she looked gorgeous, but it wasn't our

Debbie.'

'I don't see the problem though. She obviously looks at things differently now they have the business and so has grown up – no more wild child working the clubs of Tenerife – so good on her.'

'But Sarah, that was only the start. It's not just her looks that had changed, it was also the fact that her bubbliness had gone, and she barely spoke. I complimented her on how she looked and Steven – or Stephone, or whatever he's going by – jumped in before Debbie could answer. He said it was all his "creation", which made me feel uncomfortable, and every time I asked Debbie a question he answered for her. And then, when it came time to order, he told her what food she would be eating! He ordered her lean lamb cutlets and I said, "Debbie, you don't like lamb" but again he answered, "yes, she does" and that was the end of it. And while all this was going on he was getting her to take photos of him – not just one or two but dozens. Ones where he was holding the menu, then with the view in the background, then by the huge fireplace. After she took them he would go through and study them before editing the ones he deemed acceptable and putting them on social media. And Debbie just sat there and let him dictate to her. Oh, Sarah, it was horrible! I didn't know what to say or do. I just wanted to come home and bring Debbie with me.'

Sarah didn't know what to say; she was shocked and struggling to take everything in. The placid woman her mother was describing couldn't be her sister. No one ever told Debbie what to do. So what had changed? Sarah could see how upset her mum was and knew she needed to say something to reassure her.

'But the important thing is that she's happy with him. Everyone grows up eventually and different things become important in life. She has the business and her flat—'

'No, darling, she doesn't have her flat. That was sold to buy the business and they now live in a rented house. When Stephone the peacock went to the bathroom I quickly asked if she was happy and do you know what she said? She said that the business was doing well so it didn't matter if she was happy or not. I'm so worried about her and I don't know what to do.'

****

That night in bed Sarah couldn't sleep, too preoccupied thinking about her sister. Debbie had always been confident and though they didn't get on that well when they were teenagers there was always a mutual respect between them. The woman her mum had described tonight was not the sister she knew, and it was disheartening to know she was letting Steven control so many aspects of her life. And why did she even need a makeover? It didn't matter what Debbie did with her hair or what she wore because she always looked stunning – the complete opposite to Sarah whose hair always looked a mess. And as for clothes, well ... they never looked good on her, but that was down to her carrying a few more pounds than she should. Perhaps that was the reason Alexander had gone looking elsewhere. He probably wouldn't have if he had been with the other sister, she thought sadly.

Chapter 3

Debbie couldn't really believe what she was doing. After her conversation with Steven last night she'd called Jenny and Rebecca to tell them about the Portugal villa and her plan to leave for her mum's. She'd had the bare necessities packed but her friends had convinced her to load up her car with as many designer outfits and accessories as she could fit, saying they were worth a lot of money and she could sell them to keep herself going until she found a job.

The journey flashed by in a blur as she was still feeling numb, confused, and sad – along with a hundred other emotions – but as she saw the sign for her hometown she suddenly felt calm and relieved. She was in a safe place now and she just knew being back with her mum would be good for her soul.

She had purposely left her mobile behind and as it was nearly mid-day she thought about the fact that Steven would likely have tried phoning her a dozen times already today, only to be met with silence. Good. She was done jumping at his every command. She was free.

As she got to the end of her mum's road she suddenly felt exhaustion set in. She just wanted to sleep for as long as possible, something she hadn't done for such a long time. Getting closer she noticed a car on the drive and worried that her mum might have visitors, but that had always been a risk as this was a surprise visit. Hopefully her mum would soon guess something was off and wrap up the visit so they could be alone.

No sooner had she turned the engine off than

there was her mum at the front door.

'Hello, darling, this is a lovely surprise.'

'Hi, Mum, can I stay for a while? I've left Steven and I have nowhere else to go.'

'Of course, Debbie, this is your home. I must admit it's a relief to hear he's out of your life. I've been so worried.'

'Thank you, Mum, and I'm so sorry you've been worried. That's the last thing I wanted.'

'You have nothing to apologise for! Now, there's something I need to tell you before you come in: Sarah has also moved back for a while as she has left Alexander. You actually just missed her; she's gone for a walk. She's putting on a brave face for me, but I can tell she's upset about it all. But she can speak for herself, so I'll say no more. Come in, come in. I'm just so happy you're here.'

Debbie locked the car and followed her mum indoors, floored by this news. Sarah had left Alexander? Why? How? She also couldn't help but groan a bit as she'd hoped to avoid Sarah finding out about her and Steven so quickly.

I just know she'll start lecturing me at the first opportunity about getting involved with Steven in the first place.

She brushed away the unkind thought. Perhaps she'd be better off not jumping to conclusions. After all, this news about Sarah's split from Alexander suggested she didn't know her sister as well as she'd thought...

'I'll put the kettle on, shall I? To think I have both my girls back – how lucky am I? This will be just like the old days... But no, it won't, will it? Because your dad won't be here,' she finished forlornly.

'I'm sorry, Mum, I wish he was, and not just because we all know he would be able to put things right – he always could. I miss him ... but at least he isn't here to see what a mess I've made of my life.'

Sat drinking their tea Debbie was focused on the clock – though it didn't seem to be moving – waiting for her sister to walk through the door so she could get telling her about Steven over with.

'Hi, Mum, I'm back. Do we have visitors? There's a car on the drive that's jam packed with bin bags.'

'In here, Sarah. We do indeed have a visitor and just like you they are here to stay for a while.'

'Hello, Sarah,' Debbie said as her sister joined them.

'Debbie! What are you doing here?' Sarah asked, surprise evident on her face.

'The same thing as you, I suspect. I broke up with Steven and didn't have anywhere to go.'

'Right, I'll leave you two to have a chat while I get us something to eat. Before I go, though, I want to say that I know you're both here because you've had a horrible time, but this is a chance for a fresh start for both of you, and though I hate to see you down, it's so lovely for the three of us to be together again.'

Gina closed the door behind her and Sarah turned to Debbie.

'So, shall I go first? I might as well as my story is quite simple: Alexander had an affair with one of our customers, so I've left him.'

'I'm so sorry. I always thought you two were the perfect couple and you had a lovely life together. Do you think it's just a blip in your relationship and perhaps now he realises he's made a mistake you can put it behind you and move on, start again?'

'No, it would never be the same because I can't trust him anymore and the knowledge of what he did would always be there in the background. No, I'm moving on, but I have to admit I don't know what to do next. I know, me – organised and in control Sarah – without a plan. That's a first.'

'True, but it's also the first time we've really had something in common because I don't know what to do with my life either. I thought it would be scary to leave but the minute I walked into this house it was such a relief, and for the first time in such a long time I feel I can breathe freely.'

'Now that's where we're different. I'm all panicky and feel short of breath. I don't know, I worked so hard building our business up and now I've walked away, leaving it all to him. Have I made a mistake? Should I have stayed and taken over the business? I honestly don't know... Oh, I'm such a mess. I'm glad you're feeling better about things though. You seem lighter somehow, and it reminds me of when you came back from working in Tenerife. You were so confident, full of life and ready to take on the world.'

'Yes, I was full of sparkle back then, wasn't I? It makes me sad that I let things get so toxic with Steven. Mum probably told you about the lunch we had for her birthday? I could tell she was worried, and I hated putting her through that. Thankfully she can stop worrying about me now.'

'Do you want to talk about it?'

'It would probably help if I did. Steven persuaded me to sell my flat and spend the money I made on fitting out the nail salon, with the understanding that once we started to make money, we would buy a house. And stupid me, I believed him. But last night a couple of good friends helped me to realise that's never going to happen. By the way, he's coming back from Portugal today where he's been playing golf and – without telling me – invested in a villa on a golf course with the mates he's with. That was the final straw.'

Just at that moment Gina walked back into the room with two large glasses of wine.

'There you go, girls, I hope this will help.'

'Thank you, Mum, I think it will,' Sarah said with a small smile.

'Mum, I think Steven might call here once he gets home and sees the note I've left him. He won't be able to get a hold of me as I left my phone there – there were only a few numbers I needed from it, and I've written them down – so he'll likely look for me here.'

'That's fine, darling. I can handle him. Dinner will be in an hour if that's ok for you both?'

The sisters nodded as Gina returned to the kitchen.

'Mum is so calm about all this; it's not fazing her one little bit. We're very lucky to have her,' Debbie said.

'Yes, we are. We've always been lucky, what with our lovely childhood here in this house and also our time in Tenerife with Dad's family...' Both sisters smiled as memories rushed in.

'In addition to getting a new phone tomorrow I want to get rid of these hair extensions. I also need to think about how to sell all the designer clothes in my car.'

'Designer clothes?' Sarah asked, her confusion evident.

'My friends made me bring them as a sort of security. If I can sell everything – shoes, handbags, the lot – it will help to tide me over until I figure out my next steps. There's nothing left in my savings account as the last of the money went to his golf weekend away.'

'Do you think he'll turn up here? Perhaps we should move the car.'

'I don't think he would come tonight because he would have had a few drinks on the plane.'

'Ok, and the car is in your name?'

'Yes, it's a lease.'

'That's the priority for now then. If you give me the name of the leasing company, I can deal with that in the morning. We also need to find out if there are any utility bills in your name and sort out new bank accounts for you. I have a good friend who is a solicitor and I'm sure he'll be happy to give me some free advice if we hit any stumbling blocks. If I take care of that stuff, you'll then be free to go through all the clothes, shoes, and handbags. Does that sound ok? The quicker they're sold the better—' Sarah's dizzying organisation was cut off by the sound of the phone ringing and both sisters listened in as Gina picked up the receiver in the next room.

'Hello?'

'Is she there? Put her on the line now.' Steven was shouting so loud they could hear him clearly.

'I'm sorry, you must have the wrong number.'

'It's Stephone. Is Debs there? Put her on the phone.'

'I'm sorry, Stephone, I didn't recognise your voice. Are you ok? I'm afraid Debbie's not here. I've not spoken to her for about a week. Isn't she with you?'

'She's left me. I've just got back from a business trip and there's a note to say it's over between us.'

'Oh, I'm sure you're mistaken. She wouldn't just leave. She's probably at one of her friends' places. I could give her a call on her mobile just to check, if that would help?'

'She left her phone with the note.'

With that, he rang off.

Debbie breathed a sigh of relief.

'I'm sorry for that, Mum, but thank you. That was brilliant.'

'That's ok, darling, but we all know it's not the last of it. At some point he will be on the doorstep wanting answers.'

'Yes, and we will be ready for him,' Sarah said

supportively. 'Something smells nice. Shall we eat? A good home-made meal is just what we both need as we have a busy few days ahead of us.'

Chapter 4

None of them slept well and at five-thirty the next morning they were all sat around the dining table making plans. It was too early to make any calls about the lease on the car but Sarah had been looking on her iPad at online shops and suppliers of second-hand designer products. There was a huge market for the pieces Debbie had brought with her and the sisters agreed that the best way to approach things would be to consign everything to one place so that it was handled in one fell swoop. It might mean a little less money in the long-term, but in the short-term it would be a significant step in the right direction.

'I might have found somewhere. Debbie, look at this one, it's a big shop that also has an online business and they sell quite a few of the designers you have. Would you like me to email them?'

'Yes, please. The sooner everything is gone the better.'

'Right, girls, while you do that, I'll get us some breakfast. Cereal and toast ok?'

'Perfect. Do you have butter? I can't remember the last time I had it as Steven wouldn't buy it.'

'I do indeed,' Gina said happily.

'Thanks, Mum. And thanks for contacting them, Sarah. I really appreciate all you're doing to help me but I feel bad for taking up your time. Have you not got things of your own to be sorting as well? Is there anything I can help you with?'

'Thank you but no. Me being me organised to the last degree, I did it all before I left. And please don't think that's me bragging. I find it sad that I'm treating it like a job or problem to solve.'

'What do you mean?'

'At some point I have to let my emotions in and face the fact that my life with Alexander is over. I don't know if I'll scream or cry, but I know it's going to have to happen before I can move on with my life.'

Debbie didn't know what to say to comfort Sarah. They had always been so different but for the first time they were so much alike, and it wasn't just that they'd both left their partners; no, it was more than that.

'There we go,' their mum said as she lay breakfast on the table. 'You two get stuck in. Do you know, the last time I did this I had one eye on the clock so neither of you would be late for school!' she said with a laugh. 'It seems only yesterday that... Oh, there goes the phone. Don't worry, it's probably just your Auntie Iballa calling from Tenerife. She normally calls early, before the bakery gets too busy.'

Gina went off to answer the phone.

'I think it's good Mum still keeps in contact with Dad's family,' Debbie commented.

'Yes, I often wish she would visit them more though; she hasn't been since Dad died, which I find odd considering they used to go over all the time, and she always seemed happy there. I wonder what's changed.'

'I don't think she likes being there without him. She once told me she thought that being in the apartment alone would make her sad, and with Aunt Iballa and Uncle Ancor working so many hours she would be left by herself. Whereas when she's here, she has her friends to meet for coffee or lunch, or a trip to the cinema.'

'I'm not so sure, I think there's more to it—' Sarah was interrupted by a ping from her computer signifying the arrival of an email. Seeing that it was from the consignment shop she'd found, she said to Debbie, 'You should read it first, it's your things after all.'

Debbie read the email, which said they were very interested in what she was selling and asked if she could photograph and itemise everything so they could take a look and get back to her with a price.

Debbie groaned. 'That will take hours – days, even – and it would mean getting everything out of the bags. Oh, it's a right nightmare.'

'Leave it to me,' Sarah said confidently. 'If they want it and are willing to give you a fair price there's nothing stopping us visiting their showroom or warehouse to show them everything in person. I'll email them back to see if that's possible and, in the meantime, you get all the car lease paperwork together.'

****

Three hours later Sarah was pretending to be Debbie while speaking to the leasing company and in no time at all an agreement was made to take the car back. There would be a penalty to pay for breaking the lease early but that was better than holding on to it. They'd also had an email back about the clothes and an appointment was booked for two that afternoon. The only other thing on the to-do list was buying Debbie a new phone and sorting out her bank accounts.

'Right, let's make a list of bank account details and utility bills. Do you do online banking?'

'Yes, but I don't normally deal with the bills, Steven does.'

'That's ok, we can go to the bank and change things so that only you have access to your savings. Is there anything else you can think of, or you want to do?'

'Yes, I'd love to get rid of these hair extensions and buy some jeans and t-shirts – plain and simple clothes, not top of the range designer outfits. I just want to feel like myself again.'

Sarah could see the tears in her sister's eyes for the first time and though she recognised how painful all this was, she knew it would ultimately be helpful – for both of them.

Sarah's phone rang before she could respond to Debbie and though she didn't recognise the number she picked up.

'Hello?'

'Is that Sarah? Is your sister with you?'

'Sorry, who is this?'

'It's Stephone.'

'Sorry, who? Ohhh … *Steven*. Mum mentioned you'd changed your name. My sister's not with me. Is everything ok?'

'No, everything isn't ok, and I know you're lying. Your mum would have phoned you last night and told you she's missing.'

'Missing? What do you mean by missing?'

'Don't play games with me. She walked out and left me. It's unacceptable behaviour. She has responsibilities and I've invested a lot into her. She can't just go.'

'*You've* invested a lot? I think you're a little mixed up there, Steven, given that it was Debbie who sold her flat to buy you your nail salon and your golf villa, not to mention everything else. And what a very bad investment she's made.'

With that Sarah ended the call and blocked his number. Looking at Debbie she could see she looked scared. They both knew Steven wouldn't be giving up without a fight.

'Mum, if the phone goes just ignore it,' she called, 'and Debbie, text your friend at the salon

28

from my phone and give her my number to text or call if she needs to get a hold of you. It's possible he may come here so we should get ourselves ready, and we have the bank and everything else to fit into today in the meantime.'

****

It was eight o'clock in the evening when Debbie and Sarah finally pulled back onto the drive.

'I'm in the kitchen,' their mum called as they stepped inside. 'You've had a long day but dinner is nearly ready. By the way there have been no phone calls.'

'That's a relief! We'll just go and get changed and then come help you finish up.'

By the time Sarah and Debbie came back down Gina had the meal on the table – homemade lasagne with a salad.

'Debbie, I love the hair,' Gina gushed. 'When you said the extensions were coming out I imagined that would mean you'd have to cut it short but it's lovely and still quite a good length. Are you pleased?'

'To be honest, I didn't really care what it looked like as I just wanted them out, but I am pleased with the look. Dinner smells lovely. Thank you for going to all the trouble.'

'It's no trouble at all! I love to cook and it's so nice not to be preparing a meal for one. Dive in and then you can tell me all about the day.'

There was a silence as they all began to eat and Debbie seemed miles away, so Sarah decided to fill their mum in.

'They loved all the clothes at the consignment place. At first they were a little suspicious about us turning up with a car full of expensive clothes in black bin bags, but once I explained the situation

29

and showed them the Instagram photos proving they belonged to Debbie, they were fine. They took everything apart from some shoes and a few jackets I had to persuade Debbie to keep as they actually really suit her. The money has been transferred into Debbie's new bank account and we used some of it to get her a phone. Debbie sent her friend at the salon her new number and she let us know that Steven had been in and out of the salon all day, not saying more than two words to anyone.'

'Talking about bank accounts,' Debbie interjected, 'I couldn't get access to the business one. Apparently I've been locked out or taken off of it, or whatever happens. It's fine as there isn't money in it right now, but it was still disheartening to see how fast Steven moved to lock me out.'

'I'm so sorry. I'm sure it's all been taxing, darling. Still, good to get it all ticked off the list. What do you have planned for tomorrow? What else still needs to be sorted?'

'The car is being picked up and then I'll need to start looking for a job. Might as well get a move on with it, I suppose. How about you, Sarah? What do you need to get sorted?'

Another long silence descended before Sarah burst into tears, which quickly became sobbing. It was such a shock for both Debbie and Gina. This was *Sarah* crying, the one who was always in control and had everything planned to within an inch of its life. Now here she was, sat at the table, a complete mess. As the meal was finished Gina cleared the table while ushering her daughters into the lounge.

'Are you ok, Sarah? Remember that you don't have to figure out everything now. Give yourself a couple of days to process things and then you'll undoubtedly have a plan of action ready to go. You're great in these types of difficult situations.'

'Not this one. I've never had anything like this

happen to me before. All I know is that I'm just so tired and worn out. I want a rest.'

Gina walked back into the room with a pot of tea just then and quickly jumped to agree. 'Yes, you absolutely do need a complete rest. You both would benefit from lots of sleep and relaxation, and also sunshine. In fact, I think you should both go off to the apartment in Tenerife!' She smiled, warming to the idea. 'And why not? What better place to start your new lives? You could both do with a holiday away from everything and everyone and I'd be happy to pay for your flights.'

'That's so kind, Mum, but I really should focus on getting a job. Sarah, why don't you go?'

'No, I'm the same. It's a nice idea and I know the suggestion comes from a place of love but... No, I need to start looking for a job.'

'Girls, I need to be honest with you. From what I can see, neither of you is in a good place right now. The rugs have been pulled from under you in dramatic, horrible ways, so surely a short break away would only do you good? It would give you much needed time to think, recharge, and plan your new lives.'

'I think Mum could be right,' Sarah said, turning to Debbie. 'We both need time to make a plan so why not spend it in the Tenerife sunshine?'

Chapter 5

'Hello, Sarah, come let me give you a hug! Oh, it's so nice to see you. But where is Debbie?' Aunt Iballa asked, craning her neck to try and see around Sarah.

'Debbie is outside, waiting with the luggage. I've just popped in for the spare key to the apartment. I can't believe we forgot Mum's back in England!'

'No problem at all,' her aunt said as she shuffled to invite Sarah inside the bakery.

'Can I get it for you? Mum mentioned you've been struggling with your hip and I hate to see you in pain. Isn't there something the doctor or hospital could do? Or Ergual?' Sarah couldn't help adding.

'Oh no, I'm fine, and Ergual has his own life to lead. Your mum called right away when she realised you'd forgotten the key and I've put it into a bag for you along with some other supplies. It's out the back and Ruben's out there so he can show you. Will you and Debbie come for dinner tonight? We're all so excited you're both back in Kalanchoe.'

'Of course, we will! We can't wait to catch up with all your news.'

As Sarah went through the shop to where the bread was being baked the smell hit her along with so many memories of being here as a child. They were happy thoughts and a million miles away from England and what she had left behind.

'Hi, Ruben, my aunt says there's a bag here for me... Oh, sorry, I'm Sarah – Iballa's niece?' she added hesitantly as he looked at her like a deer in headlights.

Sarah could see Ruben blush and felt her own cheeks heat. Why was she introducing herself to someone she knew?

'Sorry, of course you know who I am. It just seems a long time since we were children playing together.'

Rueben nodded uncertainly and dropped a tray in his rush to point to the bag.

'I think it best I get out of your way. It's been nice to see you again, Ruben.'

Ruben just smiled in reply so she went back through to the shop.

'Thank you, Aunt. You shouldn't have gone to all this trouble.'

'It's just some milk, coffee, bread – of course – and a bottle of wine. Now, dinner won't be until eight, but come back as soon as you're settled and we can have a drink and chat before we eat. I want to hear all your news.'

'We will, and thank you again. Also, could you please apologise to Ruben for me? I think I shocked him.'

'Don't worry about Ruben. You would have only needed to look at him and he would have gone all shy,' she said with a booming laugh. 'We'll see you later.'

****

Walking through the front door of their parents' Tenerife apartment felt strange for Sarah. It had been a long time since she had been here, but she knew for her sister the feelings would be different as Debbie had lived in the apartment for the three years when she was working here in Tenerife. There was a silence as they took their luggage in, each walking to their own bedrooms.

Walking back into the main room at the same time as Debbie, Sarah felt a sense she was finally home.

'I honestly can't remember when I was last in

this apartment but nothing has changed, has it?'

'You're right. Every ornament, picture and piece of furniture is just as I remember it as a five-year-old. I still can't believe we both gave in to Mum and agreed to come here for a break before we start to rebuild our lives back in England.'

'Same. She was right though; we'll feel refreshed after lots of sleep and sunshine. It also helps that we're away from everything – you won't have the fear Steven will be tapping you on the shoulder and I can think about something other than Alexander's betrayal. That said, there is one thing I'm not looking forward to facing: cousin Ergual. I know I'm going to struggle to keep my mouth shut and I think you'll feel the same. Wait until you see Aunt Iballa. She really shouldn't be working in her condition, stood all day behind the bakery counter and walking with a stick. The agony on her face when she put one foot in front of the other... It's so sad and when I mentioned Ergual she made an excuse for that cousin of ours. He hasn't changed one bit since he was a kid. I can remember, back when we were six or seven, him screaming when he didn't get his own way, and from all accounts he's still doing it now, in his late twenties.'

'I can imagine. The stories I could tell you about him when I was working here ... you would be gobsmacked. But enough of him, let's go do some food shopping, get unpacked and ready for dinner with Iballa and Uncle Ancor. It will be very interesting to hear what he says about Ergual. No doubt he'll be defending him like he always has done in the past.'

****

Shopping done, Sarah went for a lie down on her bed for a couple of hours but Debbie wanted to take the opportunity to enjoy the last of the sunshine and so went on to the balcony, sliding into her favourite seat right in the corner – the last place the sun's rays would hit before it disappeared from view. It felt odd to be alone for the first time since arriving at her mum's house. So much had happened in the last four days and now she had finally stopped, she could reflect on it all. Although she felt sad and confused, she had to admit that she didn't miss anything – the rented house, the salon, Steven, and certainly not her image. For the first time in a couple of years she felt she could actually breathe.

She enjoyed the silence for a while and then headed inside to get ready and wake her sister.

****

'Ready?' she asked Sarah a short while later. 'If our dear cousin is there and says anything to wind us up, let's try not to take the bait. It's the only way to win.'

'You're probably right,' Sarah agreed.

Walking through Kalanchoe to their aunt and uncle's bakery, they both giggled as they passed the play park in the middle of the little town, memories flooding in.

'This was always such a happy place for us, wasn't it?' Sarah asked wistfully. 'The hours we spent on the swings, not a worry in the world ... and then we grew up and now we are both in a mess.'

'Come on, this isn't like you at all! And if I'm not mistaken, isn't it you who for the last few days has tried to pull me up with positive words? You need to take your own good advice and show me that fighting spirit. After all, you'll need it in a minute. I can see Ergual's flash car parked outside the bakery.'

They walked across the square and around the back of the bakery to the little private courtyard, where they were greeted by Iballa.

'Come in, come in! I am so happy my two gorgeous nieces are back in Tenerife. Let me give you a hug, Debbie! Now, sit down, let me get everyone a drink. Your uncle will be back soon; he's just gone to get some supplies and deliver an order.'

'We are both excited to be here but please sit down and let me get the drinks,' Debbie insisted.

'Yes, you need to get off your feet,' Sarah echoed her sister.

'I'm ok. Once I have the hip replacement all will be well.'

'And when is that going to happen?' Debbie asked.

'Well ... it's difficult,' Iballa said hesitantly. 'I need to go over to Gran Canaria for the operation but with the business ... well, your uncle wouldn't be able to come with me. I really don't want to be there by myself, so I'll just wait until there's an opportunity for both of us to go. But enough about me, tell me your news! Your mum didn't say a lot on the phone, only that you both needed a rest and time away from the UK. Has something happened?'

'Mum's right, we do both need a rest – or should I say we need to stop, take a breather, and sort ourselves out. We've both split up with our partners – on the same day, oddly! – and so now we need to think about what we want to do next. Oh, here comes Ergual. Hi, Ergual, how are you?'

'I'm great, thank you, which is more than I can say for you two. Haven't you both gotten old looking.'

'Don't be so rude to your cousins!' Iballa was quick to admonish him. 'They have been traveling all day and they are understandably tired. Now, while you three catch up I'll get us a drink. Is wine ok for everyone?'

'That would be great but I'll give you a hand.

Lead the way.'

'Thank you, Debbie, that's so kind of you.'

Left alone, Ergual eyed Sarah speculatively.

'So why are you really here?'

'We both needed a holiday. We've just split up with our boyfriends and this was the best place to come, especially given how worried Mum has been about Aunt Iballa. And she was right to worry. Iballa looks in so much pain. Thankfully you're here to take over and run the café and bakery while she is in bed recuperating after the operation. They are so lucky to have you, Ergual.'

That knocked the smile right off his face.

'Thank you for this, Aunt Iballa,' Sarah said, accepting the wine from Debbie. 'I was just saying that you're lucky to have Ergual as he can look after the café and bakery so you can have the operation you need.'

'I'm not going to be working at a bakery! What would my friends say?' Ergual said with a sneer.

It was clear that Sarah had hit a nerve as Ergual was on his feet and gone back indoors in a flash. A little smile on Debbie's face was all Sarah needed to confirm she'd scored a hit, but Iballa's face told another story – a very sad one. Perhaps she shouldn't have upset her cousin...

Thankfully the silence was soon broken with their uncle arriving.

'Uncle Ancor, hello! You haven't changed one bit.'

'Hello! How are my two favourite nieces? And welcome home to Kalanchoe! I've looked forward to this for so long and it's just such a shame your mum didn't come with you. We could have been all together again.'

Before they could say anything Ancor was hugging them tightly and crying. They both knew how much he missed their dad, his brother, and they hugged him back, sharing his grief. After a while he sat down and wiped his eyes. Iballa poured him a glass of wine and started to make conversation about the apartment and Kalanchoe. Everyone could tell she wanted to lift the conversation and when she said she would go off and finish getting dinner ready both Sarah and Debbie asked if they could help. She insisted she would be fine, but the sisters weren't so sure.

'She looks in so much pain,' Sarah said to her uncle once Iballa was out of earshot. 'Surely the quicker the operation is done the better?'

'Yes, I know that and Iballa knows that, and I would go with her today to the hospital if she'd agree, but she won't close the business. She says the only day in the last goodness knows how many years it has been closed is Christmas Day, and she would be letting her customers down if she closed it for however long it took her to get the operation and recover.'

'But can't Ergual step in and help for just a few weeks? He only has to stand behind the counter and serve... Oh, but no, you wouldn't be there either so there would be no one to bake everything,' Debbie said.

'There is Ruben, of course, but you know how he is – very shy and not confident. The few times I've left him by himself he panicked and things went wrong. I don't know why he gets in his head about these things – he is more than capable of running that side of it – and as for your cousin... I know we are to blame. We spoiled him, but that was just because we had the bakery to run and we felt bad that he was always with his grandparents while he was growing up. Also, just as it is with Ruben, if I'm not there to give Ergual instruction the whole thing would be messed up.'

'But this is serious, Uncle Ancor. He has to be

aware Aunt Iballa is not well at all and it's not as though you'll be asking him to give up his life forever. It's just for a few weeks – a month at the most.'

'Your cousin's coming back, I think we should talk about something else,' their uncle whispered, clearly eager to change the subject. 'Hi, Ergual, have you had a good day?'

'Yes, it was a busy one,' Ergual responded.

Sarah wanted to shout 'doing what?!' but said instead that she would go and see if she could help Iballa with anything.

'By the way, Debbie,' Ergual said, turning towards her. 'I saw Pedro today and told him you've come to stay. His face lit up. You two were quite the couple when you lived here, weren't you?'

'We weren't a couple, we just worked together.'

'Yes, but everyone knew he wanted to be more than just colleagues, even though you spent your time flirting with all the blokes you saw.'

'Ergual, my job – and Pedro's, for that matter – was to get holidaymakers into the nightclub. But of course you know that as you were a customer in the club most nights, as I recall. I also remember...' she began before stopping herself. Debbie wasn't going to let herself be goaded into an argument with her cousin, certainly not in front of her uncle, even if she really wanted to share how Ergual had thrown himself at every female holiday maker that walked into the club. 'It doesn't matter,' she finished lamely.

'So, you aren't interested to know what he's up to now then? I guess not if, as you say, you were just work colleagues...'

Before Debbie could respond to his barb Sarah was back with a tray of food and Ancor started remarking loudly about how it smelled and looked gorgeous.

There was no denying that the mention of Pedro

39

did bring back memories for Debbie, and that she was curious to know how he was doing. Though he hadn't crossed her mind for years, they'd been close, and though she'd always suspected he wanted to be more than just colleagues, she couldn't go there as she knew it would inevitably end in disaster and spoil their great working relationship.

She suddenly realised she could hear her aunt talking but wasn't sure what had been said as she'd been miles away.

'Sorry, did you say something?'

'My mum said dive in and help yourself. You seemed a bit day dreamy there, Debbie, was that because I touched a nerve mentioning Pedro?' Ergual asked with a sly grin.

Chapter 6

Sarah was up first. She had slept well and suspected that that was down to all the wine; her uncle had been topping up their glasses all night. Ergual hadn't stayed long after they finished eating and the atmosphere had relaxed considerably with his departure. It had been lovely to sit and reminisce, and although some of the memories also brought sadness given that all four of them missed her dad so much, it was good to talk about him and all the good times they had all had here in Kalanchoe.

Sarah had noticed that Debbie had been very quiet, only really joining in the conversation when someone asked her a direct question. This was something Sarah knew she had to work on. She really wanted her sister to feel better with herself here in Tenerife and thought that perhaps today they could start by going for a walk and having some lunch.

Her planning was interrupted when her phone beeped with an incoming email. It was from Alexander, which wasn't all that surprising given that she had made it clear to him that she would be willing to help with any queries he might have as he transitioned into running the greeting card business on his own. She knew from experience how much there was to do with the invoices and day-to-day paperwork, whereas having always been the one on the road handling sales, he didn't have a clue.

Reading the email, she saw that today's question was straightforward: one of the companies they used needed to be paid within sixty days, and he wanted to know if he should wait until the last few days to pay, or pay right away.

'Good morning, Sarah, did you sleep well?' Debbie asked as she walked into the room.

'Yes, thanks. I won't be a minute; I just need to answer this email from Alexander... There. All done.'

'Thank you again for last night. I couldn't have coped with Ergual if you hadn't been there; he certainly didn't want to drop the subject of Pedro, making a big thing of him and me. If there had been something between us, I would have sort of understood where he was coming from ... but there never was.'

'He was clutching at straws. He just wants to stir things up and he knew he wouldn't get anywhere with me so he took advantage of the fact that you're vulnerable at the moment. I have to say though, I think a lot of it he puts on. All this business about being busy and confident doesn't entirely ring true and it's definitely something I'm going to keep an eye on. Now, forget him. Wasn't it lovely to be able to sit and chat about Dad? It's a shame Mum wasn't with us.'

'Yes, it was. Maybe we can convince her to come for a visit while we're here. In the meantime, I suppose we need to figure out what we're going to do for the next few weeks. As much as lying in the sun is good for the soul and the tan, I feel the pressure to make a plan and start sorting my life out.'

'Do you mean you might be open to working here in Tenerife again?'

'Oh no, my days of sun, sea, and sangria are well and truly over. I'm not saying I didn't love those three years working here – I did – but I was younger then and it's never good to go backwards.'

'I don't know. You really enjoyed your time so wouldn't it be a step in the right direction to start doing what you truly love again? It's worth thinking about... As for myself, today I thought I would go over to the bakery to see if there's anything I can do to help take the pressure off of Iballa, even if it means doing the fetching and carrying while she sits at the till. I'd also like to help Ancor's efforts to persuade her to close the bakery and go for the operation. I know you feel anxious about taking the next step but it's our first full day here so why not take the day to yourself to think things through before you dive into anything? Perhaps you could even meet up with some of your friends that still live here.'

'I think it's going to take more than a day to work through my anxiety, but thank you for the encouragement. I'm not really in the mood to chat with anyone so I'll hold off getting in touch with friends for now. I think I might have a walk along the coastal path, and sit and look at the sea. Also, I need to buy some casual clothes. Shall we meet back here later tonight and go and eat in Kalanchoe?'

'I'd like that. I'm certainly not in the mood for another evening with Ergual so soon!'

****

Sarah was first out of the apartment and after a slow start to the day Debbie finally left and walked through and then out of Kalanchoe towards the coastal path. Her big decision for the day was: turn left, or right? She initially thought she would head towards the quiet town of La Caleta, but she knew that wasn't the best place to get clothes and she'd be better off going to Las Americas, where there would be a lot more choice – not that she was looking for anything special. Half a dozen t-shirts for a couple of euros each would be perfect.

This walk brought back so many memories as it had been the way she went to work every day when she lived and worked here. She neared Playa

Tillandsia and smiled to herself. It was certainly not a town where she'd look for clothes as everything would be designer – exactly the type of thing she wanted to leave in her past. Thinking about the designer items she'd unloaded before leaving for Tenerife, she realised she hadn't let Rebecca or Jenny know about her impromptu trip. Pausing to sit on a bench, she messaged them both that she'd come to Tenerife for a couple of weeks with her sister.

Within seconds they'd both texted back and to her surprise they said almost the same thing – they hoped she'd have fun, and had she seen Pedro yet? She was surprised that his name had come up for the third time in less than twenty-four hours and before she could respond to the texts her phone rang with a call from Jenny.

'Hi, Jenny! Before you repeat the question – no, I've not seen Pedro,' she said with a laugh.

'Well that's a shame, but there's time yet! Anyway, that's not what I was calling for. I have to be quick as I've just popped out of the salon before my next appointment, but I thought I should tell you that Steven knows you've returned the car as he had some paperwork come in the post. He's been very snappy with all of us in the salon and when clients ask where you are he's been saying that you're on holiday, but now I think he's finally realised you're serious and you really have left for good. Shoot, I need to go. I can see my next client going in. I hope you have a good time with your sister ... but even more fun with Pedro,' she said suggestively.

Before Debbie could reply and say there would be no 'fun' with Pedro, Jenny was gone. She appreciated her friend keeping her updated and was glad to hear Steven was taking her leaving seriously. Right, time to get those t-shirts. She continued on to Tillandsia, hopeful there might be the odd discount shop she could pop into and a place to grab another bottle of water.

As she walked into the main shopping area it was clear there wouldn't be any cheap clothes here. Steven would be in his element with all these world famous designer shops – some of the prices of the shoes and handbags were extortionate – but the only thing she would be purchasing was her bottle of water before heading further along the coast to Las Americas.

She was startled from her thoughts by the sound of someone saying her name twice and she realised she recognised the voice. It was coming from behind her and she could feel butterflies in her stomach as she stopped and turned around.

'Debbie! I thought it was you crossing the road,' Pedro said, smiling broadly. 'How are you? Welcome back to Tenerife, by the way; your cousin said you'll be staying a while.'

'Pedro, hi! It's good to see you. Yeah, I'm here for a little bit.'

'Are you on holiday?'

'Yes, with my sister.'

'Oh, not with Steven? Sorry, I mean *Stephone*.'

'How do you know about him?' she asked, a bit thrown.

'I follow you – well, not *you*, but your business account – on Instagram. Jenny and I swapped social media accounts while she was here visiting you and I saw her post about the salon opening...'

Pedro trailed off, evidently realising he might have revealed too much and getting all tongue tied and embarrassed.

'Anyway, it looks like you've done so well for yourself. But then you were always good at succeeding with whatever you did. I know I learned a lot from you about so much while we worked together, and I have you to thank for much of what I have, including the house I recently bought. Perhaps while you're here we could meet up for a drink and catch up on all the old times? I work across the street in that restaurant there,' he said, pointing it out. 'I'm there six days a week so feel free to pop in any time.'

Debbie was struggling to take in all Pedro was saying as he was moving so much; he was a veritable bag of nerves.

'So, you don't work for Bentor in the club we worked at anymore?'

'Yeah, I still work for him, but he's given up the club – it's a long story – and now he has the restaurant. He'd love to see you. He's always talking about you, especially when he's upset with the staff. He launches straight into "if Debbie was here things would be done properly!"' They both laughed at Pedro's terrible impression of Bentor, and it diffused some of his nervous energy. 'Right, I best let you get on. I really hope you have a great time while you're here – you've worked so hard and achieved so much success back in the UK. No one deserves a relaxing break more than you.'

Before she could reply Pedro had turned and walked away. She felt a bit guilty that she hadn't shared the truth of why she was here – how she had split up from Steven and the business – but he hadn't given her much opportunity to interject. There was something different about Pedro; he was more ... grown up. He hadn't been a kid when they worked together, but he was more mature now than he had been even a few years ago; she could tell even from their short interaction. And she couldn't deny that he looked really, really good...

****

Two hours later she had bought six t-shirts, two

pairs of shorts, and two summer dresses, all for less than forty euros. Looking at the time she saw it was too early to head back to the apartment and as she didn't want to get involved at the bakery – it would feel a bit like stepping on Sarah's toes – she decided to find a place to stop and have a bowl of chips, simply because she could. She was starting to get used to choosing her own food again, and it seemed unreal now to think Steven had controlled even her food, even though at the time it had felt ... not 'normal', but just easier to go along with, rather than cause an argument.

She knew the perfect beach café, which was located halfway between Tillandsia and Kalanchoe, and hoped it wouldn't be too busy at this time of day. She was glad she had come out for a walk; the fresh air and the Tenerife sunshine made her feel free and floaty. Was that a word? 'Floaty'? She decided it was as it encapsulated exactly how she felt.

As she walked around a little headland, there in the distance was the café. The sight brought back more memories – of the chips, of course, but more than that of the time spent there, meeting up with friends and having a laugh, not taking anything in life too seriously.

She was grateful to find a little table right on the edge of the restaurant's terrace, which was perfect. Putting her shopping underneath the table she turned the chair a little bit to get a better angle on the view of everyone walking by, with the sea in the distance.

'Hello, would you like to see the menu?' a waitress asked.

'Actually I already know what I'd like: a bowl of chips, lots of mayonnaise, and half a lager, please.'

This was lovely. She actually felt for the first time that she was on holiday as she could hear other customers talking in German, Spanish, Dutch, and, of course, English. Yes, this was just how she remembered things. The lager arrived in an ice cold glass and not long after the chips arrived. Her first mouthful brought back even more memories and she was pleased they tasted just as good as they always had.

'Was everything ok?' the waitress asked when she came to collect her empty plate a while later. 'Can I get you something else?'

'Yes, the same again! No, I'm only joking, sorry,' she rushed to add when the server seemed to take her request seriously. 'That was more than enough and just as good as I remembered.'

'You've been on holiday to Tenerife before, then?'

'Yes and no. I've been coming here since I was a baby and then I worked on the island for a couple of years. My aunt and uncle have a bakery in Kalanchoe.'

'That must be Ancor and Iballa; I know them well. They're a lovely couple and they work so hard. So you must be Geronte's daughter? I was so sorry to hear he'd died. I went to school with him when we were children and he always had such a lovely family. Well ... most of them.' She grimaced. 'Sorry, I shouldn't have said that. It's just that I don't see eye to eye with your cousin Ergual. Please, when you see your aunt and uncle, give them my regards. I must get on now though. Customers to serve.'

Debbie was surprised the woman had openly shared that she didn't get on with Ergual. Perhaps when her cousin was next having a go at her – as it seemed inevitable that he would – she could bring it up and find out what had happened. After paying the bill she texted Sarah to say she would be back at the apartment in an hour, and to ask if there was anything she needed to pick up. Sarah texted back and said some crisps or nuts to have with a glass of wine before they went out might be nice.

****

Once back in Kalanchoe Debbie headed to the little supermarket, but as she was crossing the town square, she spotted her cousin coming in the other direction. He was the last person she wanted to get into a conversation with but there was no avoiding it now they'd seen one another.

'Hi, Ergual, are you ok?'

'Why shouldn't I be?'

'I was only making conversation,' she said defensively.

'What is your and your sister's game? Why is she interfering in the bakery, trying to be all goody good? I thought you'd both come for a holiday, not to work.'

'We are on holiday, but Sarah feels sorry for Iballa and wants to help.'

'My mum and dad are just being polite,' he sneered. 'They don't actually want you around. And the bakery is mine, so you can both keep your hands off of it.'

'We don't want the bakery and taking it from you is the last thing on our minds. But why do you care about Sarah helping out anyway? You clearly can't be bothered to do it yourself. Perhaps you should be grateful instead of getting so territorial.'

'I meant that the bakery will be mine when my parents retire. Listen to you. Here I thought the old Debbie had disappeared – you were quiet and so sad looking last night at dinner, like you had all the troubles in the world on your shoulders – but I see the fighter has returned, the Debbie who likes to boss everyone around. I remember what a relief it was for Pedro when you left. He could finally get his life back after all those years of you controlling him.'

Debbie was shocked and upset at Ergual's allegation. That wasn't how her and Pedro's working relationship had been! They were a team. Ok, she might have been the one who led the ideas on how to get customers into the club and then get them spending money, but Pedro had always been more than happy to go along with things and let her lead ... hadn't he? She'd had such a pleasant day and now she was starting to feel down again. Had she messed up Pedro's life?

Trying to shake off Ergual's cruel taunts, she quickly hurried back to the apartment.

'Hi, I'm back! How was your day?' Sarah asked as she stepped inside.

'Ok, thanks. I bought some clothes, so it was a success. How did you get on at the bakery?' she asked.

'There is so much to tell you! Pour the wine first while I go get rid of the smell of bread, and then I'll explain and hopefully between us we can figure everything out.'

Once they were back in the lounge with a glass of wine each, Debbie filled Sarah in on her conversation with Ergual.

'He was really nasty to me. What have we ever done to upset him? As kids we always gave in and played the games he wanted, and even as teenagers we went where he wanted to go. And when I worked in the club he never had to wait to get in and the drinks were always free.'

'It honestly makes no sense. Maybe he's dealing with something we don't know about?' Sarah offered, giving their cousin the benefit of the doubt.

'Maybe,' Debbie said, more than a bit sceptical.

Or maybe their cousin was just one of those people who was never happy.

'You said you had lots to fill me in on about the

bakery?' she prompted Sarah.

'I really don't know where to start. Aunt Iballa is really struggling so I tried to help as much as possible. Basically, she sat on a chair and I served the customers. The shop was busy and once word spread to the locals that I was there it got even busier. Everyone popped in to ask how Mum's doing and so many wanted the chance to say they were sorry Dad had passed, which felt odd as it was five years ago. I have to admit that it was lovely to talk about him though, and to hear stories about the time he spent here.'

'That all sounds pretty standard, to be honest. What is the thing you mentioned that we need to figure out?'

'Ok, as the day went on I found it odd and a little annoying that Uncle Ancor kept coming into the shop and interfering with things. Yes, I understand I'm new and don't really know the way everything operates just yet, but it was as if he had to check every little thing I did. And when I went back into the bakery, I noticed he was the same with Ruben. Ruben has worked there for years so it's not as if he doesn't know what he's doing, but neither he nor Aunt Iballa answered Uncle back, so I didn't feel I could say something, even though I *really* wanted to.'

'Oh dear. Could you imagine if Ergual was working there as well? The atmosphere would be terrible! He and Uncle would be arguing all day long.'

'I think you're right. Maybe it's a blessing Ergual has no interest in stepping in? It's definitely something to think about... But we'll save it for another day. Tonight we are going to have a nice night out and switch off from everything.'

Chapter 7

Sarah was up early and off to the bakery again. Ergual telling Debbie that she wasn't welcome by Ancor and Iballa was a load of rubbish as she couldn't count the number of times they had thanked her yesterday.

'Good morning, Uncle Ancor! No Iballa today?'

'No, believe it or not, because you were coming back today I've persuaded her to take the day to rest. I've also made an appointment with the doctor for this afternoon, which she has agreed to. Thank you again for stepping in. It's so kind of you to help when you should be here enjoying your holiday.'

'Don't be silly! It's my pleasure. Can I ask you something though? I think I know the answer already, but I need to make sure it's the right one. It has been suggested that you're only being polite in letting me pitch in, and really my help isn't welcome or needed. Is that true?'

Sarah could see Ancor looked uncomfortable and knew he was likely aware of the exact person the suggestion had come from. Was he going to make excuses for his son?

'You and your sister are very welcome here, always. You are family, and to have you back in Kalanchoe is wonderful. And for you to give up your holiday to help us here in the bakery? It is very much appreciated and anyone who says otherwise does not know what they are talking about. Now, are you sure you will be ok running the shop if I go back and carry on baking with Ruben?'

'Absolutely. Leave it with me, I'll get everything sorted.'

Sarah was very glad to know where she stood.

The next five or so hours flew by as older customers who remembered Sarah and Debbie from childhood welcomed her back and shared stories about when her dad had worked in the bakery. During a lull, when there was no one in the shop, she found herself looking over into the shut café. It was such a shame that it was closed and it showed how unwell Iballa really was if she couldn't manage the eight or so tables.

'Everything ok out here, Sarah?' her uncle asked, startling her from her worrying. 'I'm going to head off to take Iballa to the doctor now. Ruben is in the back preparing things for tomorrow, if you need anything, and I'll be back before it's time to close. It shouldn't be too hectic as the busy part of the day is over, though there are a few orders to be picked up. They're over there on the side. All have been paid for and are clearly marked. Oh! One other thing: ignore the phone if it rings. It will only be customers ordering for tomorrow and it will go to answer machine so I can deal with the requests once I'm back.'

'There's no rush, Uncle. I promise we'll be fine. The important thing is you get Iballa sorted.'

Once Ancor had gone Sarah decided to get a bucket of hot soapy water and give everything a good clean as some areas – especially those that were harder to reach – were just a little dusty, probably because Iballa couldn't get down to do it. Now, to find a bucket...

'Hi, Ruben,' she called, stepping into the kitchen. 'Do you know where I can find a bucket to use for cleaning, please?'

Ruben nodded silently and walked out of the back door and then came back with a blue bucket.

'Thank you! By the way, I don't bite … and despite whatever you've heard from Ergual, I swear I've not come to take over the bakery. I'm only here to help my aunt.'

'Ergual's not said anything about you. In fact, he's not spoken to me properly for years. He doesn't like me,' Ruben said.

He speaks!

'Between you and me, Ruben, I would be quite happy if he didn't speak to me either! Is that a smile I see?' she asked cheekily when she clocked his grin.

Rueben shrugged his shoulders and Sarah laughed. She'd take what progress she could with the near-silent baker.

After filling the bucket with water Sarah headed back into the shop and pulled out everything from the bottom shelves. This wasn't really the holiday that she had planned, but saying that, nothing was planned in her life at present. One minute a trip to Tenerife was an offhand suggestion from her mum, the next she was here. It was all very spur of the moment, and perhaps that was exactly what she needed...

'I was just going to make coffee while I'm waiting for some baguettes to bake. Would you like one?' Ruben called from the kitchen doorway.

'Yes, please, that would be lovely! I've nearly finished here and I need to change the water anyway before I tackle another area, so I'll come fetch it in just a moment.'

Going into the back and emptying the bucket she was pleased with what she had achieved.

'That one's yours,' Ruben said, pointing to a mug, 'and there are some biscuits there. They should be cool enough to eat now.'

'What a treat! Thank you. At this pace, I'm going to be going back to England a lot heavier than when I arrived,' she joked.

Ruben just nodded and Sarah knew she'd have to be the one making the conversation as he wouldn't.

'You've worked here for quite a few years now, haven't you? My dad used to say that Ancor and Iballa would never be able to keep the bakery going if it wasn't for you.'

'That's very kind of him. Your dad was a nice man and I was so sorry to hear he'd died. It upset the family here very much.'

'Yes, I know. In a way we're still getting used to him not being around.'

Suddenly Sarah could hear someone in the shop, and it sounded like they were coming towards the kitchen.

'Where are my mum and dad?' Ergual demanded as he crashed through the door.

'Your dad's taken your mum to the doctor,' Sarah replied calmly.

Sarah could see Ruben was uncomfortable and had started to fiddle with a rack of baking trays.

'How very cosy this is, the two of you back here chatting, drinking, and eating my dad's profits. Wait until he finds out what's been going on behind his back.'

Sarah was determined not to get into an argument with Ergual and not to rise to the bait this time, but one thing was for sure: before her stay in Tenerife was over, she would be saying something to him that would really knock him into place once and for all. So instead of letting her cousin have it, she just smiled and had another biscuit.

'I'll leave the last one for you, Ruben,' she said when she was done. She took her now empty cup to the sink to rinse it and only then turned back to her cousin. 'Was there something else you needed?'

His face was a picture, but before he could answer someone rang the little bell in the shop.

'Looks like I have a customer. Break time over, back to work! But then, it's not really work if I'm not being paid, is it? Nope, just a family member helping out when there is a crisis.'

Sarah moved to walk back into the shop but Ergual pushed in front of her and was gone.

'I think I am well and truly in your little "disliked by Ergual" club now, Ruben, and I wouldn't be surprised if there were a lot more members here on the island of Tenerife as well.'

****

A while later the last of the orders had been picked up and there wasn't much left to do. The day was coming to an end at the bakery, which was odd for Sarah as she always remembered the little café staying open until late in the evening when she was young. It was where she and Debbie, and their mum and dad, always ended up at day's end, sat chatting and playing. It was such a shame to see it closed now, especially as she knew that although the café was very small, it did bring in a good income for her aunt and uncle.

'I'm back,' Ancor announced as he wafted through the door. 'Has everything been ok? No problems?'

'No, everything has been fine. All the orders have been picked up and there are a few new orders for tomorrow that have been handed in. How have you got on with Iballa?'

Sarah could tell by Ancor's face that things weren't good.

'I'm just going into the back to check Ruben's ok, and everything is sorted for tomorrow, and then I'll explain everything. We should be fine to close as there won't be many people around now.'

While Ancor went into the back Sarah started to

clear away what bread and cakes were left in the display case and wiped down the racks.

As she took the last of the stock into the back she found Ruben taking his apron off and picking up his bag to leave. Once again, it was left to Sarah to start the conversation.

'Thank you for all your help today, Ruben, I couldn't have managed without you. Ruben runs a very good bakery, Uncle, and I think you could quite easily be taking more days off as everything is in safe hands with him.'

'Um ... thank you,' Rueben said with a blush. 'I best be going. Goodbye.' With that he was gone as fast as he possibly could without actually running from the room. Apparently he was the type who was uncomfortable with praise.

'Everything is done apart from cashing out, Uncle. But first I need to pay for some biscuits Ruben and I had.'

'Thank you, but you know you don't have to pay for anything. You're family! And of course neither does Ruben. I know he isn't a blood relative but to Iballa and me he's family—'

'Sorry to interrupt, Uncle, but I think I can hear someone in the shop.'

'Yes, you can,' Ergual supplied as he came into view. 'Dad, I have a few things to tell you about what's been going on while you weren't here. And by the way, Ruben *isn't* family, he's just a sad nobody that works here.'

'That is enough, Ergual,' Ancor said swiftly.

'I think I'll head off so you two can chat,' Sarah offered. The tension in the room was palpable.

'One minute, Sarah. You need to hear this as well. The doctor has said that Iballa's condition has deteriorated and she needs the hip replacement as soon as possible. Thankfully, there is a private hospital on the island of Gran Canaria that can do the operation next week and she's been booked in. This means that we will both be off on Sunday to get her settled before the procedure on Monday, and that she will need to be off for some time, resting and recuperating.'

'But, Dad, what will happen to the bakery while you're gone?'

'I'm afraid we will have to close. Your mum's health is more important than the business.'

'Uncle, it doesn't need to close,' Sarah interjected swiftly. 'Ruben and I can keep it open ... if you think we're capable and you're comfortable with the idea?'

'Oh, that's so kind of you to offer. I know you're both more than able to run things in my absence. I'll still need to contact the shop owners whom I deliver to and tell them they'll have to come and pick up their orders for the next little while though, as there won't be anyone to deliver them.'

'There's no need to do that, Uncle – Ergual can do the deliveries! In times like these we all need to pull together as a family, isn't that right, Ergual?'

Neither Ergual nor Ancor said a word so Sarah just picked up her bag and said goodbye.

Chapter 8

With Sarah gone off to the bakery Debbie was a bit lost as to what to do on her second full day in Tenerife. It was a little cloudy so there would be no point going to the beach, but she also didn't want to stay in the apartment, so she decided to head towards La Caleta. It would be quiet, ensure she didn't run into anyone she knew, and she would be able to get some lunch.

The walk to Caleta was nice and steady. There weren't many people around and it was lovely to stop and start, taking time to look out to sea and clearing her head, though that was easier said than done. She thought the rest period in Tenerife would help but it was actually doing the opposite as every day she seemed to feel even more tired. When she had mentioned this to Sarah yesterday, her sister had suggested that it was probably because for over two years she hadn't had anything to make a decision about; all that had all been done for her. Now she was free and every little decision had to be decided by her. It was liberating, but exhausting. Hopefully by the end of the holiday she would once again have some get up and go.

She remembered there was a sharp bend along the path a little ways up and at that point there were some seats. She decided she would stop and take in the view while she ate the pastry she had picked up earlier, and have a little break before continuing on to La Caleta.

As she plonked herself onto the seat she breathed a deep sigh. It was as if for the first time she felt truly free. Her shoulders weren't weighing her down and her head was clear. It was a welcome change, but then that nice feeling turned to a scary one. What was she going to do with her life? She couldn't just stay here on holiday forever. Annoyed that the blissful feeling had been so brief and her head was starting to fill up with worry yet again, she got to her feet. It was time to continue on to La Caleta.

After a few minutes she rounded the headland and could see Caleta in the distance. It was a little early for lunch so she stopped and bought another bottle of water and then went to sit on the rocks and watch the little fishing boats coming and going. As she was walking down to the harbour front she recognised someone coming towards her – it was her old boss, Bentor. He looked miles away and evidently had not recognised her. Should she speak or just carry on walking? Was she even in the mood to chat? Not really, but it would be rude not to say hello.

'Good morning, boss,' she called as they got closer.

'Debbie! It's so nice to see you! Welcome back to Tenerife. You should have popped into the restaurant to say hello; you'd be more than welcome. In fact, any chance you're looking for work while you're here? You can start tonight if you like,' he said earnestly.

She was a bit taken aback at his upfront offer but was saved from having to reply as he continued.

'You can pick the days and hours you want to work ... and it will allow you to spend plenty of time with a certain waiter that I employ. Pedro has had a large smile on his face since he saw you yesterday and every time the restaurant door opens he turns to look at it, hoping it's you.'

Debbie laughed off his suggestive comment as she considered how best to answer. She wasn't up for chatting about Pedro but she didn't want to talk about herself either...

'Do you have time to stop and have a drink and a chat? I don't need to be back in Tillandsia for a few hours and they can manage without me if I run late. Can I interest you in wine or coffee?'

'Coffee, please. I want to hear all about your restaurant and why you've given up the nightclub.'

'That's quite simple – age. I'm too old to be running and working in clubs. I'm also too old for a busy restaurant, really. I'd like to just give up working altogether but sadly there are bills to be paid. Come on, let's walk down to one of the little cafés by the sea and then you can tell me about your glamorous life back in England. Pedro is always showing me photos of you and your husband and your business. It's all so different from when you worked here on the island.'

'Actually, Benton, there's no husband – there's never been, actually, as he was only my partner – and now there's no business. We broke up and I've left it all behind. That's why I'm here.'

'Oh, I'm sorry.'

'I'm not! Now, lead the way to the coffee and then we can catch up properly.'

They found a couple of seats at a little café and ordered almond cake along with their coffees.

'Now, Benton, I want you to go right back to the beginning. I heard you offered Becky my old job after I left.'

'I did. She was a nice enough girl but not good with customers as she wasn't outgoing enough – it also didn't help that Pedro kept telling her she needed to be more like you – and eventually she left. There were a few others after her and some were ok but it was never the same. I wasn't getting the buzz like I used to; the music was annoying me – all that banging and thudding, no proper songs – and I had a constant headache. When I was approached about

61

selling the place and the price was right, I jumped at the offer. I said "thank you very much" and I was off.'

'So how did the restaurant come about? I would imagine that's a lot harder work.'

'Yes and no. It's very different and there was a huge learning curve, but I had some understanding of what was needed as I'd worked as a waiter for years before I had the club. The rest is history, as they say, and though it's going well I could always use another great employee. I'm not joking; if ever you want to come back to Tenerife to work, I'll happily provide a job for you.'

'That's very kind of you, Bentor, but I don't think I'll be moving back.'

'That's a shame. So, what are you doing now that you've left your partner and the business? Oh, by the look on your face you don't want to talk about it, I assume?' he added hastily.

'No, it's ok. As I mentioned, my boyfriend and I have split up. It was my choice and I'm happily moving on ... but to what, I'm not sure. I've come here for a few weeks' holiday with my sister to try and figure out my next steps.'

'That's nice that you have some time to stop and breathe, to take stock. Please, you *must* come to dinner in the restaurant before you go back. I can guarantee you'll have top-notch service – Pedro will see to that. And talking of Pedro, it wasn't until you left that I realised you were the one behind him, pushing and encouraging him. Without that prompting he does struggle to be a leader, even if he's a hard worker and overall a good employee. My point is, you were always one step ahead and looking to the future. I miss having you around, buzzing with ideas and enthusiasm.'

'Thank you, that's kind of you to say.'

There was an awkward silence and Debbie could

see Bentor looking at her as if he was studying her. She suddenly wished she hadn't stopped him in the street.

'I know it's none of my business, Debbie, but I have to say it. You aren't the same girl that I knew and enjoyed working with. It's like you've had the stuffing knocked out of you, the confidence, and it makes me sad to see you like this. Is there anything I can do to help?'

'No, I'm ok. I just need to think things through and get on with my life. And you're right, I'm not that mad, excitable girl anymore; she's gone. But that could be a good thing.'

'Let's talk about something else to cheer you up. How about I tell you about Pedro? Oh, my dear, when you first left he was so down in the dumps! There I was running a fun club for holiday makers and he had a permanent sad face. There was one point I had to sit him down and tell him that if he couldn't bring the party face to work there wouldn't be a job for him. Thankfully that worked and he cheered up when he was doing his job, but the rest of the time he was still miserable. To be honest, the happiest I've seen him since you left the island was yesterday, after you ran into one another in the street.'

'I missed him as well. We worked so well together and they were happy years for so many reasons, but times have changed. I've moved on.'

'Perhaps. But now it looks like you're saying it's time to move on again. I just hope that when you do, it's a move towards the girl I used to know and not the one that's sat in front of me now. I need to be going now, but please promise me you will come and have a meal at the restaurant.'

'Of course,' Debbie agreed with a smile.

Once Bentor had gone Debbie thought about everything he'd said. She knew Pedro liked her as he had made it clear several times when they were working together, but she had always explained that she didn't have relationships with work colleagues as it would make for a disastrous working environment if things ended badly. She also knew she would like the old Debbie back, but that was never going to happen. She had been knocked and put down so much that she didn't have the energy or the confidence to bounce back anymore.

Chapter 9

'Good morning, Debbie. Did you sleep well?' Sarah asked.

'Yes, I did, thanks. Each day I seem to be waking up later and later. Not sure if that's a good thing or a bad thing.'

'Definitely good. I'll make you a coffee and we can plan the day.'

'Oh, of course! I forgot you aren't going to the bakery for a few days.'

'No, Uncle Ancor thinks it will give Ruben a bit more confidence if he's left to do all the baking himself, so he's going to mind the shop while Ruben takes care of things in the kitchen. And then from Sunday it will just be Ruben and I – not forgetting Ergual doing the deliveries, of course.'

'Good luck with the last bit because you know as well as me that he isn't going to like that. Though I suspect he'll hate you telling him where he has to go with the deliveries the most,' Debbie laughed.

'You're probably right, but it shouldn't be like that. The family should be pulling together and to be completely honest it should be Ergual organising everything, not me. Oh, why does he need to be so difficult!'

Debbie went out on to the balcony as Sarah made the coffees and as she was waiting for the kettle to boil it crossed her mind that, ok, her sister might be sleeping better and her tan was coming along nicely, but she still wasn't moving on, and there had been very few signs of the happy, bubbly Debbie. She was just the same as she had been when she turned up after leaving Steven.

'Here you are: one coffee. Do you fancy going for

a walk after breakfast? Perhaps we could make a day of it and grab lunch – or even dinner – somewhere.'

'Yes, a walk would be nice. You choose where we go though, Sarah, as it's your day off and I know those will be rare while Iballa's having her operation and recovering.'

****

It was another hour and a half before they both went to get ready for their day out and the only thing that had been decided was that they would walk towards La Caleta. Even though Debbie was there only a couple of days ago, she didn't mind as it would be quiet and they'd definitely find somewhere nice to eat with a view.

'I'm ready!' Sarah announced, coming out of her room. 'Oh by the way, Mum texted me to say how relieved she was that we're here while Iballa is going off to have her operation. I messaged back and asked if she would like me to book a flight for her to come out but again she came up with an excuse. Apparently she's "too busy" as she has her coffee mornings with friends and then her book club each week. There's also the courses she's been taking up at the community centre since Dad passed. I think she fills her days and weeks because she doesn't want to be reminded that she's alone. It's understandable but also so sad.'

'It really is. I also think she just doesn't want to be here in Dad's hometown without him. Hopefully we can convince her to take the leap and join us. Come on, let's go and get some fresh air and hopefully at the end of the walk there will be a big bowl of pasta.'

Before Sarah had time to answer, Debbie was out the door. They walked through Kalanchoe towards the coastal road in silence, each absorbed in their own thoughts.

'Can you remember how we would run on ahead of Mum and Dad when we were here when we were younger?' Debbie asked. 'Dad always used to shout that the first one to see the sea buys the ice cream ... and even though he was never first to see it, he always bought the ice cream anyway. We were very lucky in so many ways, coming here on so many school holidays. I never took that for granted. Life is somehow simpler here, there was never any stress. Not like life with Steven. How stupid I've been...'

'No, you haven't, you just fell in love. There's nothing stupid about that,' Sarah said supportively.

They both agreed any further talk of their futures or their pasts was out of bounds for the rest of the day.

'You know, I had forgotten all about La Caleta,' Sarah said thoughtfully. 'We used to walk here so often with Mum and Dad, and always in the evenings. Isn't it strange how you only remember these things when you're doing them again? It's been years since this town has crossed my mind but I vividly remember visiting here as a kid. To come here and eat was always a treat.'

'I agree. Isn't it nice that even though we didn't always see eye to eye when we were growing up, we both have such happy memories of being here? Look! I can see the big sign for La Caleta just around the corner up ahead. Are you hungry? It's nearly lunch time.'

'I am and as you know the town better than me I'll leave it to you to find us somewhere to eat, though nothing with bread, please, as that's all I seem to have been eating these last few days.'

'Pasta it is then, and I know just the place. Hopefully they're open at lunchtime and not just in the evenings. It's at the other end of town so we can have a nice walk through the shops first or we can go the long way around by the water. What would you prefer?'

Sarah said via the water and was happy to see her sister so enthused. It was the first time since arriving that she'd seen this side of Debbie, so perhaps she was turning a corner, and the old Debbie was returning.

****

'Well, that was wonderful!' Sarah said as they finished the last of their meal. 'Thank you so much for suggesting it. I won't need anything else to eat for the rest of the day and though we agreed to catch the bus back I think we'll need to walk this meal off!'

'I'm happy to walk. Was there anything else you wanted to do here before we head back?' Debbie asked.

'I'd like to walk over and sit on the rocks at the end of the town to feel the breeze on my face, just like we did as children.'

Debbie was more than happy to do that and as they walked towards the rocks she couldn't help but think that she and Sarah had never been as close as they were right now. Perhaps it was because for once they were sort of equals – both at the starting block of their new lives – though Debbie was realistic enough to realise that once the starting gun was fired Sarah would be gone, flying smoothly into her organised life, while Debbie would probably be going backwards.

'I think if we turn here and go up the steep steps we'll be where we want to be...' She trailed off as she noticed Bentor coming towards them. 'This chap coming down is my ex-boss, Bentor,' she said as an aside to Sarah, 'And I can guarantee that the first thing he's going to ask is why haven't I been to his restaurant yet.'

'Hello again, Debbie! We're still waiting for you to come and eat and if it's not soon I'll have to deal with a waiter who has exploded with anticipation,' he joked.

'Very funny, Bentor. Sarah, this is my old boss, Bentor; we bumped into one another a few days ago. Bentor, this is my sister, Sarah.'

'Hello, Sarah, you must come over to Tillandsia with Debbie to eat at the best table in the house! We have gorgeous food, lovely wine and it's all on me because if it wasn't for Debbie being so successful and brilliant in my club, I would never have earned enough to buy the restaurant. I have to rush as I'm running late but please come, Debbie, for old times' sake.'

With that he was gone, and they carried on up the steps and then across some rough ground until they got to the rocks. This was what they both wanted and needed: a sit down and to feel the breeze before heading back.

'He seemed nice,' Sarah began. 'I know Mum and Dad said they always liked him when they visited, and it's clear he really appreciated the work you did for him. We must take him up on the offer as it sounds like it will be a lovely evening. Is there a reason you're reluctant to go? I couldn't help but notice you hesitated to agree.'

'Yes and no. I'd love to but ... well, it's a long story.'

'I have time,' Sarah said kindly.

'Ok, I used to work with a lad called Pedro and we got on brilliantly. We were a great team and I couldn't have earned as much money as I did if it wasn't for him; it was the same for him – we needed one another. The thing was, he wanted more than just a working relationship and I didn't. Well, that's not quite right. I did like him – very much – and if we hadn't been work colleagues we could have

69

possibly got together, but like I kept telling him, I don't date people I work with as it can easily become complicated.'

'But surely things are different now as you aren't working together? If you've been avoiding going to this restaurant, do you think it's perhaps because you want something to happen between you?'

'I don't know. I do really like him and when I bumped into him in Tillandsia, I did feel good, but I'm not ready for a relationship with anyone. My life is a mess that I need to sort out first.'

'But say your life was sorted and everything was good – would you be ready to have a relationship with this lad then?'

'I don't know. His life is here in Tenerife and mine is back in England.'

'Does it have to be?' Sarah asked sagely.

Now *there* was something to think about...

Chapter 10

After the long walk the day before, both Debbie and Sarah had had an early night, tired not just from the exercise but also from the mental strain of this time spent in limbo, which was not getting any easier. But today was a new day and so Sarah was up at five-thirty, sitting on the balcony with a coffee, waiting for the sun to come up. Her head was full of all sorts, her thoughts flitting from one thing to the next: what was she going to do when it was time to leave Tenerife? Where would her life take her? She was full of thoughts and ideas for Debbie, but when it came to herself she had nothing. She was also worried about her mum's refusal to visit. The apartment was here and the family was here but for some reason there was something stopping her. Had there been a family fallout Sarah wasn't aware of? It was all very confusing.

The other thing she was sort of bopping along with were the emails from Alexander to do with the greeting card business. Thankfully everything was being kept very professional. He would ask a question and she would keep her reply short and to the point. There was no aggression or emotion, though she had to admit she had thought he would be grovelling just a little bit, and was a tad disappointed that wasn't the case.

Finally there were her worries about the bakery. Would she really be able to cope while her aunt and uncle were away? But almost more importantly, would Ruben? He was so shy and had no confidence in himself. The one thing she *was* sure about was how she would deal with Ergual. One word out of turn and she would be putting him straight in his place.

Seeing the time she realised she was more than ready for some breakfast. Perhaps a little walk to the bakery for some pastries would solve her hunger problem. It would also get her out of the way when Debbie got up, so she could have some time to herself.

****

'Good morning, Uncle, how are things going?' Sarah asked as she stepped into the bakery.

'Hello, Sarah, all sorted here. Ruben is doing ok, though the same can't be said for your aunt. She isn't happy staying at home but she needs to rest ahead of her operation. Have you got time to nip in and have a quick chat with her just now? It will break up the day for her.'

'Of course I can. Will you put a couple of almond croissants and two small cheese pies aside for me, please?'

'Of course, and please try to get it through to your aunt that she needs to rest.'

Sarah walked around the back of the bakery, past the little café that looked so sad, all shut up, to Iballa and Ancor's little house. The front door was open, so she knocked and went right in.

'Hello, Iballa, it's only me.'

'Oh, hello! Come in, I'm so glad you're here as I want to check that you're sure you're ok with looking after the shop when we go to the hospital. It's not that I don't think you're capable, but you're supposed to be on holiday, resting and having fun, not working.'

'I am more than happy to do it and by the way please tell me you aren't sorting cupboards out,' Sarah said, alarmed to have found her aunt sitting on the kitchen floor surrounded by pots and pans.

'You should be resting!'

'Oh Sarah, I can't just stop doing everything. When have you known me to just be sat down? Although now you're here I'll do just that because I have you to talk to.' Sarah helped her to her feet and the two women settled on the sofa. 'Now, tell me your news. What have you and Debbie been up to?'

'No news, really. We've just been resting and taking it easy. It's all very laid back and quiet, which is just what we wanted from our break. It's just a shame that Mum hasn't come with us. That would have been lovely.'

'Yes, but your mum hasn't wanted to visit us here in Tenerife since your dad died, and I very much doubt anyone will be able to change her mind.'

'But why? Up until Dad died, they were here all the time. They loved it! I knew she would miss him not being here with her, but she loves the apartment and the sunshine, and she has friends here.'

'Yes, all of that is right, Sarah, but she's feeling guilty, which both your uncle and I have told her is a load of nonsense.'

'Sorry, I don't understand. What has she got to feel guilty about?'

'Nothing whatsoever. She feels bad that she encouraged your dad to move to England when they first met and has convinced herself that he – that they – should have stayed here in Tenerife. Then maybe— Oh, that sounds like Ergual, and I've just remembered I need to iron some clothes he needs.'

That made Sarah's blood boil. Her aunt could hardly stand up and here she was going to iron clothes for her son, who was quite capable of doing it himself. She knew that if she hung around any longer, she would be telling him so, so it was best that she leave. Saying goodbye to her aunt, she headed back to the bakery.

'Uncle, I'm back. I'll just pay for my things and be off.'

'You will not be paying for anything because you're family. Now, was Iballa sat resting? Probably not. In fact, I wouldn't be surprised if she was cleaning the oven.'

'Close. She was sorting out the kitchen cupboards. There really is no stopping her! Now, thank you for your generosity. I'd best be off.'

As she turned to leave Ruben came out of the kitchen, a blush quickly stealing across his face with one look at Sarah.

'Hi, Ruben, are you looking forward to running the place together?'

Before Ruben could answer, in walked Ergual, who had obviously heard what Sarah had just said.

'I think you've got a little mixed up there, cousin. *I'll* be running the bakery when Mum and Dad are away, and so you and Ruben will be working for me.'

Sarah could see her uncle was embarrassed so she just said thank you for the pastries and goodbye.

Walking back to the apartment, it wasn't Ergual that was on her mind, but what Iballa had said about Gina. She knew she had to think this through first, and she certainly wouldn't be saying any of it to Debbie, but she needed to speak to her mum about it.

'Morning, Debbie! I've got croissants for breakfast, small cheese pies for lunch, and we'll have dinner out. Are you still sure you're ok going to your ex-boss's restaurant tonight?'

'Yes, I need to get it over with. First, though, I thought I might have a few hours on the beach today. Would you like to come with me?'

'No, you go. I'm not really in the mood for the beach. I think I'll stay here, reading and puttering, if that's ok.'

'Of course it is. Shall we meet back here with an eye to being ready to leave and go out at seven o'clock?'

'That's perfect. Have a nice time on the beach!'

Once Debbie had gone Sarah started to think about what Iballa had said and she realised the only thing to do was call her mum and try to get something out of her.

'Hi, Mum, it's Sarah. Just checking everything is ok?' she said when her mum picked up the phone.

'All good here. How is everything in Tenerife?'

'Fine, thanks, but Debbie and I would love it if you came over and joined us. I think it would do us all good to share some nice days on the beach and go out for some gorgeous meals in the evening.'

'I'm sorry, darling. I would love to but I'm far too busy. I've signed up for a pottery course over the next six weeks and I wouldn't want to miss any of the classes. And talking of busyness, there's someone at the door. Have a lovely day, bye for now!'

Coming off the phone Sarah resolved to not let the matter drop. One way or another she would find out what was happening with their mum.

*****

'Ok, I'm going to give you one final opportunity to bail: are you sure you want to go to this restaurant and it's not just me persuading you to do it? We can quite easily make an excuse not to go.'

'No, I'm actually looking forward to it. I'm sure that the food will be delicious and I want to see what Bentor has created. And I can cope with seeing Pedro. At the end of the day, all we did was work together, so whatever is going on in his head is his problem, not mine.'

They had already decided they would walk to

Tillandsia and get a taxi back and although Debbie said she was looking forward to the evening out, Sarah hoped the restaurant would be busy and they would be lost among all the other patrons.

'Has your friend said what type of food he serves at his restaurant?' Sarah asked once they were nearly there.

'No, actually, he hasn't, but I'm sure there will be something on the menu we'll like. By the way, I was thinking perhaps it would be best if we don't have a starter or a desert and just stick to a main course so we won't have to be there that long. Is that ok for you?'

'Yes, whatever you think.'

Suddenly all of Debbie's nonchalance slipped away and she confessed in a panicked rush, 'Sarah, I think it's going to be a disastrous evening. Pedro will want to chat and Bentor would have told all the staff I was the best person who ever worked for him, and they will all be staring at us with the dead eye. Ugh, we're in for a very uncomfortable evening, aren't we?'

'I'm sure it will be absolutely fine, and if not, we can just leave. There are loads of restaurants around and we could easily find somewhere else.'

'No, you're right. It's probably all going to be fine and I owe this to Bentor. He was a very good boss to me. Look, we're nearly there. Let's see if we can be in and out within the hour. Would you go in first, please, Sarah?'

'Of course,' Sarah said supportively.

As they got to the door Sarah recognised Bentor and he came over to greet them. They were also in luck as the restaurant was very busy, meaning Bentor wouldn't have much time to spare for them. She found herself wanting to look around to see if there was a waiter looking at them, and she was annoyed that it hadn't crossed her mind to ask

Debbie what Pedro looked like.

'Hi, Sarah, Debbie, thank you so much for coming!' Bentor said warmly. 'I haven't got a table for about ten minutes so would you like to sit at the bar or outside while you look at the menu and have a drink?'

Before Sarah could say anything, Debbie jumped in and said outside would be fine and then turned sharply to leave the way they'd just arrived. The look on Bentor's face said it all. It appeared that, just like Sarah, he wasn't used to this different Debbie. Sarah smiled in apology and followed Debbie out.

'Are you really sure you're ok with this? Like I said, we don't need to stay. We can go somewhere else or even back to the apartment—' She was cut off by the arrival of their very bubbly server.

'Hi! Welcome to Bentor's! My name's Patrice and I'll be your waitress for the evening. Please enjoy a complimentary glass of champagne, and here are your menus. I'll be back to grab you just as soon as your table is ready.'

'She seemed nice. Do you know her?' Sarah asked once Patrice had bounced away.

'No, but she's good at her job, very welcoming and professional. The place is very nice from what I've seen and I'm pleased for Bentor. I'd still like to be in and out quickly though.'

'Can you see your friend Pedro anywhere?'

'No, but be prepared. The minute he spots me, he'll pounce. I think I'll have the steak and chips – very straightforward, no messing around.'

Sarah said she would have the same.

Ten minutes later Patrice returned as promised and took their order before leading them to their table, which was in the far corner of the dining room. Sarah went first and once at the table she sussed out the seats so Debbie would be tucked out of the way. She had to admit that this had started to feel more of a chore being here, rather than a nice night out.

'There he is. Pedro has spotted me. Let's try and make it clear we have a busy time here, with the bakery and everything else, so this will probably be our only night eating here... Oh, no, he's gone the other way. That's a relief.'

The food arrived and it was delightful. Sarah was relieved to see Debbie had relaxed a little.

'Was everything ok with your meals?' Bentor asked just as they were finishing eating.

'Yes, thank you. I really love the restaurant and it's fantastic that you're so busy,' Debbie said supportively.

'Thanks, that's very kind of you. Please excuse me, I just need to greet that family at the door. Patrice will come over and clear the plates in just a moment.'

'Would you like to see the dessert menu?' Patrice asked as she gathered everything.

'No dessert, just the bill, please,' Sarah said smoothly, but within minutes Patrice was back with two liqueurs.

'Bentor has asked me to tell you there is no bill for tonight; your meals are on the house. He also said he would come over to say goodbye before you leave. Enjoy your liqueurs!'

'Darn. We can't just leave, Debbie. We're going to have to chat to Bentor. It's only polite seeing as we haven't paid a penny for tonight's food and drink.'

'I know, but that's ok, we'll make it quick. Thankfully we're sat on a table for two and there's no way they can get two more chairs around it. Drink up, Sarah, here comes Bentor now,' she whispered before turning to her friend. 'Bentor! Thank you for everything. Are you sure we can't pay though? We didn't expect to get it for free.'

'No way! I'm not charging you, Debbie, not after all the money you made for me when you worked at the club. Now, would you like to move outside and have a drink? In another half an hour I should be able to stop and have a proper chat.'

'We would love to, Bentor, but sadly we need to head off. Sarah has an early start in the morning at our uncle's bakery.'

'That's a shame. Perhaps another evening.'

'Yes, we would love that, wouldn't we, Sarah? Oh I think that customer is trying to get your attention, Bentor.'

'See? That's why I need you to be working for me again! You don't miss anything, always having your eye on the ball.'

With that he went to the other customer and Sarah decided to pop to the bathroom before they headed back to Kalanchoe. Debbie said she would wait outside.

Sarah took a swift look around the dining room and then moved towards a very specific waiter to ask her question.

'Excuse me, which way to the lady's bathroom, please?'

'Just head to the back wall and turn to the left.'

'Thank you. Are you Pedro, by any chance? I'm Debbie's sister.'

'Hi, yes, I thought you must be. Have you enjoyed your meal?'

'Yes, it was lovely, thank you. Why didn't you come over and say hello though? I'm just curious as you and Debbie are such good friends.'

'We were good friends – best friends – once, but not anymore. She's made that very clear because she's been here for over a week and not made contact with me. That's not what friends do, is it? Please excuse me.'

He hurried away and Sarah was left a bit speechless. What on earth was going on with these two?

Chapter 11

Debbie hadn't slept well last night, and had been awake for hours already this morning. She waited until she heard Sarah leave for the bakery before exiting her room, not quite ready to discuss what her sister had told her Pedro had said. She felt dreadful because she knew it was true – she hadn't been acting like a friend. If only he could see the mess she was in, he would understand why she hadn't contacted him. But the only way for that to happen was for her to explain everything to Pedro, which would involve talking about Steven, something she was trying very hard to put behind her.

She made a coffee and went out onto the balcony. She knew she had to pull herself together. It was strange how just a couple of days ago, when she and Sarah had gone to La Caleta, she had been feeling better, a little more positive, but today she felt as if she was at the bottom of the pit again and that wasn't where she wanted to be. She was determined to put things right with Pedro but she didn't need to tell him everything, just that she and Steven had split up and she was having some quiet time to assess her life. She didn't have his number so that would mean calling the restaurant. Actually, that was perfect. He'd only have fifteen minutes to half an hour for the call – the length of one of his breaks – which would mean no time for a long, drawn-out conversation.

She was guessing no one would be at the restaurant until half nine or ten o'clock so she used the interim time to shower and get ready. She was feeling much more confident by the time she googled the phone number and called it.

'Hi, good morning, is Pedro there please?'

'Is that Debbie? It's Bentor! I'm sorry but he's not here – it's his day off today. I could give you his number? I know he'd be so happy to hear from you. I admit I had a go at him last night for not saying hello to you and was surprised to learn that he's got it in his mind that you really don't want to speak to him. I tried to explain that wasn't the case but you know more than most what he's like, always getting the wrong end of the stick. He has grown up in so many ways, but in others... Anyway, have you got a pen and paper handy? Here's his number—'

'Oh no, that's ok,' Debbie said quickly, cutting Bentor off. 'I don't want to disturb him on his day off. I'm sorry to have bothered you and thank you again for dinner last night. It was lovely and my sister and I both had a great time.'

'Debbie, just a minute. You know Pedro. Call him and explain that you aren't yourself and it's nothing to do with him. I promise he'll understand and I somehow think you'll feel a lot better for doing it.'

'Thanks, Bentor. I appreciate the advice. I'm sorry if my behaviour has caused you any problems with Pedro.'

'Don't be sorry! Just write this phone number down and call him.'

Coming off the phone one thing was certain: she couldn't call him today. Though she knew Bentor was probably right and that she'd feel better after making the call, Pedro wasn't working today and so might want to meet up. He'd know she hadn't any plans and the half hour chat she was planning would undoubtedly turn into a whole afternoon or even an evening. No, she would leave it for now.

****

An hour later Pedro was still on her mind and she was chastising herself for being so stupid. All she had to do was briefly tell him her situation and that she was sorry for being rude. If he wasn't happy with that, it was his problem, not hers. So she had made the call and they agreed to meet up in Playa Del Duque later that afternoon.

She was regretting things now.

It was four forty-five and she had fifteen minutes before she had to meet Pedro in a nearby café. Why had she let him talk her into this? But then, he hadn't had to try all that hard. She could tell by his voice on the phone he was happy she had called and when she apologised he had told her there was no need to worry, so here she was, nearly at the little beach café.

Pedro spotted her and waved, smiling warmly.

'Hi, Debbie, you look nice. What can I get you to drink? A cocktail, just like the old days?'

'No, just a Coke, please. This beach café hasn't changed at all since we used to come here, but saying that, it's only been a few years, I suppose.'

'Yes, but so much has changed for both of us.'

The waitress came across and took their drink orders.

'So, tell me all about the restaurant,' Debbie said once they were alone again, determined to steer the conversation. 'My sister and I loved the food and what a great atmosphere. The waitress who served us was lovely and friendly and we had a really nice evening. Bentor looks very comfortable in his new role. Do you find you enjoy it more than the nightclub? It's a very different type of business but it also deals with holiday makers so I guess it's similar in that way—'

'Debbie, you can take a breath, you know. I'm not here to ask awkward questions about what you've been up to since we worked together, or your future plans. I just want to have a drink with my friend and catch up. I'll answer all your questions, of course, though you might have to say them again ... and perhaps slower ... and one at a time.'

'I'm sorry,' she said, blushing. 'It's just ... I'm not really myself at the moment. I'm a bit fragile – not a word you'd ever think to use to describe me in the past, would you?'

'No, but fragile is fine and nothing to be ashamed of. I think most people are at some point in their lives, but it doesn't last and there is nothing stopping you from bouncing back when the time is right.'

The drinks arrived and it was so obvious they both felt awkward. Debbie wanted to fill the silence but her mind had gone blank, the list of questions having disappeared.

'I'm sorry for not reaching out to you the minute I arrived, but my life's a mess and I've been trying to blank it out, though not with a lot of luck. To be honest, I would love to go back to the days here on the island where we worked hard and played hard. There was very little sleep and we were always eating rubbish food and indulging in far too much drink, but we didn't worry about anything. We had no responsibilities so life was carefree and simple.'

'Yes, but we had to grow up at some point, and to be honest, we got out when the going was good, just like Bentor. He was on top and knew it couldn't get bigger or better and we were the same.'

'Yes, you're right, I suppose. I hadn't looked at it like that. By the way, you mentioned you've bought a house? That's exciting!'

'Yes, in Playa Paraíso. It's small – actually it's minute – but at least I'm not paying rent to someone. I'm happy and it's made me feel grown up.'

'How about the job?'

'That's good as well. As you know better than anyone, Bentor is great to work for and the type of customers we get are very nice. We are a bit pricier than a lot of the other restaurants in the area but we're always full. In fact, Bentor would like to expand the business. The shop owner next door keeps telling him he should buy their property and expand, but I think they know how much he wants it and so they've inflated the price. We'll see,' he said with a shrug. 'I think he has another meeting with the owners sometime this week.'

Debbie could tell Pedro was trying so hard to keep the conversation going because he'd realised she didn't want to talk about herself, and she was grateful. She honestly had never had anyone else in her life like him. Jenny and Rebecca always gave great advice but Pedro seemed to instinctively know when she just needed someone to listen, and when she needed someone else to carry the conversation.

'Shall we have another drink?' she asked. 'Perhaps I'll have a cocktail ... or how about a jug of sangria?'

'I'm up for that, but you know what happens when we have sangria – one jug leads to two ... and then three...'

They both laughed.

'And what's wrong with that? It's your day off and I think I need to explain more about my life over the last few years because it's nothing like the images you've seen of me on social media.'

The jugs soon arrived along with two Spanish omelettes with chips. It really did feel like the old days now.

'Where do I begin...? At the beginning, I think. Once I left here I went and lived with my friend Rebecca, and within days I got a job. It meant I didn't need to live off the money I had saved from working here – by the way we both did so well financially from that club, didn't we? It wasn't until I was back in England that I realised how well, and my dad advised me to use it to invest in property. It was actually one of the last bits of advice he gave me before he died.'

She could feel herself welling up. She worried she had let her dad down by losing everything, but she couldn't dwell on that right now. She needed to get this story out, preferably without any more emotion.

'I found this little flat. It was so small – just one bedroom and a lounge/dining/kitchen/ all-in-one room – but I loved it, and I spent a few months making it perfect. I was so happy there and to be honest it's probably because my life then was very similar to what it was here – work hard, play hard. I met Steven in a club one night. He was handsome and grown up, nothing like anyone I'd met before, and he made me feel different.

'The first few weeks with Steven were really fun. We went out a lot and got to know one another. The only not so good thing was he didn't like Rebecca, and she didn't like him either. Looking at it now with the benefit of hindsight, I should have listened to everything she said. I was paying for everything, which Rebecca said was a red flag, but when I asked him about it he was honest and said he had a cash flow problem, but it would soon be solved. Silly me, I believed him. Turned out the cash flow "problem" was that he didn't have any cash at all.'

Debbie topped up their glasses as she spoke. She was on a roll now.

'So, if he didn't have any money, how could he buy the business?' Pedro asked, confusion evident in his expression.

'He didn't – I did. He persuaded me to sell my flat and we rented a house, one that was far too big and grander than what we needed, but that's another story... The flat sold literally overnight and we used the money to rent the unit for the salon and refurb it. Once the business was open and the money was coming in, that's when everything really changed. When Steven changed. He was out to make a name for himself and that's what he concentrated on twenty-four-seven. Every penny that went into the till was spent on projecting the image of the perfect life. He joined an expensive golf club, claiming that was the way to promote the business, and when I was on his arm we had to look like the perfect professional, successful couple. He's the one who created everything you saw in those Instagram photos. I was a product, just like the salon.'

'I'm so sorry, Debbie, I don't know what to say.'

'There's nothing to say. I have only myself to blame as I went along with everything. And now I have nothing because I walked away from it all. Now that's all out in the open, shall we talk about something other than my past? Well, the Steven part of my past, I mean. I'll happily talk about our past... Oh, that didn't sound right! Sorry.' She blushed.

'I know what you meant. Sadly, we didn't have that sort of past together. Perhaps if we had you would never have had to go through what you've been through.' They both lapsed into silence for a moment, thinking about the deeper meaning behind his words.

'I'm going to order another jug of sangria,' Pedro announced. 'And this one will be to celebrate your new start.'

'What do you mean?'

'You are a survivor, Debbie, and though it may feel like the end of things, I promise this is only the start for you. And perhaps that new start could be here, back on the island of Tenerife.'

Chapter 12

'Good morning, Deb—' Sarah came to an abrupt stop when she saw her sister's face. 'Are you ok? You look dreadful.'

'I can assure you, I feel a lot worse than I look. I had far too many jugs of sangria last night.'

'Oh dear. But did you at least have a nice time?'

'Actually, I had a lovely time. I met up with Pedro. I explained why I hadn't been in touch, and that I wasn't ignoring him, and we had a real laugh. I'm paying the price today with my head though. How was your day at the bakery? Isn't it today that Iballa and Ancor leave for Gran Canaria?'

'Yes, at lunch time. I'm going over to the bakery just before they leave. All the baking will have been done by then and Ruben will be able to spend the afternoon preparing for tomorrow while I mind the shop. That's when the fun will really start – Ruben, Ergual, and me, one happy working family,' she said sarcastically. 'It's going to be disastrous, I just know it, but he's their son, and he has far more right to say how things are done than I do.'

'I think you're wrong as I suspect Ergual will keep out of the way; anything to avoid doing actual work. I keep meaning to ask, is Ruben still very shy? He was always such a quiet boy. I remember when we were children he was always there in the group, whether it be on the beach or here in the park in Kalanchoe, but he was always at the back of everything we did, and of course Ergual was always teasing him. I feel bad now I'm older that I didn't stick up for him.'

'To be honest, I think it's still the same between them as they don't talk. But I can assure you that if

Ergual says one rude or horrible thing to Ruben while Ancor and Iballa are away, I'll not be putting up with it. He's a really nice man and he doesn't deserve that. Now, can I get you some medication for that bad head?'

As Sarah went to get the headache tablets Debbie thought about how her sister's face had lit up when she mentioned Ruben. Was she reading more into this than there actually was, or could Sarah be a little keen on Ruben?

'There you go, one glass of water and two tablets. I'm glad you had a good time, even if you're paying the price for it now. Do you think you'll meet up with Pedro again before the holiday is over?'

'Yes, I think so, but using the word "holiday" doesn't seem right. You've been working most of the time and I'm, well ... procrastinating. We sort of arrived here with no plans and I think we're just putting everything off and using staying here as an excuse not to be sorting out our futures.'

There was a big silence and Debbie wasn't sure how to carry the conversation on, so she made an excuse and said she would have a shower to try and make herself feel a bit better.

****

The morning had flown by and Sarah was now on her way to the bakery. The first thing she noticed when she arrived was that Ergual's car wasn't parked in the usual place. That was good; it meant he wouldn't be around so the afternoon should be very straightforward.

'Hi, Uncle. Are you all packed and ready to leave? You do know you don't need to worry about anything here while you're away, right? Ruben and I will be fine.'

'Of course you will be! Ruben knows what he's

doing – probably better than me at this point – and as for you, Miss Organised, I'm sure you've got everything mapped out. I remember when you were a little girl coming to Kalanchoe your mum and dad always said you were just like a calendar, every day and hour planned. I know the bakery couldn't be in better hands, but I have to admit that I am worried about Iballa. She seems to think we'll head off to Gran Canaria, get the operation done, and then she'll be able to do what she did twenty or thirty years ago, clamouring all over and running things on her own. But the doctor and I have told her she'll need to rest when she's first back in Tenerife, which means no going out, cleaning, shopping, and certainly no working in the bakery until she has fully recovered. She will need looking after and I don't know what I'm going to do as I can't be by her side and in the bakery at the same time.'

It was a lightbulb moment for Sarah. She knew the perfect person to look after Iballa while she recovered – Gina! It would kill two birds with one stone: Iballa would be looked after and Sarah and Debbie would have got their mum back in Tenerife. She was excited by her plan but knew Ancor was anxious to get back to Iballa and be on their way so she would wait until later to share her idea. For now, she had to take control and let Ancor go. He had a plane to catch.

She waved goodbye as he went and got the cases and Iballa into the car and after a few last words, they were gone. This was it, she had a bakery to run. It wasn't a bit like her to be nervous, but she was. She couldn't let her family down, which meant that the business had to be just the same when they came back as when they left it.

****

Surprisingly the afternoon was quite busy as a lot of locals were popping in to see if her aunt and uncle had got away ok. Finally, the last of the orders had been collected, a few more orders were taken for the next few days, all the bread and cakes had been condensed to one shelf, and the bakery had been cleaned up. There was just the till to cash up and the floors to mop, and Sarah took a moment to thank her lucky stars that there had been no sighting of her cousin yet today.

'Here are two more orders for tomorrow, and one for the next day,' Sarah said to Ruben as she stepped into the kitchen. 'I think we're nearly done for today. Is it ok if I get the bucket and mop?'

'That's ok, I'll bring it out into the shop. I've already done in here, so I'll do the floor out there as well.'

'Thank you— Oh! That sounds like the shop door; I thought I had locked it.' She rushed back into the bakery to explain to whomever had arrived that they were closed, and was disappointed to find her cousin, rather than a customer.

'Hi, Ergual. Do you know if your mum and dad landed ok?'

'I've come for the takings,' he said, ignoring her question. 'I've not got time to chat. Unlike you two, who seem busy talking rather than working.'

Sarah was a little taken aback by his insinuation but knew that the best way to deal with Ergual was to kill him with kindness, something he wouldn't be expecting whatsoever.

'That's good you're taking the cash. I didn't really want to leave it here or take it back to the apartment. If you just give me five minutes to cash the till up you can have it.'

'No, you don't need to do that, I'll just take the money out.'

'Sorry, but your dad has instructed me to fill out

91

the accounts book for each day so just bear with me.'

'Why are you being difficult? Oh, I know. It's because you don't trust me with the cash, isn't it?'

'Of course I trust you. It's your mum and dad's business. It's not like you're going to spend their hard-earned money, is it?'

Without waiting for a reply Sarah went and checked the till receipts and counted out the float money, noting everything down in the ledger. It only took a minute or two and when she was done she put the day's takings in the lockable cash pouch and handed it to her cousin.

While she was dealing with the finances, Ruben had appeared and started to mop the floor.

'Look at you, cleaning up for the boss,' Ergual said with a sneer. 'Tomorrow you'll be bringing an apple for the teacher. You're so sad, Ruben, trying to get in Sarah's good books. You're wasting your time though. By the time Mum and Dad get back she will have sussed out what a useless waste of space you are.'

'Ergual, you've got the money, now go. And one other thing, if you ever come in here and talk to Ruben like that again you will regret it. That's not a threat but a promise because I can assure you, you will see a very different side to me if you continue being so cruel to your father's faithful employee.'

He was out that door like a flash. Ruben hadn't looked up during the heated exchange, just carried on mopping, but Sarah could see he was smiling.

Once the floor was mopped and everything was checked for tomorrow, Sarah and Ruben gathered their things to leave.

'Has Ergual always been this cruel to you?' she couldn't help but ask.

'He's jealous of me. It's a long story; I'll tell you when we've got more time.'

'I have plenty of time now. How about we go for

92

a drink, both to celebrate our first day running the bakery between us, and so I can find out more about that cousin of mine?'

Sarah was telling the truth – she did want to find out about Ergual – but she also really wanted to get to know Ruben a little better. She suggested one of the little restaurants in the square overlooking the park, saying it wouldn't be busy yet as it was only late afternoon, and was pleased when Ruben agreed.

Once they had sat down and ordered two beers, Ruben looked uncomfortable. Sarah was aware that perhaps it wasn't a good idea to dive straight in with lots of questions. No, she would talk about the bakery instead, which she knew he would be comfortable with.

'So, are we organised for tomorrow, Ruben? Is there anything else I need to know?'

'No, everything is sorted. I suspect we won't be that busy tomorrow as Ancor did so much prep before he left. It will be the day after that things pick up. We have lots of orders, and most of them will need to be delivered, so I think if I get ahead with them, it will be just a question of whether Ergual does as promised and picks them up to deliver them.'

There was another silence. The beers had arrived, and they both seemed to be drinking them very quickly.

Sarah had started to talk about Kalanchoe and how lovely it was compared to the very busy and flash Tillandsia, when Ruben interrupted her.

'About Ergual... It's all a bit silly, really. The conflict between us goes way back to when we were both at school together. On weekends and school holidays I used to help out in the bakery – cleaning, lifting, carrying, all those types of jobs. It was good pocket money and both Iballa and Ancor were so good to me – and still are – and it was nice to feel

93

like I was actually good at something. You see, I had a problem with my reading. I was a lot slower than the other kids, and falling behind at school as a result. Once I started working in the bakery, Ancor noticed that I was struggling and started to help me. Ergual didn't like that we were spending so much time together, but the thing was, the jobs I was doing in the bakery, *he* could have done. He just didn't want to.'

'Of course he didn't. He wanted the money without doing the work. Sorry, Ruben, I shouldn't have interrupted you. Carry on, please.'

'I knew he resented me but he kept it to himself. Or at least, he did, until one of the kids at school mentioned how lucky I was working at the bakery and said he wished he could find a weekend job like that. Ergual told everyone that I wasn't working at the bakery and the only reason I went there was because his dad was teaching me to read. It caused everyone to laugh and take the mickey out of me, which hurt.'

'That's horrible, but sadly it doesn't surprise me. The stories I could tell about when my sister and I came here on holiday and what Ergual was like...' She shook her head.

'Somehow Ancor found out about it even though I hadn't said anything. He questioned me and although I kept quiet, he ripped into Ergual and made him apologise to me, which, as you can imagine, made things a hundred times worse between us. From that day on things have only gotten worse. I find it's best to just say nothing and even though it appears to everyone that he scares me and I'm not brave enough to stand up for myself, he and I know who is the winner and who is the loser in this situation. I find it all very sad for him, really. He has no purpose – is that the right word? Yes, purpose. The bakery could be so much bigger and better if he was involved with a positive attitude. Both Ancor and Iballa are tired and worn out, and if Ergual stepped in he could have a wonderful successful business. If only he could see that.'

'That's what my sister and mum say as well. But as much as I love my aunt and uncle, they have brought the situation upon themselves by spoiling him. There's something else I've noticed this last week as well, which had never crossed my mind before: my uncle doesn't really trust anyone to do a job. He has to interfere, even with my aunt, and I know – and he knows – that you can do the job with your eyes closed, but he still checks up on you all the time. You're very sweet to allow it, but I feel if my cousin was working there he would be different from you and he wouldn't put up with it, which would undoubtedly cause arguments with my uncle. But putting that to one side, perhaps instead of letting Ergual get his way you should go back at him and put him in his place.'

'No, I won't ever do that. It would put Ancor and Iballa in an awkward position, in the middle of the two of us. No, I'm fine letting Ergual think he's the winner as I know differently.'

'I admire you so much for thinking like that. I'm afraid I wouldn't be able to keep my mouth shut. One comment from him and I would fly off the handle and give him what for, regardless of the circumstances.'

'No, you wouldn't, Sarah, you're far too nice a person to upset anyone. I remember even as a little kid you were always nice to everyone when you came here on holiday. I used to look forward to you coming to stay, just like I'm looking forward to working with you while Ancor and Iballa are away.'

Sarah could tell he really meant what he'd said. It made her blush.

Before she could respond, her phone rang.

'Sorry, Ruben, it's my mum. I need to take it.'

'That's ok, it's probably time I get going anyway.'

After a quick goodbye, he was off. The phone had stopped ringing so Sarah called her mum back.

'Hi, Mum, sorry, I was just talking to someone. How are you? What have you been up to?'

'I'm sorry to bother you, I was just anxious to know if Iballa had gone or not. I've had my doubts she would.'

'Yes, they've gone. All is fine for the time being, thankfully.'

'That makes it sound as if you think something is going to happen. Is something wrong?'

'Yes, we have a huge problem ahead of us and I really don't know how we'll cope, but that's nothing for you to worry about.'

Sarah had sowed a seed and now she needed to build on it. This was her one and only chance to get her mum back here to Tenerife, and though she felt a bit bad tricking her, it was the only way and so had to be done.

'What do you mean? Cope with what?'

'Well, it's like this. Once Iballa is discharged from the hospital she will need a lot of help back here. I can't do it and neither can Ancor, and as for Ergual ... we both know he won't be anywhere in sight. I thought of suggesting to Debbie that she step in, but as you know she's not in that good of a place at the moment, so we're pretty much scarpered. I suppose we'll struggle through. It's just ... I don't trust Iballa to rest. The minute our eyes are turned she will be up on her feet. If only there was someone who could help...' She purposely let the suggestion hang.

There was a silence on the end of the line and Sarah knew her mum had put two and two together and realised she was the best person for the job. But would she decide to come without Sarah actually asking? Only time would tell.

'Oh, I need to go – there's someone at the door. Please keep me up to date with how everything is going with Iballa, and give my love to Debbie. Bye for now, darling.'

She hoped her mum would come around because her hesitance only made Sarah more curious to know why Gina wouldn't come and visit the family here in Tenerife.

Chapter 13

Debbie could hear Sarah leaving to go to the bakery as she awoke. It was still very early so she decided she would make a drink and then go back to bed. As she was waiting for the kettle to boil she thought back to last night when her sister came home and told her about her drink with Ruben. She was surprised how relaxed and happy Sarah had seemed. She hadn't seen her like that for years, and she was happy for her.

Back in bed with a cup of tea she pondered what she was going to do with herself today. Another walk, perhaps? If she headed towards Tillandsia she could see Pedro and they might be able to pop out for a coffee or an ice cream between his shifts. She was just about to text him when her phone went off with an incoming call from her mum. Thankfully, because of the conversation with Sarah last night, she knew she needed to use the opportunity to push the idea of Gina coming to look after Iballa.

'Morning, Mum! I know what you're going to ask but we've had no news yet on Iballa as the operation isn't until later today.'

'Thanks, darling. And how are you?'

'I'm ok, thanks. Just taking each day as it comes. I think I'll be back with you soon as there's nothing really keeping me here. I need to get a job and start again and hopefully this time I won't mess it up. I also have to admit that I don't think I want to be here when Iballa gets out of hospital. She's going to need a lot of looking after and as I'm family it would only be right for me to take it on, but I don't think I could handle the responsibility while I'm still trying to sort myself out.' She waited, hoping her mum might make the offer Sarah so wanted her to make.

'Do you ... do you think I should come over and nurse her for a few weeks? I wouldn't have a problem with all the hands-on things, it's just... No, I would be the best person.'

'I think it sounds like a great idea. Sarah will be so relieved as she's been worried sick about what's going to happen.'

'Ok, get her to call me and I'll tell her myself. I'll ring off now. Have a nice day, darling.'

Once off the phone Debbie texted Sarah to tell her about the call. It would be so nice if her mum did come over to Tenerife, though she was a bit worried about how she would cope coming back to the apartment that she hadn't been to since Dad had died. There were so many memories for her here.

Perhaps Debbie could freshen things up so that the memories were maintained but the space felt fresh? She could get some paint and it would only take a few days to brighten up the walls... Yes, if it would make her mum smile, or make it easier for her to return to the apartment, it was worth it.

****

There were lots of people around as she headed off along the coastal path and into the centre of Tillandsia. The town was starting to come alive with summer tourists and she could see the lights on in Bentor's restaurant.

'I'm sorry, we aren't open yet...' Bentor began, before realising it was Debbie.

'Hi, Bentor, I haven't come to eat, just to see if Pedro will be free between shifts today. Is he around?'

'Yes, he's just out the back. Pedro! Someone to see you,' he called through a doorway. 'So, have you two sorted your differences? What am I saying? Of course you have! He's been a different person since you spent his day off together.'

'Hi, Debbie. Is everything ok?' Pedro asked as he joined them.

'Yes, thanks. I was wondering if between shifts you wanted to go and have something to eat?'

'I can do better than that,' Bentor interjected. 'Why not take the afternoon off ahead of your evening shift? We can manage without you over lunchtime. Go and have some fun, you two.'

The word 'fun' made Debbie blush.

'Are you sure, Bentor?'

'Of course, I'm sure. Why don't you have a day on the beach? It will give Pedro time to persuade you to stay and work,' he said with a wink.

'That sounds great!' Pedro said. 'I have a few things to finish preparing, but I'll only be a few minutes. Back in a flash.'

'While Pedro's getting himself ready, I've something to show you. Come with me,' Bentor said with a secretive smile as he went out the front door.

Debbie followed and watched as he fumbled for his keys and walked to the shop next door, which was empty. It looked a right mess from the outside.

'Come in, I want to show you my vision.'

It seemed the neighbours had finally agreed to a price that worked for Bentor.

Debbie looked at the two buildings and assessed how he might knock the wall down between them and make the restaurant bigger.

'Welcome to the new extension,' he said with a flourish as he unlocked the door. 'The restaurant is great but it isn't currently big enough for the amount of business we attract. We pride ourselves on not rushing the customer, but that means that the tables aren't getting turned around quick enough, which limits how many people we can seat on any one night. But I've had an idea. I've taken the lease on this property and I'm going to knock the dividing wall down. Now, I could just add more tables, but I thought instead I would make it a cocktail bar area where customers could have a drink before their meal and then, once they've finished, they can come back in for coffee or a drink. That way, people can linger over after dinner drinks as long as they like and we can simultaneously cycle people through the tables at the restaurant a bit faster. What do you think?'

'I think it sounds great. How exciting!'

'Yes, it's definitely exciting, but I have to admit I'm a bit nervous taking on another property...'

Before she could reassure Bentor, Pedro appeared and Bentor shooed them out of the space, saying, 'Go off and have a nice day.'

They both said goodbye and headed out the door towards the beach.

'That was kind of him to give you the day off, but then, you're good to him as well, so it works both ways. He was telling me about his idea of turning the other premises into a cocktail bar. That's exciting.'

'Yes, I'm really looking forward to running it,' he said confidently. 'Now, the big question of the day is: a sun lounger or towel on the sand? That's a question we'd never have asked a few years ago, is it? We wouldn't have dreamed of paying for a lounger!'

'You're right. All the more reason for us to treat ourselves!'

They decided on loungers on the quiet part of the beach and on the way they stopped and bought some bottles of water.

'I really enjoyed our time together the other day, Debbie; it felt just like the old days. I don't think I could drink like that very often though, given the bad head I had the day after. To think we used to party all the time!'

'I know what you mean. Over the past few years I haven't thought much about my time working here in Tenerife but they really were good days. We had a laugh and it was all about making sure the customers in the club had a good time and a holiday to remember.'

'Yes, and lots of them kept coming back, so we obviously did something right.'

'Of course we did – we're professionals!' She laughed. 'And now we're on the edge of new adventures. You have the new cocktail bar to look forward to and I have an exciting new future back in England.'

'So you know what you're going to do when you go back?'

'No idea whatsoever. I was being a little sarcastic – sorry – but I'm thinking perhaps some kind of office work? Something nine to five, Monday to Friday, ideally where I don't need to be dealing with the public. My days of happy smiles are over.'

'But you're so good at interacting with people! I know you've been through a horrible time, but it really is ok to bring the old Debbie back. I'm sure it would help you to move on with your life.'

'Thank you, but I don't think I want her back. I've moved on from Steven making every decision for me so perhaps it's time for a new Debbie – a sensible, more serious Debbie that doesn't mess her life up. Now enough about me. Tell me more about the new cocktail bar.'

'You're going to regret asking that question because I could go on forever about it! The bar will feature a bespoke cocktail barman and I'll meet and greet the customer, explain the menu, and take their drink orders. I'll also take their food order so that they'll be at the table in the restaurant for a shorter period and we'll be able to get more covers turned around faster. I'm really excited about it and can't wait for it all to happen. In a way I'll be my own boss and it will be like my own business. I have to say, none of this would have happened if it wasn't for you, Debbie.'

'What do you mean? I didn't know anything about it until today.'

'I learned so much from you when we worked together, how to deal with customers, being one step ahead and foreseeing what's going to happen.'

'That's rubbish; you did all that yourself! You were always good and I'm really excited for you and the new job. Now, do you think it's warm enough for a swim? Silly question, of course it's not, but then that's never stopped us before,' she said, standing. 'I'm not racing you to the sea like the old days though. Let's have a nice slow stroll down to the edge of the sea.'

As they walked across the sand Debbie felt happy. Pedro was so lovely to be around, not telling her what to do or putting pressure on her to decide what to do with her future. It felt as though he was giving her permission to take her time to sort things out.

As they neared the water there was a little drop in the sand and all of a sudden she slipped. Pedro caught her, his arms around her waist and their faces almost touching, and for a brief moment neither of them moved. As she finally stood up and he let go of her she felt a flash of heat go through her. She couldn't deny that it felt good to be in his arms.

'I'll try and get in the sea without any more mishaps,' she joked, trying to ignore the sudden tension between them.

'You can fall as much as you like. I'm here to catch you.'

They swam for around twenty minutes or so and

every time she glanced towards Pedro he was smiling back at her. It had been such a long time since anyone had looked at her like that and for the first time she was genuinely pleased her mum had insisted she and Sarah came to Tenerife.

Once out of the water they both lay in the sun drying off. There wasn't any conversation but she wondered if that was because everything had been said without words when she'd slipped and he'd caught her.

After a while she saw Pedro look at his phone.

'I was just checking the time. Do you fancy something to eat? I'll need some food before I go to work, and I really need to be at the restaurant by five-fifteen as Bentor is taking the night off and he'll want to brief me first. We could get a pizza or a bowl of pasta?'

'Yes, that would be nice. What time is it now?'

'Three-thirty, so it gives us just under two hours if you'd like to make a move.'

They got themselves ready and headed off the beach and back towards Tillandsia.

****

Pedro said he knew the perfect restaurant in one of the side streets and they shared a big pizza as Debbie said she would probably have something later with Sarah, so only needed a couple of small slices.

'It's been a lovely day, thank you, Pedro. I've really had a good time and I think I legitimately switched off from everything. Have you enjoyed yourself?'

'Yes, thank you, more than you would ever know, but I'm going to have to make a move. Bentor will want to take off soon.'

'Come on then, I'll walk back with you, and we

can thank Bentor together. And you never know, he might suggest it again another day!'

'That would be nice.'

They both smiled all the way back and found the restaurant was empty of everyone except for Patrice, who was there getting things sorted for the evening rush.

'Has Bentor left yet?' Pedro asked.

'No, he's next door in the empty unit, measuring things up,' Patrice explained.

'I'm going to have to go and get changed. Thank you again, Debbie, for a lovely day.'

'No, thank you, Pedro, it's done me well. I'll just go and thank Bentor as well before I head back to Kalanchoe.'

With that Pedro leaned towards her and kissed her on the cheek before turning and heading out the back of the restaurant. She stood there a little dazed and Patrice gave her a big smile.

'I've never seen him like this before. He's always talked about you and so has Bentor. There's a lot of love for you in this restaurant, Debbie. Excuse me, I think that's the phone. Hope you have a lovely evening!'

Debbie could feel herself go red and quickly turned to leave, only just remembering that she was planning to nip in and thank Bentor for giving Pedro the day off. As she went towards the empty unit she saw the door was open and Bentor was stood just inside with a writing pad and pen.

'Hi! I just want to thank you for giving Pedro the day off. It was very kind of you.'

'It was my pleasure. He's a good lad and never asks for anything. Have you had a nice time?'

'Yes, we have, and he is so excited about his new job.'

'What do you mean? He hasn't told me he's leaving.'

'Sorry, I meant his new job here, running the cocktail bar for you.'

'Oh dear, is that what he's told you? I don't know where he's got that idea from; it certainly wasn't from me. I'm going to have to talk to him. He's a great lad – a hard worker, and loyal – but you know better than anyone that he's not a leader, he needs to be guided and for the new cocktail bar I need someone who thinks on their feet and makes decisions in a split second. Basically ... someone like you. Well, not the you that's stood here now, but the old Debbie, the one full of confidence, who sparkled and could control and own any room with her presence. If you think you still have that in you, you would be perfect for the job. We both know you would be good – no, great – at it, and more importantly, that you would love it. In fact, I think it's just what you need to get your life back on track.'

Debbie was shocked and a little taken back. She couldn't possibly consider Bentor's offer. Her life wasn't here in Tenerife running a cocktail bar. No, she needed something stable – something boring – something that would allow her to quietly put the shattered pieces of her life back together.

'Thank you, Bentor. I'm very flattered but I'm afraid it's not for me. Look, you're busy and I need to be heading home. Thank you again for giving Pedro the day off.'

Debbie didn't give him time to answer before she was out the door and on her way, back along the coastal road to Kalanchoe. She knew she had made the right decision. Her life wasn't here in Tenerife running a cocktail bar. No, her new start would be in the UK

Chapter 14

As she neared the bakery Sarah could see the lights were on. It was only just gone five-thirty in the morning but Ruben was already there, just like yesterday. No doubt the first batch of bread would be in the ovens and he would be on to preparing the next. She knew how determined he was to keep up with everything and not let Ancor down while he was away.

Today would be a bit different to yesterday as there were lots of deliveries to be made to the little shops around the island, which meant Ergual would be in and out of the bakery all day – something she nor Ruben were looking forward to. Ergual would probably be equally unhappy as he would be working all day, something he clearly wasn't used to, but she hoped he would rise to the challenge because if he messed up he would be letting his parents down, which wouldn't go down very well.

'Good morning, Ruben! Oh my, look at all the bread cooling. You must have arrived hours ago. What time did you start?'

'About two-thirty, but it means we're ahead, and it will make for a smoother day.'

'Well, thank you. I know my uncle will be very grateful. Now, what would you like me to do to help you?'

'It would be a big help if you labelled the boxes for all the deliveries and put the paperwork for each order on or in the individual boxes. Some of the bread has cooled enough to go in so if you could start some of the packing as well, that would be great.'

Sarah felt positive. Ruben had really stepped up

to the mark, which was good to see, and it was a huge relief that the responsibility for keeping the business going wasn't just left to her.

****

Looking at the time she saw that it was nearly eight o'clock and time to open the shop. The first lot of the orders were ready to be delivered and when Ergual got back from delivering them, the next batch would be done and ready to go. The shelves in the shop were full and there was just enough time to make a quick coffee before things got busy.

As she handed Ruben his coffee, she heard the shop door open and recognised the heavy footsteps that followed as Ergual's. That was a shock – he was early! She and Ruben had joked that it would probably be lunch time before he turned up.

'Good morning, Ergual. How are you today?'

'Don't good morning me. You should be in the shop and yet I find you – yet again – in the kitchen. I better not have to wait for the orders; I have a busy day ahead.'

Sarah bit her lip. She so wanted to have a go at him but any family disagreement could wait as the business had to come first.

'The first batch of orders is ready. They're over there on the side, all clearly marked, and once they've been delivered the next ones will be here waiting for you,' Ruben said calmly.

'Listen to you! You sound just like Sarah, giving instructions and acting like you're in charge. You both need to realise that while my parents are away, *I'm* in charge, and I say what happens.'

'Ok. I've baked and prepared the orders, just as your dad instructed, so whether they are or aren't delivered isn't my problem. If you'll excuse me, I have more bread to be getting on with.'

Ergual's face was a picture as Sarah went out into the shop and a moment later he started to put the orders in the van.

One thing was for sure though, it wouldn't be the end of this. As far as her cousin was concerned, no one had a right to put him in his place, and especially not Ruben.

****

It was a few hours before Sarah could leave the shop counter as all the locals were coming in for their bread and to find out how Iballa was. Ruben had brought out more bread and cakes and also mentioned that the rest of the day's orders were ready and waiting for Ergual. Her cousin had already popped back once to pick up the second batch of deliveries but he hadn't spoken to either of them. Ergual walked in, picked up the boxes, and left straight away. Thankfully there would be only one more time he would have to come back.

Looking at the clock in the shop Sarah suspected it would start to slow down now, with just the odd customer here and there for the rest of the day. Ruben had started to prepare the dough for tomorrow and as she took some of the now empty trays back into the kitchen, Sarah felt good. It had been a successful day – and a real team effort – and her aunt and uncle would no doubt be very pleased.

'As you started so early, Ruben, why don't you leave once all the prep is done? The shop will just tick over slowly all afternoon and I can cope with that. It would also ensure you'll be out of the way – and out of the line of fire – when Ergual comes back for the last batch of orders, because I'm sure he's not going to want to let you get away with what you said to him this morning. I also think it's time my cousin and I had a little chat. I'm not putting up with his antics any longer. I want to know what his problem is with me.'

'It's likely the same as it is with me, Sarah. He's jealous of you and Debbie.'

'What has he to be jealous of? He has a lovely life here in Tenerife – he's not working so he can enjoy the gorgeous weather, he drives a flash car, and most of all, he has the bank of mum and dad supporting him.'

'Yes, he has all that, but there's something you and your sister have that he lacks: your independence.'

'But he could be independent if he wanted. All he has to do is get a job, and I'm sure Ancor would love to have him work here in the bakery.'

'But could you see Ancor and him getting on working together? I can't. They would be arguing all day long. Even after all these years Ancor tells Iballa how to do her job, and she puts up with it because she's just like me in that we don't see the point in pushing back. But it would certainly be a different situation with Ergual.'

'You're probably right. Talking of my cousin, I think that sounds like the van pulling up. He must be back for the last of the orders.'

Sarah dived back into the shop and busied herself wiping down the shelves. Ergual marched in silently and spent a few minutes putting the orders into the van, and then left just as silently. There had been no eye contact, let alone any conversation.

'He's gone,' she called to Ruben. 'He's probably saving everything up for when he comes to collect the money when I close the shop. If you're done you might as well head off now. Thankfully it shouldn't be such a busy day tomorrow, so you won't need to be in so early.'

'Are you sure you don't want me to stay? I don't mind. I have nothing else to be doing and perhaps we can go for a drink after work again. I enjoyed that.'

'No, I'll be fine. I enjoyed having the drink with you as well. Perhaps we can grab that drink on a day when we've not had such a busy one? Oh, that looks like a customer coming towards the door. Thanks again, Ruben, have a lovely evening.'

By the time Sarah had served the customer Ruben had gone. Before she could think further on his invitation, her sister walked into the shop.

'Hello! What brings you here?'

'I'm off for a walk over to La Caleta to clear my head but first I wanted to know how things have gone here today. Did Ergual turn up to do the deliveries?'

'Surprisingly, yes, and he was even early. It's been a very smooth day but that's all down to Ruben starting so early and getting everything organised.'

'He's out to impress you, Sarah. I'm a bit shocked though – you're the organiser and you've let someone else take the lead with it. That's a first! Right, I'm off. I'm not sure what time I'll get back to the apartment so I'll text you later.'

'Are you seeing Pedro?'

'No. Actually that's the reason I'm going to Caleta and not to Tillandsia – I'm trying to avoid him.'

'Why would you want to avoid him?' Sarah asked, confused.

'Because I know something he doesn't, and I don't want to be the one to tell him. It's all a bit complicated so I'll tell you about it later. Have a nice rest of your shift.'

'Oh, I will. Ergual will be back soon to collect the day's takings and it's time we put the cards on the table. Wish me luck.'

'It's not you that needs the luck, it's him! He's met his match with you, Sarah. Have fun.'

As Sarah waved goodbye to her sister her eyes went to the locked up café. It was such a waste, it being closed. It was also sad because the café was a big part of her childhood. Whenever they were here on holiday her dad and uncle had sat there late into the night putting the world to rights while her mum and aunt gossiped about people they knew. It all seemed so long ago now. What she would give to have those years back again.

Snapping out of those thoughts she got busy sorting and cleaning the bakery, and preparing the boxes with the paperwork for tomorrow's orders, just in case Ruben did come in early, as she knew it would be a big help to him.

By the time she had finished it was time to close the shop so she cashed out the till and prepared the day's takings for Ergual. When he failed to appear she waited a while before deciding it was possible he wasn't coming back at all and decided to take the money with her to keep it safe.

Once back in the apartment she had a quick shower and then sat in the late afternoon sunshine reading her book. She had forgotten all about Ergual and the bakery's takings until her phone rang.

'Where is it?' Ergual almost growled the question.

'Hi, Ergual, I've brought the takings back to the apartment with me to keep them safe. You're welcome to call around for them or I could bring them with me tomorrow. It's up to you.'

There was a silence on the other end of the line and she suspected he was warring with himself. Coming here would put him on Sarah's territory and that might make him feel uncomfortable.

'I'll be there in ten minutes,' he finally said.

'Ok, see you soon.'

Sarah went and got out of her dressing gown and put on a pair of shorts and a t-shirt. She topped up her glass and got another glass ready. She would offer her cousin a drink and hopefully he would say yes, and they could possibly have a conversation without all the digs.

There was a knock at the door and Sarah told herself to be calm, they were both adults.

'Hi, come in, I'm just having a glass of wine. If you want to go through onto the balcony I'll fetch you one.'

Ergual looked surprised but did as she suggested.

'Did everything go ok with the deliveries?' she asked as she joined him and handed over a glass. 'You'll be pleased to know there are only a couple tomorrow, so I think it will all fit in the van in one trip.'

'Yes, it was all ok, and as I've been to most of the places before with Dad when I was younger, I knew where they were.'

'That's good. Have you heard from your mum and dad? How was the operation?'

'Yes, apparently everything went ok. To be honest, my dad didn't give me many details as he was too busy asking about the bakery. I told him you had everything under control.'

'Thank you, but it's Ruben who's keeping the ship sailing, not me. I'm just there to help him out.'

'He doesn't like me; he never speaks when I'm around.'

'Perhaps he's just shy. He was at first with me too, but now we get on fine.'

'Yes, I've noticed the way he looks at you. He fancies you. See? You know it, you're blushing. It's such a shame you'll have to let him down gently. After all, what would someone successful like you want with the likes of him?'

'You've got two things wrong there, Ergual. I'm not successful – I have nothing now, no home, no job – and Ruben would make someone a lovely partner. He's kind, helpful ... everything a person would want.'

Sarah could see Ergual was thinking about what she'd just said but before he had time to reply, Sarah changed the subject. She was ready to put her cards on the table; she wanted to know why her cousin disliked her so much.

'Ergual, can I ask you something? I'm not saying it to create an argument or to fall out, but because I want to put things right, apologise or do whatever it takes to make peace. Why do you not like me? To be brutally honest, you've been horrible since I've arrived in Tenerife, always snapping at me. I've come here to get over a cheating boyfriend and losing a business I worked so hard to build, and I'm only working in your dad's bakery so your mum could go for a much-needed operation. I'm just trying to be helpful.'

Sarah could feel herself getting upset, explaining her situation out loud. There was a long pause, but Sarah would wait as long as it took to get an answer out of her cousin.

'I'm no different to you than I am with anyone else. Ok, it might come across as if I'm snappy, but that's just how I am.'

'Yes, but why?'

'What do you mean, "why"? It's just me.'

'I think it's something deeper, but I'm not sure where it's coming from. You have so much going for you, far more than I'll ever have.'

'Rubbish. I don't have anything – no job, no independence, nothing.'

'Would you like a job?'

'Is this the part where you tell me the bakery's there, waiting for me? I can't do it. It wouldn't be mine. I would be just like Ruben, working for my dad. No, actually I would be worse because he would be thinking more of him than me. And what would my friends think of me working in an old fashioned bakery?'

'So you're jealous of Ruben because your dad shows him attention? Don't you see that if it wasn't for Ruben your mum and dad would struggle even more than they already do? And as for your friends, they would see how lucky you are to be working in the family business, which one day will be yours. The hard work building the business has been done by your grandfather and your dad, but now it needs to be moved on and made more successful, and that's something you could lead. You could reopen the café, modernise it and bring it into this century. Ergual, you could be one of the most successful businessmen here in Kalanchoe if you put your mind to it and put a lot of hard work in. You're missing a huge opportunity and not just for yourself but for your parents as well.'

Chapter 15

Walking back into the apartment after another day in the bakery, all Sarah wanted to do was have a long shower and sit on the balcony with a large glass of wine. It had been a couple of days since she'd had the conversation with Ergual in the apartment and the few times she had seen him since there had been barely any conversation at all. He came in, picked up the deliveries, and that was all. There was the odd 'thank you', which was new, but how long that would last was anyone's guess.

As Sarah kicked her shoes off and put her bag down on the kitchen worktop, she realised she'd forgotten her phone at the bakery. She was so mad at herself. She would have to go back for it. This was so out of character for her. Perhaps the Tenerife life was having an effect on her.

As she got nearer to the bakery, she could see Ergual's car was outside and oddly the café light was on.

Unlocking the bakery door, she could see her phone on the side. She would just quickly grab it and go, and hopefully before Ergual realised she was there.

'Sorry, we're closed,' Ergual called from the café space.

'It's only me. I forgot my phone and I've just popped back for it. Have a lovely evening.'

She was just about to turn and go back out the door when he spoke again.

'Have you got five minutes to spare, Sarah? Please?'

That was a first – a please from her cousin. Perhaps the conversation in the apartment had done some good after all. Bracing herself she made her way to the open door of the café.

'I've been thinking a lot about what you said the other day. What did you mean about bringing this place into this century?'

His question took Sarah by surprise. What was going on here? Before she could answer, he continued.

'I worked here in the café once, quite a few years ago. Not for long, though, because my dad was forever peering over my shoulder and interfering, telling me I was doing things wrong. I tried to make a few small changes to make things more efficient and it didn't go over well. For example, all the cups and saucers are kept back there next to the coffee machine and the hot water, which is fine and works, but the cutlery is kept in a drawer at the other end of the counter, so you'd have to dash over there for teaspoons every time. I thought it was madness as surely it's common sense to have them together.'

'I agree.'

'On the second or third day I moved the cutlery to the drawer under the coffee machine. It made life so much easier and quicker.'

'I think I know what you're going to say, Ergual. I take it your dad didn't like it?'

'Yep. He was really annoyed, shouting about who did I think I was changing things, and saying that the business had been successfully operating for years and here I had come along trying to change everything. You would have thought I had done a major thing like rearranging the tables or scrapping the menu. All I did was put some teaspoons with the coffee cups, and that was the end of me working in the family business.'

'That's so sad, Ergual. I'm really sorry for you but I'm also angry with Uncle Ancor. He could have such a better business and life if he just let you get involved, and if you had been working here Iballa wouldn't have spent so many years in pain. He is just so stubborn.'

****

Two hours later Sarah was sat on the balcony with her second glass of wine when she heard Debbie coming in the front door.

'Hi, have you had a nice day? Did you see Pedro?'

'No, I've only been to the beach. He's texted me a few times over the last two days, but I've made excuses. Actually, I could use a bit of advice.'

'I'm certainly in demand tonight. First Ergual and now you! Go and change and then I'll explain,' she said, laughing when she saw Debbie's incredulous expression.

'So, tell me what advice our cousin wanted,' Debbie said when she was settled next to her sister. 'Hopefully it was how he could go about being nice to people.'

Sarah filled her sister in on the conversation with their cousin.

'We're talking about Ergual here, right?' Debbie asked once Sarah had finished. 'I really can't see him working at the bakery because it would be too much like, well ... hard work! He'd have to be there six – possibly seven – days a week from first thing in the morning, when he doesn't usually get up until lunchtime. I think it's more likely that he will try and get Uncle to sell it to bring in more money.'

'I don't think so. The more I'm at the bakery the more I can see what the real problem is and it's not Ergual, it's Uncle Ancor. He's so stubborn! Just because something worked well fifty years ago, it doesn't mean it's the right thing for this day and age. The problem is that Aunt Iballa and Ruben have always kept their mouths shut and don't challenge him, so he's very set in his ways. I can see myself coming to a point where I'll go back at him the same as Ergual has over the years.'

'Oh, dear. It's all very strange because this is a thing with the family we've never noticed before and we probably never would have if you hadn't gone there to help out.'

'Yes, I agree entirely. It's going to require some serious thought. Now, how can I help you?'

'You know how Pedro and I had the day out together, which was lovely, and he talked to me about the new cocktail bar Bentor was opening at the restaurant? Well, he told me he was going to be running it and I was really happy for him. When we got back I went to thank Bentor for giving Pedro the time off and I mentioned to Bentor how excited Pedro was about the new job, but he said that wasn't going to happen. In fact, he offered *me* the job of running the cocktail bar! There's no way I'd take the job here in Tenerife but I feel bad that here's me not wanting it, and Pedro is the opposite. Should I tell Pedro I was offered it and turned it down?'

'But why have you turned it down? It's the perfect job for you and the new start you want. It's away from England and you have the apartment here to live in so it sounds ideal. Ok, I can see Pedro will be disappointed he hasn't got the job, but he gains so much more than the job if he has you back on the island.'

'I turned it down because Bentor wants the "old Debbie" to manage it, not me as I am now, and to be honest, I suspect that she's gone, never to return.'

'I disagree. I think the minute you start she would come back with a vengeance! I'm so jealous, I wish my life would fall into place like yours. Instead, I'm in a worse state than I was when I first came here to sort everything out. I know I've got the bakery to think of but I can admit I'm ultimately just using that as an excuse not to be planning everything. Oh, I don't know. Do you think I should have just forgiven Alexander, put it behind us, and carried on?'

'No, of course not! It would be like you were saying you forgave him. And if he got away with it once he could do it again. Come on, Sarah, you're the sensible one between us. You just need to get your lists finished and you'll figure it all out.'

'I know you won't believe me but there are no lists, no plans, nothing. I really have blocked my future out of my head. The only thing in it is the bakery, you, and Mum. I'm refusing to let anything else in.'

With that Sarah burst into tears. Debbie was shocked and she wished she knew what to do. How could she help? The shoe was well and truly on the other foot now.

'Oh, Sarah, I'm so sorry, I don't know what to say. I'm no good in these situations. Let me get us another drink and shall I cook us something or should we go out to eat? I'm babbling on, sorry. Look, I'll get the wine. That seems like a good place to start.'

Debbie took her time pouring the wine. She also filled a couple of bowls with crisps. Perhaps it was silly for both of them to have escaped here. They had both run away, coming to Tenerife, when they should have just stayed home and sorted out their lives.

'There you go. Wine always helps, I find. It shouldn't, but it does. If it's any consolation, there is a silver lining in all of this – the fact that we have one another. Not that I would wish this on either of us, but don't you think it's brought us closer together? I think the relationship we have now is better than we've ever had and that makes me feel good.'

'You're right, and thank you. That's a kind thing to say and a good way to look at it. I have to admit though, there is the odd time when I miss Alexander. Oh I know I shouldn't, but life was easy then, just one straight path with no ups and downs or highs and lows. Everything was planned and there were no uncertainties.'

'I suspect that what you miss is the planned, organised life, not Alexander himself. And once you have structure back he will never cross your mind again. But listen to me, trying to give advice. How bonkers is that? Come on, we need to talk about something else apart from our pasts. Ooh! I know what I wanted to say to you – that business with Iballa saying Mum feels guilty about taking Dad to England. It doesn't make sense at all.'

'I was thinking the same because if it was up to Mum, she would have loved to stay here in Tenerife when she first met Dad. Living and working on the island would have been her dream. No, I'm one hundred per cent sure it was Dad's choice to leave.'

'I agree, but if that's the truth, then what is Mum's problem? Why has she refused to come and visit since Dad's death? There's something we're missing here, and I think it's right under our noses.'

Chapter 16

Last night in the apartment had been a real downer for Sarah and Debbie and even today in the bakery Sarah was struggling to be upbeat and positive. She could tell she wasn't herself as even Ruben was quiet with her and keeping out of her way. To be honest, she just wanted the day to end. Ergual had popped in a couple of times to pick up orders but hadn't said more than two words to either her or Ruben. The one thing that she was pleased about was the fact that Debbie was planning to sort out all the arrangements for their mum coming to stay. It gave Debbie something to focus on and distract her, which was much needed.

The one thing Sarah wasn't prepared for when she agreed to look after the bakery was the amount of people who would want to talk about her dad. It was lovely how everyone had nice things to say about him but the constant reminders of him just made her miss him more, especially on days like today when she was feeling low. Oh, she just needed the day to end and then tomorrow she would give herself a good talking to and snap out of this mood. Looking at the clock she saw that it was nearly two-thirty, which meant it was time to start clearing things away, and condensing what bread and cakes were left in the display. As she went to get a bucket of soapy water she took the opportunity to apologise to Ruben.

'I'm so sorry about today and I promise you I'll be back to normal tomorrow. It's just that everything seems to have caught up with me and though normally I could snap out of it, today I can't find the energy so I've been a miserable old thing.'

'We all have days like that,' Ruben said kindly, 'and it likely doesn't help that every other customer who walks into the shop asks about Iballa, so you have to keep repeating yourself. I have the same problem walking home from here; everyone stops me to see how the operation has gone.'

'Yes, and also people want to talk about my dad and though their intentions are good, it's emotionally draining. I just need to switch off from it all and I'll be fine. I need to escape from Kalanchoe for a bit, I think.'

'I can help with that. How about I borrow my dad's car this evening and we go up to a little village in the hills I know? There's a restaurant there where we won't be stopped and asked any questions, plus the food is gorgeous.'

'I would really like that, but would I be able to go back to the apartment and shower first?'

'Of course!' Ruben smiled and she could see she had taken him by surprise by saying yes and being so enthusiastic.

'Right then, let's get cleared up. I think we could stand to close early today as all the orders have been picked up and you're all prepared for tomorrow. Fingers crossed we'll be out of here before Ergual comes for the takings.'

****

Stood in her bedroom trying to decide what to wear, Sarah still couldn't believe she had agreed to a date with Ruben. Ok, he hadn't technically used the word 'date', but that's what it was. This wasn't like last time when they went for a drink after work. No, this was planned.

She was on the third dress in as many minutes and decided it had to do. The indecision was making her crazy! Putting the final touches on her makeup she prepared to face Debbie, who was treating her night out as the beginning of a big love affair.

'You look gorgeous!' Debbie said with a squeal. 'How on earth have you managed to get a tan when all you've done since we've been here is work? And where are you going on your date?'

'It's not a date, just a meal out to get away from Kalanchoe. Ruben's taking me to a restaurant up in the hills somewhere – I didn't ask where – just to get away from everyone stopping me and asking questions.'

'Lovely. I'm pleased you're getting away and having some fun.'

'I think it will be nice and a complete change, which is the part I'm looking forward to the most. Before I go, I've been meaning to ask if you've decided what to do about Pedro. You can't keep putting him off.'

'I know. I need to stop making excuses and see him. Tomorrow it is his day off so I'll text him and see if he wants to spend the day with me.'

'That's a good idea, and of course the answer will be yes.'

'Enough about me. This is your night away from all of it and you look lovely so go and have fun. And I mean it! Enjoy yourself, you deserve it.'

As Sarah closed the front door behind her she felt so nervous. She had been working with Ruben for days now and it wasn't as though she didn't know anything about him. But thinking that ... did she really know him apart from the fact that he worked in the bakery and didn't get on with Ergual? She got to the main gate and could see him stood next to a red car. He looked very smart and she was so glad she had gone to the effort of looking nice.

'Hi, Ruben, are you ok?'

'Yes, are you ready to go and are you still happy to go up to the little village?'

'Yes, definitely.'

'Then hop in. It should only take twenty minutes to get there, and I must warn you it's a bit rustic – the restaurant that is, not the village.'

'It sounds perfect. I'm looking forward to seeing it and of course food is involved so really, what's not to love?'

'Most of the village residents have shops, restaurants, or businesses around the island, but choose to live up in the village as they have more land than they would living in a town. Plus there's the best bit: it's really quiet.'

It surprised Sarah how talkative and relaxed Ruben was. It made her feel more and more comfortable. As they drove along the roads were getting less busy and there were fewer buildings either side.

'I'll warn you, Sarah, a few of the older locals who don't leave the village very often will likely be intrigued to know who you are. But I promise it's all in a nice way. They're just not used to seeing me up there with anyone other than my family.'

'That's fine. You have four siblings, right?'

'Two of each and I'm right in the middle, child number three. It was a very busy but happy time when we were all young. My parents didn't have a lot of money and they worked long hours so we children sort of entertained ourselves.'

'That's nice. I just have the one sister. Sorry, of course you already know that, from when we came here on holiday.'

They both laughed.

'It's a shame the bakery is keeping you busy and you can't spend more time together, as that must have been the purpose of your holiday?' Ruben suggested.

'That's ok. She's keeping busy as well. She's actually just started repainting the apartment. The place hasn't had anything done to it for many years so Debbie's going to work her way through and freshen up every wall with a coat or two of paint.'

'It sounds like you both have come for a rest and holiday but have ended up working. That's such a shame! You need to make sure you both have fun at some point,' he said kindly as they made a turn.

'Here we are! See what I mean about the space up here? You wouldn't get so much land down in the towns. The only downside is that you need to have transport to go anywhere. Right, hold on, the road – or should I say "track" – is a little rough and bumpy. I did warn you it's rustic,' he added before they finally pulled to a stop.

'Yes, but also gorgeous! Look at the tables under the trees; it's very romantic.'

Ruben had parked the car next to half a dozen others and before they were able to get out a man had come out to greet them. He clearly knew Ruben and asked how his parents and family were.

'Sarah, this is Alejandro, he owns the restaurant.'

'Welcome! Is it your first time to Tenerife?'

'No, I've been coming here all my life. My aunt and uncle own the bakery in Kalanchoe.'

'Ancor and Iballa! I know them. How are they?'

'Fine, thank you.'

Sarah wasn't going to mention Iballa's operation as the whole point of coming up here was to get away from all the questions.

'Please come this way. Now, would you like to eat indoors or out here under the trees?'

'You choose, Sarah.'

'Outdoors, please. It's such a lovely evening so it would be a shame to sit indoors.'

Alejandro led them to a little table in the corner of the garden. There were menus there already and he asked them what they would like to drink.

'As I'm driving, I'll just have a small glass of white wine please, and for you, Sarah?'

'The same, please. Thank you.'

'You're sure this is ok here for you?' Ruben asked as Alejandro went to grab their drinks.

'Definitely. It's a lovely place and I'm sure the food will be delicious.'

They both picked up their menus and the conversation stopped momentarily. Sarah didn't have a clue what she was reading as her mind wasn't on the dishes but on the situation she was in. She couldn't help but smile.

'What are you smiling about?' Ruben asked.

'Oh, nothing really, now talk me through the menu. What should I be eating? You must have some favourite dishes.'

'I absolutely do. I never have fish here – I save that for when I'm down somewhere by the sea – and I would definitely recommend that whatever you have you must get the Canaria potatoes to go with it. The lamb stew is lovely, it's slow cooked and just melts in the mouth, but go for what you want as everything is nice.'

'Are you both ready to order?' Alejandro asked when he came back with the drinks.

'I'm having the lamb,' Ruben said confidently. 'I know I have it every time I come here, but it is just so good.'

'As you like it so much, I'll have the same,' Sarah said, smiling.

Their order taken, Sarah went off to the restroom to wash her hands and stopped to speak to Alejandro on the way back.

'You have a lovely restaurant. It's so peaceful up here in the hills and I'm so glad Ruben suggested coming here.'

'Thank you, that's very kind of you to say. If you don't mind me mentioning it, Ruben is a very nice young man, and I don't think I've ever seen him look so happy as he does tonight.'

Sarah could feel herself blushing and gave a smile before heading back outside to Ruben. Before she sat down she moved her chair slightly so she wouldn't have to be looking at him straight on. She made an excuse that she wanted to take in the view of the garden and she hoped Ruben believed her. She couldn't tell him the truth, which was that it felt a bit too intensely romantic to stare into his eyes across the table. When the food arrived she ordered another glass of wine and Ruben had some water as he was driving.

'This is gorgeous, Ruben, the lamb is just so succulent. Most of the time when Debbie and I go out to eat I have fish or pasta, so this makes such a lovely change. As does this restaurant. My dad would have loved it up here. He was always one for escaping somewhere quiet – that's why as children we went over to La Caleta a lot – and of course his favourite thing was to sit in the bakery café at night chatting to Ancor.'

'Yes, it was a huge shock and a massive upset to Ancor when your dad died. This might sound silly but I think a bit of Ancor died as well. He gave up a little with the bakery, certainly, but he's also lost a lot of his get up and go spirit, and I know Iballa worries about him. I think it will do both him and Iballa a lot of good seeing your mum. It will help having someone different for them to chat to.'

'Yes, I hope so. Getting my mum to come here has been a huge effort, but that's another story. Now, tell me about you. I know about your family but do you like working at the bakery or would you sooner be doing something else? Are you staying because you know Ancor can't manage without you?'

There was a silence as Ruben seemed to take forever to drink his glass of water. Had Sarah pushed him into a corner with all her questions? Should she apologise and change the subject? Just as she was about to speak he finally answered.

'I enjoy working in the bakery and especially for Ancor and Iballa. They have been so good to me; they treat me well and pay me a good wage with bonuses, which is lovely because it means I can help my parents out with a little extra cash from time to time. I suppose the reason I stay is because I don't have any ambition in me to do anything else. But I don't see that as a problem as not everyone can take on the world. Some of us are plodders and I'm happy plodding.'

'You're definitely not a plodder! You're more than capable of running the bakery with your eyes closed and one hand tied behind your back. It's not your fault Ancor treats you as if it's your first day. He seems to forget all he's taught you and instead of interfering he should just leave you to get on and run things.'

'Thank you, that's very kind of you to say. One of the first things I learned working at the bakery is that Ancor is very ... let's just say he's not open for suggestions and likes to do things the way they've always been done. I'm not sure, perhaps change scares him a little.'

'Yes, I hadn't realised until this visit how controlling my uncle is. Having witnessed it for myself it makes me feel a little sorry for Ergual. I understand now why they aren't working together, but it's still sad.'

'Yes, it is, especially with how much Iballa has been suffering with her health the last few years. But sadly I don't think anyone will ever change Ancor. But enough of that as we've come up here to get away from any bakery chat. Tell me about your life in England ... but only if you want to of course,' he quickly added.

'I don't mind telling you about it, Ruben. I've always had ambition, tons of it – probably far too much, if I'm honest. I wanted a fabulous, successful business and Alexander and I were heading that way until he messed up. But I'm beginning to think it was my ambition that pushed him to it. Perhaps it would have been better if I had followed your lead and been more of a plodder. I'm sorry, I don't want to put a downer on our evening. Debbie is also going through a major upset in her life and she's not coping very well so I spend my time trying to make her feel better, which doesn't leave a lot of energy for putting a positive spin on my own situation and uncertain future.'

'That's kind of you to be there for Debbie, but you also need to think of your own future.'

'I know, but I really haven't a clue where to start. I also don't know if my ambitious days are over. Perhaps instead of the success I've always dreamed of, all I need to be happy is a simple life, a quiet, steady one.'

There was a silence and for the first time since Ruben picked her up the smile disappeared off his face. He suddenly looked quite serious.

'Sarah, you could have that quiet, steady life in a heartbeat. You could stay here in Tenerife, have Iballa's job running the bakery with Ancor, and we could drive up here every night to eat dinner. Now, is there any chance you'll consider turning your chair back towards me so I can look into your gorgeous eyes?'

Sarah's heartbeat raced as she looked at Ruben. Was he suggesting that he wanted to play a part in the future he'd just described for her?

Chapter 17

Debbie was so cross with herself. She had fallen asleep before Sarah got in from her date with Ruben last night and her sister had already left to go to the bakery before she woke up this morning, meaning she would have to wait until tonight to find out how it went. She supposed she could nip around to the bakery on her way to meet Pedro but it would likely be very awkward for Sarah to speak as Ruben would be in the next room. No, she'd wait it out. She just hoped their night out was a success.

The plan was to spend most of the day on the beach with Pedro. Once the sun went down they would go for something to eat and she was excited to spend the time with him. She'd already decided that she was not going to mention the job offer from Bentor. She wasn't taking him up on it so there was no need for Pedro to know anything about it.

It was a shorts and t-shirt day but she put a bit of effort into her hair because she wanted to look nice for Pedro. Once her bag was packed with everything she would need she sent a quick text to Pedro to say she was just leaving, and she would see him at the beach café in forty-five minutes.

As she headed out of Kalanchoe and onto the coastal path it suddenly hit her how comfortable she was starting to feel here. It was just like the old days when she was working here. Was that because she was off to meet Pedro? Or just because she actually had a day of activities planned rather than how she usually spent her time: sitting around and moping. Whatever it was, she was feeling happy.

As she got near to the beach café her phone beeped with a text from Pedro to say he would be a little late as he had to take something into the restaurant first. She decided to wait for him inside with a coffee.

She grabbed a table and when the waitress came to greet her and take her order, she realised it was the same woman who had served her the last time she was here. The woman who had mentioned she didn't get on with Ergual.

'You're back!' the waitress said with a smile. 'What can I get you?'

'Could I just have a black coffee, please? I'm waiting for someone and they shouldn't be long.'

'Of course,' she said, hurrying off to grab it.

'There you go, one coffee,' she said, stooping to clear the table next to Debbie's. 'So, have you decided whether or not to stay on the island? Perhaps your old job would have you back.'

'Oh no, I couldn't go back to that. It was in a club and with the kids getting younger every year it would make me feel so old!' She laughed. 'Anyway, the owner I worked for sold it and now has a restaurant in Tillandsia.'

'You must mean Bentor.'

'Yes, that's right, do you know him? That's probably a silly question, isn't it? Everyone seems to know everyone when they work in the restaurant industry here.'

'So true. Bentor is one of the good ones and I'm really happy for him. He works hard and treats his staff as if they are family. Please excuse me, I think I'm needed over there and that sounds like your phone.'

Looking at the screen Debbie saw it was her mum calling.

'Hi, Mum, everything ok? I expect you're getting excited about coming over here? Not long now.'

'Yes, just a few more days and I think I'm all organised and ready. I'm calling because it suddenly hit me that I don't know if Iballa knows I'm coming. More importantly, does she know I'll be there to take care of her? Because when I spoke to Ancor yesterday he didn't mention it.'

'I'm not sure, Mum. I've not said anything to Aunt or Uncle, but I thought Sarah might have. Either way, I'm sure it's fine. I know they will both be so excited to have you here. Oh, sorry, I'm going to have to go as Pedro's just arrived. I'll get Sarah to give you a call tonight.'

'Thank you, darling, and please give my love to Pedro. Have a nice day.'

'Hi, Pedro, my mum sends her love,' she said, waving her phone. 'I'll just pay for my coffee and then I'm ready to get going.'

They had decided to go on the same bit of beach they went to the other day as it had been nice and quiet. Pedro had stopped and bought some treats for them to eat but he wouldn't say what they were and the anticipation was nearly killing Debbie by the time they got to their part of the beach and found two sun loungers.

'Before you get sand on your hands, here is your first treat,' Pedro said as he opened his bag and handed Debbie a paper bag.

'Aww, you remembered that a bacon and cheese croissant is one of my favourite things! Thank you so much.'

'Of course, I remembered! It was the one thing you loved to start your day with.'

'Yes, and it's my first one since I've been back. I had hoped my uncle's bakery would have started selling them, but sadly no.'

'Is your sister still at the bakery or has Ancor come back?'

'No, she's still there and enjoying it. I think it has something to do with Ruben working there.'

'He's a nice chap, very clever.'

133

'Yes, he is, but what do you mean by clever?'

'I guess I just mean that he plays the game. He enjoys his job but doesn't get involved with all Ergual's dramas. Your cousin is so spoiled that even friends of his tell him so. He really needs something to focus on instead of spending his days going between businesses where his friends work and having coffees and lunches. He's wasting his life away.'

Neither of them had anything to add to that so they sat and ate their croissants, chatting about the beach and the weather for a bit until they decided to go in the sea.

'I promise I'll be careful this time, and they'll be no slipping,' Debbie joked.

'That's not a problem. Like I said, I'm here to catch you.'

He smiled, and she knew he meant every word.

****

They swam in silence for a while, exchanging the odd glance, and once back on the sun loungers drying off in the gorgeous sunshine, the conversation was all about the old days when they had worked together. They reminisced about big nights in the club, the parties they went to, and, of course, the bad heads from all the partying. Debbie was thankful there was no mention of Bentor and his new cocktail bar, and presumed that meant that Pedro hadn't yet been told that he wouldn't be running it.

'Treat number two,' Pedro announced, jolting her out of her thoughts.

'Sorry, what did you say?'

Pedro pulled out a bag and handed it to her.

'What's this?'

'Open it and see.'

She did and then nearly squealed with delight.

'My favourite sweets! I've not had these since I worked here.'

'I thought so. That's why I was late meeting you; I nipped into Las America, to your favourite sweet shop.'

'That's really kind. You didn't need to do that.'

'I wanted to. It all adds to this lovely day.'

'I'm well and truly spoiled. Please tell me you don't have a big bowl of chips with a ton of mayonnaise on them in your bag as well,' she joked.

They both laughed.

Debbie knew she looked just as happy as Pedro. This was the perfect day.

****

A few hours later all the sweets had been eaten between them as Debbie had insisted Pedro should share them with her.

'Did you want to go to a café for some chips, Debbie?'

'Thank you for the offer but I'm quite happy staying here for a few more hours if that's ok with you. I'm not saying chips won't be involved later in the day though.'

'Sounds good to me. It's so nice having you back here in Tenerife and more than that I hope being here is helping you to recover.'

'"Recover" really sums it up, doesn't it? I was damaged by the last few years and as my time here goes on I'm happy to say that I think less and less about Steven. I think once Mum gets here and Iballa comes back from having her operation any thoughts of England will be few and far between.'

'Does that mean you might decide to stay here? I know I shouldn't put you on the spot like this, it's just ... I would really like it if you did stay. You could take Bentor up on his offer of a job!'

Did this mean that Pedro knew about the job offer? But why was he being so nice about it when he really wanted it?

'Sorry, what do you mean?'

'Bentor would love to have you back and has always said there would be a job for you in the restaurant if you want it. Perhaps you could have my job when I go and run the cocktail bar!' he said, getting excited by the idea.

So he didn't know about the offer after all.

'No talk of my future, please, Pedro. I don't want to spoil our lovely day.'

'Sorry I didn't mean to pressure you. I was just hoping we could have a lot more special days like this.'

'So do I, Pedro. I really do.'

Chapter 18

After being out with Pedro the day before Debbie was spending the day getting as much painting done as she could. Thankfully in the Tenerife heat the walls dried so quickly she was able to go back and give them a second coat within hours. With a bit of luck all of the lounge and kitchen area would be finished before her mum arrived in two days' time, as she wanted the place to be sparkling and clean.

It had been nice to spend time on the beach with Pedro and they'd had a lovely meal afterwards where they had sat at the table for ages. The day just flew by, and she was already looking forward to Pedro's next day off.

The one thing that niggled was the fact that she still hadn't been able to chat to Sarah about her night out with Ruben. It was so odd. Here they were in the same apartment but they were constantly like passing ships. Thankfully, all would be revealed later on as she'd had a text from her sister confirming she'd be home for dinner tonight. Sarah had also told her she had told Ancor about Gina coming to stay and help look after Iballa, and he had said they were both over the moon about it and couldn't wait to get back to Tenerife.

Several hours later the lounge was finished and everything had been cleaned to an inch of its life. Gina's room was all made up and ready for her, and it would just need a wipe around with a damp cloth in the morning before she arrived.

Debbie had a quick shower and was just preparing to go food shopping when her phone beeped with a text from Pedro thanking her again for a lovely day yesterday and saying he couldn't wait until they could do it all again. She messaged back and said she was looking forward to it as well. As she had her phone in her hand she texted Sarah to ask if pasta would be ok for her tonight. The text back said 'yes' in capital letters next to multiple emojis of wine bottles.

As she locked the apartment door behind her she thought to herself that just a few months ago she could never have dreamed about the relationship she and her sister now had. It made her feel really like everything was falling into place. The horrible two years were slowly disappearing into the past, though she still didn't know what the future had in store for her.

****

Back in the apartment she put all the shopping away then poured a glass of wine and went and sat in her favourite place on the balcony. Sarah should be back soon and she couldn't wait to hear all about her date. She also wanted to tell her about the time she had spent with Pedro. Looking at her phone she saw she had a text from Rebecca asking how she was and for the first time here in Tenerife she could answer positively by saying she was really good.

'Hi, Debbie, I'm back!' Sarah called as she came through the door. 'Well look at this. You've finished the painting – congratulations! This room looks so fresh and light ... and somehow bigger.'

'I've enjoyed doing it and to be honest it took no time at all. I'm just hoping Mum will be ok with it. How has the world of bread been today?'

'Ok, actually. Let me just get rid of the smell of the bakery and then I'll be back to tell you all about it. I also want to hear about what you and Pedro have been up to.'

'Forget me and Pedro; I want to hear about your

138

date up in the hills with Ruben!'

'Oh, I'm not sure I'm ready to talk about that...' She winked. 'Only joking, let me get showered and changed.'

Debbie's phone beeped again a few minutes later, this time with a text from Jenny. She had obviously heard from Rebecca and wanted to know if Debbie's feeling 'really good' had anything to do with Pedro. The message made her laugh.

'What are you laughing about?' Sarah asked, running her hands through her wet hair as she stepped out onto the balcony.

'Oh, nothing, just my friends back in England wanting to know why I'm happy all of a sudden.'

'I could ask the same, but I think I know the answer.'

'Enough of that. I want you to tell me about dinner with Ruben.'

'We had such a lovely evening. The food was phenomenal, and the setting in the village with the views was perfect. It was nice to get to sit and chat with Ruben and we've been getting on really well at the bakery ever since. I think it really annoys Ergual as he makes a face at us every time he comes to pick up an order, but I swear it's just timing. We aren't laughing and joking all the time but it seems to happen right at the moments when he walks in. I think Ruben gets a kick out of it,' she said ruefully.

'I need more details about the meal, Sarah!'

Sarah laughed. 'I already told you! We had a wonderful time and Ruben was so different – chatty, not shy or nervous. I think we'll do it again at some point; we just need to juggle things when Mum comes. Talking of that, I know she'll be spending a lot of time with Iballa but we need to pin her down at some point and get to the bottom of what happened in the past and why she won't come here.'

With that there was a knock at the door. Sarah

went to answer it and seeing it was Ergual she realised she should have grabbed the bag with the day's takings from where she'd dropped it when she got home, so she wouldn't have to invite him in.

'Hi, Ergual. Come in, I just need to get the money for you.'

'Thanks, I also have news – Mum is on the mend and she could be back here in a few days. There's also something else—'

'Why don't you go through onto the balcony to say hi to Debbie?' Sarah said, cutting him off. 'I'll just grab the money for you. I won't be a minute.'

'You've been decorating,' he said as he stepped into the apartment, taking in the refreshed walls. 'It looks like a different room entirely, very modern.'

'Debbie's been busy giving everywhere a fresh look. I think she just has our rooms left to do.'

Sarah went to her room and Ergual walked out to see Debbie.

'Hi, Ergual, how is Aunt Iballa doing? Any news of her return to Tenerife?'

'Dad's hopeful they'll be back in a few days. I love what you've done with the apartment.'

'Thank you,' she said, a bit surprised by the compliment. 'I can't believe how quick it was to do. That's great news about Iballa. Mum will be here this week so the timings have worked out ok.'

'Here you go,' Sarah said, handing over the cash pouch. 'You mentioned you had something to tell us?' she prompted.

'My dad thinks that as Gina is coming you should have time off, away from the bakery, to spend with her, and so he suggested that until he gets back, I should work in the shop.'

This was a shock to Sarah. Of course this was the way things should have gone from the start, but given how well she'd been doing – not to mention how much she was enjoying the time with Ruben –

she was hesitant to walk away.

'Oh … are you sure? If you don't mind me saying, communication is so important in the role and with you not really talking to Ruben... And I'm sorry, I don't mean this in a horrible way, but I'm not sure you would enjoy talking to the customers either.'

'You're right, I would hate everything about being there. But if I don't do it my dad won't be happy.'

'Look, there has to be a solution that pleases everyone. Why don't we sort of do it between us? You could pop in for an hour or so each day and that way you would be doing what Ancor asked. There must be little jobs that you could do around the bakery and I know the shut up café could do with a sweep and a dust, especially the outside part. That way you wouldn't need to deal with customers or Ruben.'

There was a silence and Sarah could see he was thinking about it.

'Are you sure? I have to admit I have noticed how the café looks a mess, very sad and neglected.'

'Can I butt in?' Debbie ventured. 'It's such a shame the café isn't open. It brings back so many memories of happy times. Perhaps when Iballa is fitter and able to move around they might reopen it.'

'It's so dated and old fashioned though. My dad's never done anything with it.'

'That's because he's been so busy with the bakery; he doesn't have a spare minute. It just needs someone to show an interest in it and modernising the place would bring in a good income,' Sarah said.

'Change the café? You must be joking. That's never going to happen, not as long as my dad has a say. Look, I need to be going. So the plan is you just carry on as you've been doing, and I'll pop in each day and work to tidy the café up?'

Sarah nodded.

'Fine.'

With that he left. No 'thank you' or 'goodbye' or anything.

'I admire your patience, Sarah. I don't think I could be as nice to him after he's been horrible to you and Ruben these last few weeks.'

'I know, but like the old saying goes: two wrongs don't make a right. It's just so annoying that he and Ancor don't see that he could be running that café and earning a good income from it.'

'Well, that's never going to happen, by the sounds of it.'

'I don't know, I'm beginning to think there's a lot more to what's going on at the bakery than what we see on the surface. I think we see things with Ancor perhaps differently than they actually are...'

Chapter 19

It was the day Gina was scheduled to arrive and as Sarah was working in the bakery it was left to Debbie to meet her at the airport, which wasn't a problem.

She was waiting at the bus stop to get the bus into Las Cristianos, where she would then get another one to the airport – coming back, they would just get a taxi – and reading a text from Pedro asking when they could spend some more time together. She really wished she could give him an answer but until her mum had settled in and they knew what was happening with Iballa, she couldn't. She thought it would be easier to explain that on a call so while she was waiting for the second bus she gave him a ring.

'Morning, Pedro, how are you?'

'I'm fine, just walking to work. It's nice to hear your voice. Are you excited to see your mum?'

'I am, actually. It will be nice to have her here on the island, but I'm feeling a little bit like Sarah, in that having her here will mean finally starting to face up to our future. Mum is sure to ask what we've decided we want to do when we leave the island, where we'll live and work, that sort of thing. I'm not saying she will be putting pressure on either of us, it's just that she worries, and we'll need to reassure her we're both ok.'

'Well, I'm not sure about Sarah, but I think you know what you want, Debbie, and that's to stay here in Tenerife.'

'Oh, so that's what you think? And can I ask where you got that impression from?' she said with a laugh.

'It's obvious. We enjoy our time together and when you talk about Tenerife you always have a smile on your face, whereas when you mention England, you look sad. I rest my case.'

'I've never thought about it like that. I need to go, the bus has just pulled up and there's nothing more annoying than listening to someone talking on their phone on a bus; it drives me mad. By the way, you're going to work early today. Everything ok?'

'Yes, apparently Bentor needs to have a chat with me before the other staff get in. I think it's probably about the cocktail bar and how he's going to break the news that I'll be overseeing it. I know one or two won't be happy but that's life. Enough of that though, when are we going to meet up?'

'Thanks for reminding me, that's why I called you in the first place – to say that I'll have to let you know once we know what my mum is up to. I have to go. Hope you have a nice day.'

Debbie took a deep breath as she took her seat on the bus, very aware that this was not going to be a good day for Pedro. He would be so disappointed and feel really let down by Bentor, but hopefully he would soon get over it, and as long as Bentor didn't mention he had offered her the job, things would be ok.

The bus was packed with people, bags, and suitcases, and she was beginning to think she should have got a taxi. At the airport she waited until everyone else got off first and then headed towards the arrival hall. She noticed there was a long line of waiting taxis so at least once her mum was through security they would quickly be on their way back to Kalanchoe.

The plane had just landed so she found a place to stand where she could see the arriving passengers. Stood there, it suddenly hit her like a big thundercloud: the last time she had done this

144

was when she worked on the island and waited for her mum and dad, who had come to visit. Oh how she missed him, and how lovely it would have been if he was arriving now alongside Mum. She felt a lump in her throat and tears in her eyes. She fumbled in her bag for a tissue at the same time her phone rang so she grabbed it to answer. In her haste she didn't bother to look at the caller ID, but just accepted the call.

'Hello?'

'You think you're so clever, don't you? Well it hasn't worked.'

'Pedro? What's wrong? What are you talking about?'

'Oh, come on. All the time we've spent together you've been asking questions about Bentor's new business, all so you can jump over my head and get the job that was promised to me.'

'That's absolutely not the case. I can explain but not at the moment as my mum's just walking towards me. I have to go but I'll call you later.'

She quickly took a deep breath and pulled herself together before hugging her mum who she couldn't help but notice looked very tired and worn out.

'It's so lovely to see you, Mum! Let me take your case and bag and we'll go out and get a taxi. How was your flight?'

'It was fine, darling, and don't you look well. I'm pleased to see that the rest and the sunshine have certainly worked for you.'

As they got in the taxi and told the driver where they were going Debbie's phone beeped with an incoming text and as she expected, it was from Pedro.

No need to explain. I'm just glad I now know where I stand.

She didn't reply because she didn't need the

hassle at the moment but also, she hadn't done anything wrong. Bentor was the one who offered her the job, so it was him Pedro should be getting angry with, not her.

'Nearly there,' she said to her mum. 'Sarah shouldn't be too late getting back from the bakery and hopefully by tonight we'll know when exactly Ancor and Iballa will be back in Tenerife.'

'Dare I ask how things have been with your cousin? Has he been causing any problems?'

'Ergual is a very interesting case. Once we've sorted you out in the apartment, I'll fill you in on your nephew. Please can you drop us by the big gate?' she added, addressing the cab driver. 'Mum, I'll get your bags. Here, I'll give you my key so you can open up the apartment.'

As the taxi driver got the case and bag out of the boot, Debbie's eyes were on her mum. She really looked like this was the last thing in the world she wanted to do. Debbie paid the driver and followed her mum to the gate. She knew returning to the apartment without Dad would be difficult for her mum, so she thought it best to leave her by herself for a few minutes and took the luggage into her mum's room.

'I'm just going to change my clothes,' she said when she rejoined her in the entryway. 'I won't be a moment and then I'll make us a cup of tea before filling you in on everything.'

'I think I'll change as well, actually. And would you mind if I lie down for a bit? I'm quite tired.'

'Of course! Can I get you a drink first?'

'I'll just take a glass of water in with me, but thank you, darling.'

Debbie changed her clothes and went out onto the balcony. There had been no mention from Gina about the freshly painted walls. Had she done the wrong thing in redecorating? Had it upset her

146

mum? She texted Sarah to say they were back and Gina was looking very tired and had gone for a nap. She added that they would probably have a difficult evening ahead of them given their mum's mood.

****

The afternoon ticked along and there was no sign of Gina. As Debbie was debating whether or not to finally wake her, she heard the bedroom door open, followed by the bathroom door opening and closing. So she was awake. Debbie went to put the kettle on just as the apartment door opened. Sarah was back from work.

'You have perfect timing. I've just put the kettle on, and Mum just got up. Do I spot a bag of bakery treats in your hand? This is becoming a habit.'

'Yes, and it's an extra big bag of pastries today as Mum's here. And a cup of tea sounds perfect. I'll just go and shower the smell of the bakery off. It was so hot in there today with all the ovens on all the time... Hi, Mum! Don't hug me yet, I'm very hot and smelly. Just give me five minutes and I'll be back refreshed and ready to chat.'

'Did you have a nice sleep, Mum?' Debbie asked as Sarah rushed off. 'If you want to go sit on the balcony I'll bring your tea out to you along with something delicious. One of the perks with Sarah at the bakery is all the goodies she brings back with her!'

'That sounds lovely, darling. Is there anything you'd like me to do? By the way, I'm so sorry I haven't mentioned or thanked you for what you've done with the apartment. I can't get over how bright and fresh it looks. Your dad and I always talked about updating the place but once we got here time sort of ran out on us.'

'I was happy to do it. With Sarah at the bakery it

147

gave me something to do with my time, and it was so easy. I've just got mine and Sarah's rooms to do and then I'll be finished. Now you make yourself comfortable. I'll just be two minutes.'

As Debbie put the pastries on a plate she could hear the shower going. It was good Sarah was back as conversation would be a lot easier.

'There you go, Mum, one tea. I thought we could go out to one of the restaurants here in Kalanchoe tonight, if that's ok with you?'

'Oh, I think it needs to be an early night for me. You and Sarah should go though.'

'Are you sure?'

'Yes. Now tell me all your news. Have you been to the beach much? You have a lovely tan.'

'Yes, quite a bit, but it might also be from afternoons spent here on the balcony, which is a real sun trap.'

'I'm back,' Sarah announced as she joined them, giving their mum a big hug.

'Thank you for the cakes,' Debbie said, taking a bite.

'Tell me all about the bakery, and more importantly that nephew of mine,' Gina encouraged.

'Where do I start? The bakery is ticking over nicely. I'm not really doing a lot, just serving, and all the real hard work is being done by Ruben. Ergual is also playing a part, doing the deliveries, and as the time has gone on he's becoming less rude. There's been a little hiccup in the proceedings though. Ancor wants me to take time off from the bakery to spend with you while you're here, and he wants Ergual to run the shop in my stead.'

'Imagine it,' Debbie said, 'all the hard work Sarah has put in over the last few weeks while Ancor and Iballa have not been here and now Ergual is going to go in and upset everything – and that would be before he even comes in contact with the customers!'

Tears suddenly appeared in their mum's eyes and she looked so sad.

'Is everything ok? Is there something wrong?' Sarah asked anxiously.

'I'm ok, darling, it's just odd being back here. My head is a little all over the place as my thoughts go back to the past. I can't help but think how life would be if things had been different.'

'What do you mean?' Debbie asked.

'If your dad and I had stayed here in Tenerife and not moved back to the UK. But enough of that. I want to hear all about what you've been up to.'

There was an awkward silence and before either of the sisters could speak Gina answered her own unasked question.

'Would I be right in thinking you've both filled your days keeping busy with the bakery and the decorating? Is that because you don't want to think about or plan your futures, or is it that you think leaving Alexander and Steven was the wrong thing to do? Are you regretting those decisions?'

Another long silence ensued, both sisters waiting for the other to speak first.

'My darlings, please take your time with this. There's no point rushing into anything because the last thing you both need in years to come is to have regrets. I know that from experience.'

Chapter 20

Sarah was at the bakery very early. She hadn't slept at all even though it had been very late when she and Debbie went to bed. They had talked for hours about Gina getting upset and had both come to the conclusion that something had definitely happened in the past – before she and their dad had moved to England – to have upset her.

'Good morning, Sarah,' Ruben said, startling her. 'You're here early ... not that it's a problem, of course. Are you ok?'

'Yes, fine, thank you. I just couldn't sleep.'

'Has your mum settled in ok? It must be nice for you and your sister to have her here.'

'Yes, she has. By the way, I have some news. The good news is that Ancor and Iballa will be back in a couple of days, and the not so good news is that we have help in the bakery today. Ergual is coming to work with us. He's going to sort the café out by giving it a clean... Why are you smiling like that?'

'You know why. For a start, Ergual doesn't know one end of a broom from another, and for the other, he's never done a day's work in his life, apart from delivering a few orders. There is no way he's going to lower himself to be a cleaner. I suspect he'll storm in here, wait until all the baking is done, and then send me in to do the cleaning.'

'I'm going to stop you right there, Ruben. That's not going to happen. Something tells me that as much as we don't want him around, when he is here, he will get on with sorting the place out. Now, time to get the show on the road.'

'Before we get going, there's one more thing. As Ancor will be back soon does that mean we won't see one another? You have your mum here and before you know it your holiday will have flown by, and you'll be heading back to England.'

'I don't really know what to say, Ruben, as I'm not even sure how long my mum will want to stay. But I can say that while I'm here in Kalanchoe, even if I'm not in the bakery, I would still like to see you and spend time with you... I think that's the door,' she said, turning towards the shop. 'Hi, Ergual, you're early.'

'Yes, I thought I would get the cleaning up done on the café terrace before everyone comes out and starts asking me what I'm up to. You know how nosey the regulars all are. Now, where are the things I need?'

Sarah smiled as Ruben led him to the cleaning cupboard and silently pointed everything out. She couldn't wait to see the transformation in the café.

****

'Thanks again, Ruben, I'll see you in the morning and I promise I won't be in as early to disturb you,' Sarah said as the day came to a close. Ruben had cleaned up and was preparing to head off to meet his mum and dad.

'You weren't disturbing me. It was nice having you here. Have a nice evening, Sarah.'

As Sarah finished tidying up the now silent bakery, the door opened and in walked Debbie.

'Hi! I've nearly done here so I'll walk back with you. How is Mum today? Has she mentioned how she's feeling or why she got upset?'

'No, but she did go out for a walk. I offered to go with her but she said she would be ok by herself, which I'm taking as a positive. I've just nipped out for some shopping as she wants to eat in the apartment tonight.' She paused, her eyes going to the shop window. 'I think that Ergual has just pulled up in the van. I'm not in the mood for him so I'll go and get the shopping and see you back at the apartment. Good luck.'

'Thanks, it will probably be short and sweet though. I might even be back before you!'

'It's a race,' Debbie joked.

Sarah was ready for her cousin. The till was cashed up and there were just a few things to switch off before she could make her escape.

'Hi, Ergual. Today's takings are all ready for you. They're over on the counter there. Were the deliveries all ok? There are quite a lot for tomorrow; I think it'll be at least three trips.'

Ergual didn't respond, just stood at the door. She could see he looked uncomfortable for some reason. Had something happened? As he hadn't made a move to go over and pick up the day's takings, she did it instead.

'There you go. Well, I think I'm done here for the day so I'll be heading off.'

'Do you have a few minutes to spare?' he suddenly asked.

'Of course,' she said, even if she didn't entirely mean it. 'What do you need?'

'Would you come into the café with me? I'd like to show you something.'

'I saw all the bags of rubbish you carried around the back and I have to admit that Ruben and I took a peek in while you were out. It's looking really good and I think your dad will be pleased.'

'No, it's not that.'

With that he opened the connecting door and she followed him through.

'It's looking so much better, Ergual, you have really done a great job to improve it.'

'Yes, it's cleaner, but it's also still very old fashioned and dated. If this was your café, what would you do with it?'

'Well, given that it hasn't changed at all since I was a child, I don't think a simple coat of paint would help. It needs a few things ripped out, such as the old shelves on the back wall, and the mirrors and pictures that have faded in the sun. Once that was done, I think I would possibly have to have a few of the walls redone as that stipple effect is well horrible. I know it was probably the height of fashion when it was first done, but there could potentially be some nice brickwork hidden underneath it. For the outside terrace, I'd get smaller tables as those are far too big. You just need enough room on them for a couple of coffees and some plates of cake. Am I going on too much?'

'No, you're fine, and I have to agree with you. It's so dated and needs more than paint. What do you think about the kitchen?' he asked, leading her in that direction.

She followed him into the kitchen and they both stood looking around the room. It was huge, and again very dated. It crossed her mind that, if tested, most of the equipment would likely be condemned, but then a lot of it hadn't been used for decades because they didn't serve full meals.

'This really takes me back. Can you remember when we were children – and I mean really young – how this was where all the family meals were cooked by our grandmother? If I close my eyes, I can still smell the food. Those were special times, easier times ... happier times.'

She started to cry and before she knew it Ergual had pulled a chair over for her to sit down.

'I'm sorry. I didn't mean to get upset but life really was simpler then, not like now where my life's a complete mess.'

'Don't be sorry. I have to agree that life was better then. Being a child was far easier than having to deal with things as an adult. Being a grown-up is a nightmare.'

With that they both laughed and for the first time she actually felt sorry for him, but she knew that wouldn't last long because no doubt he would start to be nasty again.

'Now, this kitchen. Apart from getting rid of everything in here and starting again, I was thinking it's far too big. The bread and cakes are cooked next door in the bakery so an oven isn't really needed, so perhaps we could replace it with a couple of microwaves and a hob or grill for warming things up. And of course we'd have a coffee machine, but none of that would take up much room.'

'Are you thinking of making the kitchen a lot smaller?'

'Yes. If that wall came down,' he said, pointing, 'we could add at least six to eight extra tables, if we go with the smaller ones, as you suggested.'

'That's a really good idea and would work well. Why don't we continue this outside? I could do with some fresh air as it's really stuffy and claustrophobic in this kitchen.'

He unlocked the door out onto the little terrace and once out there he turned to look at the front of the building. She turned around as well.

'It could look really nice with a little love and attention, and become a lovely little business and more importantly, a very profitable one,' she said.

'Yes, but I know what you're probably thinking – that the last person to ever make a success of it would be me – nasty, rude Ergual.'

'No ... well yes...' she fumbled. 'Look, cards on the table, Ergual. You've made it very clear that you don't want to work in the bakery and you don't like being in Kalanchoe. You also don't really like people... No, that's unfair of me to say. What I mean is that you aren't naturally one for dealing with customers, and if you did decide to take this on, everything would have to change. You would have to become a completely different person and the big question is whether that's possible.'

'Yes, that is one of the problems. But we both know there's an even bigger one: my dad.'

'Surely not. He would be happy to have you run the café.'

'Yes, but his problem would be change. He wouldn't allow even a picture to be taken down, let alone a wall. In his mind it has to stay the same as how his grandfather had it.'

'I'm sure you're wrong, Ergual. He would be happy the business was reopened and making money.'

'No, he's always been opposed to the idea of change. It was the main reason your dad left and moved to England. He was bright and could see things had to move with the times, but Dad and Granddad were having none of it and still to this day he hasn't changed his opinion. Thanks for giving me the time to talk through some potential options. You've given me a lot to think about.'

As Sarah said goodbye and started to walk back to the apartment, she was confused. How had she never known this about her dad and uncle? Whenever she'd seen them together, they were so close and happy. She had never seen or heard them have a cross word. No, Ergual must have got it all wrong. But had he? Could this be something to do with her mum not wanting to come back to Tenerife?

Chapter 21

'Good morning, Mum, did you sleep ok?'

'Yes, thank you, darling. You come and sit down. Sarah left really early today and it made me think what long hours Ancor does at the bakery.'

'It's not like this every day. I think they just have a lot of orders to send out today. Now, what do you want to do today? Shall we go to the beach? Perhaps some shopping? We could have a walk and some lunch out, anywhere you choose.'

'How about I make you a coffee and we sit on the balcony and chat? You can tell me why when I phoned from England and talked to you it was always "Pedro this" and "Pedro that", but now I'm here you change the subject every time I mention his name. Has me coming here upset the apple cart? You go and sit down and decide how much you're comfortable sharing. I'll only be a couple of minutes.'

Debbie was shocked. She thought she had hidden everything quite well, but her mum had picked up on it. It wasn't that she didn't want to tell her mum about Pedro, it was just that she didn't want her mum worrying about her.

'There you go, darling, a coffee and some toast.'

'Thank you. To answer your question, Pedro and I were getting on brilliantly and enjoying days out together when he had time off. Everything was lovely and then one day Bentor offered me a job running a new cocktail bar he's opening. Of course I said no because my life isn't here, it's back in the UK, but Pedro found out and he freaked out. His problem isn't really with me, but with Bentor. I just wish he would see that.'

'So why is he cross with you? I don't understand.'

'Because he thought the position was already his and when he found out I was offered the job and didn't tell him, he accused me of spending time with him purely so I could work my way into the job, not because I wanted to be with him.'

'Oh dear, that's such a shame. You've been such good friends for many years, so you would think he'd give you the benefit of the doubt.'

'What do you think I should do about Pedro?'

There was a long silence before eventually Gina spoke.

'I actually don't think Pedro comes into the equation. My question is: why aren't you accepting the job? We both know you could do it with your eyes closed, but more than that, darling, you would love it.'

'I didn't accept it because my life's back in England, not here in Tenerife.'

'Are you sure? The job is perfect and you have a home here, something you don't have back in the UK. You're on the mend now and this would be a fantastic next step. Promise me you'll at least think about it?'

'Ok, I'll think about it,' Debbie said hesitantly.

'Good. Now we just have to figure out something for Sarah. Your sister is doing everything possible to block out what happened with Alexander and she's avoiding facing up to the future. I'm not saying she hasn't been a huge help to Ancor and Iballa, and I know she's loved doing it, but under all that toughness she gives off is a very shattered young lady who is scared. She's not as strong and resilient as you are. I also don't like that she's still in contact with Alexander, helping him with any issues he has with the greeting card business. Now, I think we should go out for the day. A walk to La Caleta and a little lunch will give us time to put a plan of action together.'

'A plan for what?'

'How we can help your sister and point her in the right direction – aka the complete opposite one from Alexander.'

****

They took their time walking to La Caleta and for a while at least there was no talk of either Sarah or Debbie's future. They did touch on the past and how they used to do this walk when the girls were young, but Debbie avoided asking if her mum was comfortable being back on the island. All in all there were a lot of things not being talked about, and that shouldn't be the case. Things needed to be addressed.

'Shall we find somewhere for a coffee and a cake?' Debbie ventured.

'A nice table outside looking out to sea would be perfect. Lead the way.'

They found a little café that only the locals used – little groups of elderly men chatting away all around them – and as they ordered Debbie could see her mum was in deep thought. She knew why though – this was just the type of place she would have come with Debbie's dad. They would sit for hours and her dad would inevitably join in chatting to the group of men. Debbie wanted to ask her mum if she was ok and whether she wanted to talk about it, but she didn't want to push her. Everything in its own time.

'Debbie!' a voice called from behind her and she turned to find Bentor.

'Hi, Bentor. Mum, you remember my old boss, Bentor, don't you?'

'Of course, I do, darling. Hello, have you got

time to sit and have a coffee with us? I've heard all about your new restaurant, it sounds so exciting.'

'It really is and I'm happy with how it's going.'

'Do you miss the nightclub?'

'Oh no, not one little bit. I'm far too old for all that noise now.'

Debbie wanted to ask Bentor why he had told Pedro about offering her the job, and if she had been here by herself, she would have, but it didn't feel like the right time with her mum there so she just let them carry on chatting.

'So, are you staying long, Gina?'

'I'm not sure. My sister-in-law is coming out of hospital and will need looking after but we don't know yet how long her recovery might take.'

'Well, you must come to the restaurant for dinner one night with Debbie and Sarah. I'm sure you would enjoy it.'

'Oh, definitely! I'm also looking forward to coming to your cocktail bar when it opens; I've heard a lot about it. If you'll both excuse me, I just need to pop to the bathroom. It will give you time to talk about the job you offered Debbie, and when she'll be starting.'

Debbie wanted to shout at her mum but before she could say anything Bentor spoke.

'So, your mum thinks you should take the job then? But of course you don't think you should – and you're likely annoyed that I let slip to Pedro that I had offered it to you.'

'How could you let a thing like that slip out?'

'I'm sorry, it was just … he was going on about when was it going to open and who would replace him in the restaurant and then one of the other staff overheard him and asked why they hadn't been offered the cocktail manager job, saying it wasn't fair. I'd had enough of the squabbling so I said neither of them would be having the job and that of course led them to asking who would. I said I hadn't got anyone yet as the woman I offered it to had turned me down, and, well ... that was it. Pedro instantly guessed it was you and I couldn't think of a lie quick enough. I'm sorry if it's caused problems for you, Debbie. I really didn't mean to tell anyone but they pushed me into it.'

'It just upsets me that he thinks I was using him for information with the intent of stealing the job out from under him.'

'But if you aren't taking the job then surely he can't be mad at you. It's me he should be mad at. Unless ... you're still considering it? You must be interested to have discussed it with your mum.'

'No, I just mentioned the upset with Pedro, and she said she thinks the job would be good for me.'

'I have to agree with her. You're perfect for the role. Your mum's coming back so I promise I won't mention it again. Gina, it's been lovely seeing you and hopefully I'll see you again before you leave. For now though, I need to be getting going.'

'It was so nice to see you again as well, Bentor.'

Bentor left and for a few minutes there was silence.

'Darling, I don't want to spoil the day, but I feel I need to say two things. First, the job is perfect for you, and second, if Pedro likes you and wants to have a relationship with you it shouldn't matter to him that you were offered the role. If it continues to be an issue for him, I have to say he's not the right man for you.'

Chapter 22

Today was the day Ancor and Iballa were coming back from Gran Canaria. Sarah and Ruben had been at the bakery very early as they knew it would be Ancor's first stop and they wanted to make sure everything was spotless and show that the standards hadn't dropped since he had been away. Thankfully it wasn't a busy delivery day so they could get well ahead with everything, prepping the orders for the following day before giving the bakery a deep clean.

'I've made you a coffee, Sarah, I'll leave it here on the side,' Ruben said when they were nearly finished.

'Thanks, Ruben.'

'We need to make sure to move that rack back before we leave,' he said, pointing to a rack that Sarah had moved to improve flow within the shop.

'Do you think so? It works really well there as it keeps all the orders out of the way of all the stock we have for sale. It stops any confusion.'

'I agree with you but Ancor won't like it. I know it's easier to manage and work around the way you have it but the orders have been over there on the other side since the bakery opened all those years ago and, well ... you know what your uncle's like. He doesn't like change. Everything needs to be put back to the way he had it.'

'Do you know what, I'm just going to leave everything as I've put it. It's called pushing my luck,' she joked. 'It will be interesting to see when I come back if things have moved back.'

'I'll miss having you here.'

'I'll miss it as well but with you doing the baking and Uncle running the shop I'm not really needed –

unless he goes back to doing the deliveries, then I'll come in for a few hours, I expect.'

'Oh, he will definitely do the deliveries. There's no way he'll trust Ergual to continue with that. Everything has to be done Ancor's way, even if it might not always be the easiest way.'

Ruben went back into the bakery and she started to think how right he was. Perhaps Ancor's resistance to change could explain why Ergual acted the way he did.

'Hello, Sarah. Sorry, I didn't mean to make you jump.'

'Hi, Mum. Not your fault – I was miles away. Are you off next door to Iballa's? I'll fetch you the key.'

'Yes, I thought before I start to prepare a meal for their return I would give the house a good clean. Ergual's picking them up from the airport tonight. I have to admit that I'm hoping he doesn't join us for dinner. The last thing we need is an atmosphere while Iballa's not feeling one hundred per cent.'

'I know I might regret saying this and it will come back to bite me but ... I'm starting to feel sorry for Ergual.'

'Are you? You know, your dad always said his behaviour was down to Iballa and Ancor spoiling him.'

Sarah grabbed the key from where it was stored in the back of the shop.

'There you go, Mum. Have fun and I'll see you later.'

'Fun isn't the word I would use as I'll probably have to deal with all the mess Ergual has made while they've been away. Have a nice rest of the day.'

****

Five hours later and the day had flown by. Both

Sarah and Ruben had cleaned everything to within an inch of its life and there had been no time for chatting.

'I'm off now,' Ruben said as he packed his things. I've really enjoyed our time working together. Perhaps before you go back to England, we could have another night out together?'

'Yes, I'd really like that. We deserve a night out to celebrate our success.'

As Sarah watched Ruben leave her phone rang. Seeing that it was Alexander, she declined the call. She wasn't in the mood to speak to him and though she had agreed to help him with the business, it was meant to be by text or email only. Although there had been a few times these last few weeks she would have loved to hear his voice, the bakery had thankfully kept her too busy to act on the impulse. She needed to be looking to the future, not the past.

'Hi, Ergual. I have the takings here for you; I just need to put them in a bag. Are you off to the airport now to collect your parents?'

'Thanks for this, and yes.'

'Have you had any more thoughts on the café since we spoke about it?'

'Yes, and then I put them right out of my mind as there's no point even mentioning it to my dad as I know he won't budge. He just wants to keep the whole business as if it's a museum. Right, I best get going.'

He looked sad as he closed the door behind him, and Sarah realised this was a side of her cousin she had never seen before.

****

'I'm back!' Sarah called as she came through the door.

'Hi, Sarah,' Debbie replied.

'You look nice, where are you off to?'

'Thank you. I thought it was only right that I came with you to dinner tonight. It's not fair for you to have to sit there and take all the digs from our cousin by yourself. Hopefully Iballa will be tired from the journey and will want an early night.'

'Thank you, you really don't know how much that means.'

'Are you ok?' Debbie asked, concerned.

'Yes, well, no ... but I will be. I just need to do what you've been doing: sit down, relax, and start rebuilding my life now I don't need to be going to the bakery anymore. And speaking of the bakery, can I ask you something? Did you ever hear Dad complain about or criticise Uncle Ancor over the years?'

'No, but I'm not sure I really understand what you mean.'

'To be honest, neither do I. I know you'll think I've lost my mind but I'm starting to feel sorry for Ergual.'

'How come? As far as I'm concerned, he brings it all on himself by being so horrible.'

'That's the thing – I think he's not actually as horrible as we always thought. I think he might be being held back ... by Uncle Ancor. There are definitely a lot of questions I need to find answers to...'

****

'Here they are, my two favourite nieces! Come and sit down, girls.' Ancor poured them each a drink as they settled in.

'Now, Sarah, tell me all about the bakery,' Iballa said. 'Not the boring things, but rather who has asked about me and the operation – and especially who has not.'

'Aunt, *everyone* has been asking. I'll tell you, if everyone who came in inquiring had bought something, instead of just asking after you, you would be able to retire some two or three times a day. At one point I felt it would be easier to just put a note on the door with your updates! You were dearly missed and it's clear that you're thought of very highly by the residents here in Kalanchoe.'

The smile on Iballa's face was huge and it was clear that she was more than pleased that people cared. But Sarah knew that wouldn't be the end of her questions. She would undoubtedly want to know every bit of gossip that she had missed since she had been away.

'Uncle, you sit and chat to Sarah about the bakery and I'll go into the kitchen and help Mum,' Debbie offered. 'I'm sure you have lots to talk about.'

'I'm off to the bathroom while you talk business and how much money has come in,' Iballa said, getting to her feet.

'Do you need a hand to get there, Aunt?' Debbie asked.

'No, thank you. The hospital has told me I need to keep moving and I'll be fine. I have this frame to help me along.'

'Here are the takings and the cash book,' Sarah said, handing them over as her sister and aunt left the room. 'I've updated the order book and have all the delivery notes for you here. There are also a few invoices that have come in, which I've marked with the dates they arrived. That's about it, really.'

'Thank you, Sarah, that's the practical things taken care of. Now tell me, have you enjoyed it? And how have you and Ruben got on? Has he been a help to you?'

Sarah realised this might be the time to dig a little deeper with her uncle. She had done him a huge favour and he was so grateful – perhaps she could use that to her advantage and could push her luck a little.

'It was great, and I couldn't have done any of it without Ruben. He has been the one running the show, really, as I've just stood in the shop. And of course it goes without saying we couldn't have managed without Ergual's help either.'

'Well, the first bit about Ruben I agree with, but I don't believe my son helped whatsoever. He's a complete waste of space.'

'No, Uncle, you're wrong. Ergual did all the deliveries and he was always asking if either Ruben or I needed a hand with anything, and of course he's been into the café and cleaned it up. The amount of rubbish, leaves, and dirt he's cleared from the terrace... It looks like a different place!'

'I'm shocked. Ergual, cleaning? That's a first.'

'Yes, he's been very concerned to ensure that the bakery has been ticking over ok while you've not been here. I was saying to him the other day that it's a shame the café is closed, but then I can see and understand why that's the case. It's very old fashioned and the kitchen is far too big, so the space isn't being used to its best advantage. That said, I'm sure with just a little bit of money spent on it to bring it up to date – a few alterations here and there – and it could be a gold mine, don't you think, Uncle?'

There was a long silence and the start of a bad atmosphere, but she trusted that her uncle wasn't going to argue with her given she had helped out in a huge way by keeping the bakery open while he hadn't been there.

'Sarah, there will be no changes to any part of the bakery, especially the café. It's staying just as it was the day your grandfather and his father started the business. They worked so hard to achieve what they did and I'll not be destroying their hard work.

Now, I'll tell you the same as I told your father, nothing – and I mean nothing – is going to change while I am still alive. Now if you'll excuse me, I'll go and see if your mum and sister need a hand in the kitchen.'

Chapter 23

Sarah was up early and had heard her mum leave to go over to help Iballa. After last night and what Ancor had said about nothing changing at the bakery, she wouldn't be going anywhere near there today. No, a day away from everyone and everything was just what she needed, though what the day would consist of she wasn't really sure.

Picking up her coffee and phone she went out onto the balcony. Perhaps today should be the day she looked through the job sites to see if there was anything that took her attention near to where her mum lived. She knew she would have to have an open mind and look at everything. Who knew, maybe something might jump out at her, something new, exciting, and challenging... Yes, challenging was the right word. She needed a career that taxed her brain, one that she could really get her teeth stuck into. One thing was for sure though – it wouldn't involve greeting cards. Thinking of that, she realised that it had been over a week now since Alexander had emailed her for help with anything. Perhaps he had finally gotten to grips with running the business by himself. That made her feel a little sad, but she knew it shouldn't because what she needed was a solid break from him, meaning no more contact. They both needed to move on, something that would have been able to happen naturally if they didn't have the business keeping them connected.

With all of this going around in her head she hadn't heard Debbie getting up and was startled when she walked out onto the balcony.

'Good morning! You're up early,' Debbie said.

'Yes, I heard Mum go and, well … I was wide awake, so I got up.'

'I've had a restless night,' Debbie said wearily. 'This might sound funny but, in my head, I feel this break – holiday, whatever it is – has come to an end even though I'm still here. I think it's time to sort myself out and plan the future so I can move on.'

'Strange you say that, Debbie, as that's exactly how I feel. I was about to start looking through employment websites to see if anything jumped out at me. I need a little inspiration as I'm not sure where to start.'

'Little inspiration? I need a whole lot of it. I really haven't got a clue what I want to do, though if Mum had her way, I would be here working for Bentor, running his new cocktail bar.'

'Are you not tempted to take him up on the offer? I'm not suggesting that's what you should do, I'm just wondering if it's crossed your mind.'

'It's not the Pedro thing that's putting me off, it's the job itself. The thought of having to be, for a better expression, "the hostess with the mostess" and all smiles... I couldn't do it. I know that sounds stupid, but I haven't got it in me to be that person. Not anymore.'

'I get that. Look, do you fancy a day away from here? We could take a walk and find a headland, and just stand there and scream; let everything out.'

'Yes, a day away would be nice, but it has to involve food and more importantly no other people.'

'That would be perfect.' Sarah laughed. 'We sound like two bitter old spinsters. We just need a couple of cats, and we'll be sorted!'

'If only sorting out our lives was that easy. Right, I'm off to get ready. I call the bathroom first.'

As Debbie went off Sarah smiled at her declaration. It reminded her of when they were teenagers and always fighting over the bathroom.

They had come a long way from those days and getting close to her sister again was one of the good things that had come out of all this. It was something a couple of months ago she would never have dreamed would ever happen as they had grown so far apart, going months without bothering to get in contact. Now it was almost as though they couldn't manage without one another, but – and it was a big but – soon it would be time for them to both go in their different directions and start to rebuild their lives.

Before Sarah went to get ready she quickly looked at her emails, just to check if Alexander had contacted her and somehow she had missed it, but no, there was nothing. He could obviously manage without her help. She was free of him, and she realised she was glad.

****

Two hours later the sisters were sat on a bench looking out to sea. They each had a large ice cream as Debbie had insisted that this was how they would start their day. There was a lovely breeze, which was so welcome.

'Debbie, you know all the business with Steven telling you what to wear and eat and how you should look? Was it a gradual thing or did it start right away?'

'It was slow, and to be honest, in the very beginning I didn't even notice it was happening. We would go clothes shopping and he would suggest things and even though I thought some of the clothes he picked out weren't me, I liked that he was interested in how I looked. And when we went to restaurants he would suggest food for me to try, which I thought was just him trying to expand my horizons. And selling the flat I was sort of ok with as it meant we were going to have our own business together, which was exciting.'

'So does that mean the problems started once you had the salon?'

'Yes. It took quite a while to set it up, what with choosing all the fixtures and fittings, interviewing staff, that sort of thing. We hired my friend Jenny and about a week before we opened she and I were in the salon alone and she asked which fixtures and fittings I had chosen. I realised none of the final fixtures had been chosen by me, so I lied. But she wasn't daft, she knew I hadn't had a say in anything; everything was Steven's idea. Then, three days before the opening, Steven said we had to get ourselves some clothes to wear for work, so we went off to one of these designer outlet villages...' She trailed off, distress eating away at her.

'Are you ok, Debbie? You don't need to talk about it if you don't want to. I'm so sorry I asked, I shouldn't have brought the subject up.'

'No, it's fine. You see, that's when my life changed forever. It was – and still is – frightening how much money was spent that day, the day he "created" me. I was just another fixture or fitting for him to decorate and I was stupid enough to let him do it. The following day he took my identity away with the hair extensions and the makeup. That was when I said goodbye for good to the old Debbie.'

'Yes, but now you're back to being the real you.'

'But I'm not really, am I.'

'You could be. Look, it's none of my business as I haven't been through what you have, but Debbie, take the job you've been offered with Bentor. You say you aren't having it because you can't bring that happy bubbly person back, but what if you can? Don't you want to prove to Steven – and more importantly, to yourself – that he hasn't won?'

'I just feel so silly and stupid that I let him do

what he did to me.'

'Ok, I get that, but surely you want to leave all that behind you? Ultimately, you're the winner because you walked away. You're the strong one, in charge of your own destiny. You just need to give yourself that final push to really move on and that's what this job is – it's an opportunity. An opportunity Bentor gave you because he believes in you. And you know as well as I do that he's got so much riding on this new cocktail bar, and there's no way he would offer you the position if he didn't think you were capable of doing a truly amazing job with it. Now enough of all this. Let's head around the coast to La Caleta. I want... No, that's wrong ... I *need* pizza and chips and a large glass of wine ... or two.'

****

They walked for the next forty minutes in silence, until they finally spotted the sign welcoming them to Caleta. It crossed Debbie's mind that they could possibly bump into Bentor again, but she could deal with that if she had to.

'Shall we have food first and then a walk around?' Sarah asked.

'Sounds good to me,' Debbie agreed.

They found their favourite pizza restaurant and grabbed a table out on the street to watch the world go by. The pizzas came quickly and apart from a little chit chat about the town and the food, they ate in silence, both lost in thought. Once they were done, they paid the bill and headed up the steep steps away from the town to the cliff top, to sit and watch the boats before heading back to Kalanchoe.

'I love it here,' Debbie said, taking a deep breath of sea air. 'It's well worth the trek up the steps and across the rough bit of land. I always feel as if I'm on the edge of the world when I sit here as all you can see is the sea in front of you.'

'We're so lucky to have family living here, don't you think?' Sarah asked. 'As a kid I took it for granted but now, as an adult, I feel very lucky that we have the apartment to come back to and all this on the doorstep.'

'I agree, even though the family thing isn't always straightforward,' Debbie joked. 'Now, we've talked about me. How about you? What do you think the future holds for you? Have you made any plans?'

'I don't have a clue. I think I'll live with Mum to start with and find a job, although doing what, I have no idea.'

'Can I tell you something Mum said, and please promise me you won't tell her I told you?'

Sarah nodded hesitantly.

'She said she was worried about you. That really shocked me as you're always so in control and organised, with everything planned to within an inch of its life. And what scares her the most is the thought of you going back to Alexander.'

'We've talked about the old you, Debbie, well ... I think the old in control and organised me has gone as well. In fact, I'm beginning to think she was my downfall. I was so organised with Alexander and the business and that's what drove him away. All those lists of jobs that had to be ticked off at the end of every day... And where did all that get me? Sat here feeling sorry for myself. No home, no job, nothing.'

'Oh, Sarah, you don't have nothing! You're clever and intelligent and you just need to find out what direction you want to go in and then you will fly at whatever you choose.'

'Do you know what? I've loved working in the bakery these past couple of weeks. It was different. Nice, relaxed and – most importantly – fun.'

173

'Yes, but do you think it's possible that that was largely because you were spending time with Ruben who, using an old word, is "smitten" with you?'

'You're funny. Yes, I really enjoyed working with him and we got on well, but it was more than that. Working at the bakery has helped me to look at things so differently. It's shown me that it *is* possible to have the perfect work/life balance and there's time for fun as well – just like you did when you lived and worked here. I've never really had "fun".'

'But you built up a very successful business. That didn't happen overnight and is something to be proud of. You worked hard and though Alexander might have been the face of the company, *you* were the brains behind it all. He could never have succeeded without you and that shows. Look at how many times a week he's contacting you for help. Even now, you're basically still running the business.'

'He was.'

'Sorry?'

'He *was* contacting me, but it's now been over a week since he's messaged me with a question, and to be entirely honest ... I'm missing it.'

'I promise you it's a good thing that the strings have been cut. It's time for you to fly. See, that's made you smile!'

'I'm smiling because this is a bit of role reversal, which I don't have a problem with. I can see a lot of the old Debbie coming out – the fighter, the survivor.'

'Yes, I'm good at telling other people how to live their lives. I just have a problem with living my own. There's one question you haven't answered though, and that is – and to be clear, I don't really want to ask it because I think you will give me the wrong answer – would you take Alexander back, even after all he's done?'

There was a long silence before Sarah spoke but they both knew what was coming.

'The way I'm feeling at this precise moment... Yes, I would welcome him with open arms. How sad is that?'

Chapter 24

Sarah awakened to the sound of the apartment's front door being closed. That must be her mum going over to help Iballa get washed and dressed for the day. She couldn't hear Debbie moving around but that wasn't that surprising given they did have a late-ish night, sat on the balcony chatting once Gina had gone to bed. She couldn't believe she had told her sister she would take Alexander back, but she couldn't lie to Debbie and that was how she really felt.

After she made a coffee she went out onto the balcony and noticed her mum had left her phone behind. She knew Gina would panic if she didn't have it, and then rush back, so she would have to take it over to the bakery once she'd finished the coffee.

****

'Hi, Uncle.'

'You're up and out early, Sarah, is everything ok?'

'Yes, Mum left her phone behind in the apartment so I've brought it over before she starts panicking. Are you back into the swing of things?'

'Oh yes, everything is fine, thank you.'

'Right, I'll nip around the back and give Mum her phone. See you later.'

Sarah couldn't fail to notice that everything had been moved back to how it had been before, but then it was Ancor's business and not hers, so he had the right to do whatever he liked. As she walked around the side of the building she saw Iballa was sat at the courtyard table.

'Hello, Aunt, you're looking well. How are you feeling?'

'I'm fine, but as you can see, I'm not allowed to do anything. One foot out of place and your mum comes down on me like a ton of bricks!'

'That sounds like her!' Sarah laughed. 'Speaking of Mum, is she around? She left her phone in the apartment, so I brought it over.'

'She won't be long. She's just nipped out to get some vegetables and fruit as apparently that will help my recovery. I've said wine would help it more, but they tell me it doesn't go well with my tablets, so veg it is. Sit down and chat with me until your mum comes back – but please don't give me any instructions on what not to do. Between your mum and Ancor, I can't breathe!'

'I promise I won't. I meant to say, Ergual really was a help when you were away. I know Uncle doesn't think so, but he was.'

'Oh, I don't know what goes on in that lad's head. I try to talk to him when Ancor's not around, but he keeps so much inside. He just needs a purpose in life, something to get up for every day. Ancor did tell me he swept up a lot of the rubbish in the café, which is a huge help. Hopefully once I'm back on my feet I can reopen it.'

Was this an opportunity for Sarah to dive in and talk about updating the café? She knew her uncle's views on that, but did Iballa think the same or should she just leave it because it was none of her business? She decided to go for it.

'Aunt, don't you think it would be the perfect job for Ergual, running the café? I'm sure he would make a good job of it... Why are you smiling?'

'Because we both know my son and customers don't go well together. And we both know Ergual wants to modernise it, but that will never happen while Ancor is here. Ergual isn't the first one to mention it. Your dad tried to persuade him many times and it never happened.'

'But most of the equipment doesn't even work! I get that he doesn't want walls knocked down, but who keeps broken equipment? What would happen if one of his ovens broke and couldn't be fixed? He would replace it. So why not do the same with the café?'

'I see your point, Sarah, but Ancor just doesn't like change.'

'But it could be a little gold mine! I'm sorry, I shouldn't have brought the subject up. Shall we talk about something else?'

'Yes, perhaps we should. Since it's just the two of us, tell me about Ruben.'

'What about Ruben? You know him far better than me.'

'Oh, Sarah, don't be coy. You know what I mean. Since Ancor's been back he's noticed a difference in Ruben. For one thing it's "Sarah this" and "Sarah that" and he has really taken control with Ancor being in the shop. So tell me, how did all that come about?'

'He had to take control as you and Uncle Ancor weren't here, and I know nothing about the baking. I don't know, I guess we just worked well together.'

'Yes, and outside of work I hear you were spotted having a drink with him in a bar one evening.'

'That's right, we did.'

'And?'

'And what?'

'Oh, come on, Sarah, surely you didn't just talk bread and cakes! Oh, here comes your mum. I think there's more to your story so don't think you're going to get away without telling me at some point.'

'Hi, Mum, you left your phone behind in the

apartment, so I've brought it around for you,' Sarah said warmly, glad for her mother's timing.

'Thank you, darling, that's kind of you. Can I make you a drink?'

'No, thanks, I'll leave the two of you in peace. Have a nice day.'

So, what was she going to do now? How would she fill her day? She decided to head towards Tillandsia as it would make a nice change of scenery and she wasn't in the mood for shops.

She was just heading out from Kalanchoe when her phone beeped. Stopping to take it out of her bag she saw the name on the screen was one she hadn't seen for at least a week: Alexander. She felt her heart beat faster. Her first thought was that he probably needed her help, but she read the text and the question was unexpected: could she find the time for a quick chat? He needed advice and it was too complicated to explain in a text. She wasn't sure what she should do but she did know she shouldn't reply right away as she didn't want him to think she was at his beck and call.

Putting her phone back in her bag she headed off towards the coastal path. When she stopped at the little junction a familiar van pulled up and Ergual leaned out the window.

'Can I give you a lift somewhere?' he offered.

'No, it's ok. I'm only out for a bit of fresh air. How are things now your mum and dad are back?'

'I'm still doing the deliveries as Dad's in the shop, but it's ok. By the way, did you mention the café to him? Because he made a comment about you saying how hard I worked cleaning it. He also muttered something about you calling it old fashioned and in need of modernisation. He reckoned you sounded just like your dad. Are you sure you don't need a lift? We could chat ... if you want?'

'Ok then, which way are you going?' she said, not wanting to spoil the nice moment they were having.

'I have just one delivery to do in a little town a few kilometres away, and then I need to nip into Tillandsia.'

'If you don't mind me coming with you, it would be a nice change to go somewhere different.'

Sarah hopped into the van, and it crossed her mind that just a couple of weeks ago this would never have happened. If Ergual had seen her back then he would have driven right by. It was a welcome change; this was how their relationship *should* be as cousins.

'Yes, I talked to him and your dad wasn't happy that I mentioned the café needing to be done up. I spoke to your mum about it this morning and she said there would be no budging from him. But maybe if you took it on you could make the changes so gradually he would hardly know it was happening. Actually, that's probably complete nonsense, isn't it? He would likely spot every cup or saucer that was in the wrong place, wouldn't he?'

They both laughed a bit sadly.

'Here we are,' Ergual said as he pulled to a stop. 'I'm just going to the little shop over there with the courtyard garden. I won't be a minute.'

'Do you need a hand? I see there's more than one box to take in.'

'Thank you, that would be great.'

Sarah had never been to this little town before, at least not that she could remember. It was entirely possible she might have as a young child. Once in the shop she could see they appeared to sell everything in the world, from food to clothes to household items, and behind the counter was a coffee machine and a cabinet filled with cakes. She put the box she was carrying down next to the two

Ergual had brought in, and while he was chatting to the owner she went out the side door to the courtyard. It had clearly once been a very neglected space but now it was beautiful. The owners had brought in a dozen tables and a load of chairs and placed them haphazardly, and loads of pots full of plants hid the damaged walls while also making the space feel as though it had been reclaimed by nature.

'Ready to go?' Ergual asked.

'Yes, but before we do, tell me what you think of this,' she said, gesturing to the space.

'It's gorgeous and I know it's always busy as they're one of my dad's best customers. Sitting here makes you feel like you're in a secret garden.'

'Yes, exactly, and all they've done is added plants. No knocking anything down or painting anything. Surely your dad wouldn't object to a few plants here and there? I think it would work, don't you? And it would solve two problems because it would make it look fresh and new, which is what *you* want, while keeping it exactly the same, which is what your *dad* wants.'

Chapter 25

'Slow down, Sarah, and let me wake up properly. Also, start at the beginning, please,' Debbie said as they sank into their seats on the balcony.

Debbie hadn't seen Sarah like this before and all she could get from the babbled words was that she had spent yesterday with Ergual and something about the bakery café.

'Sorry, I think because I've been up and awake for hours my mind is overexcited.'

'Probably. Now, please go slowly, not like you're on a very fast train.'

'When I went out for a walk yesterday Ergual stopped and asked if I wanted a lift. He was in the bakery van and off to do a delivery to a shop in a small town away from the coast. While he was talking to the owner, I wandered into the little courtyard café they had adjoining the shop to wait for him, and then the idea came to me. This little café was on a bit of scruffy waste land and what the owners had done was fill the space with plants and bushes – all in pots – and created a lovely room. Don't you see? It's the answer to Ergual's problem!'

'I didn't know he had a problem, apart from the fact that he, himself, is a problem. Perhaps that's unkind,' she quickly added, seeing the look of annoyance on Sarah's face. 'Carry on.'

'You know how I told you Ancor is refusing to modernise the café, saying everything has to stay the same as the way it was when his father and grandfather started it? Well, if we add plants in a similar way to this other café, we hide the horrible walls without needing to change anything structurally. Ok, it doesn't solve the problem of getting more space into the building – that would only happen if the wall into the café kitchen came down – but it would be a start and if Ergual could make a success of it, perhaps in time Uncle would come around to doing proper alterations.'

'I don't want to put a damper on things but our cousin serving customers? I can't see it working. Also, why are you so excited about it? Could it perhaps be because it's something else to fill your time with so you don't have to think of your future?' she asked as gently as she could.

There was a silence and Debbie wasn't sure if she had overstepped the mark with her sister. The last thing she wanted to do was fall out with her and she was just about to apologise when Sarah got up and went into the apartment. Should she follow her in and say sorry? No, she would stay out on the balcony, giving Sarah space.

She finished her coffee and decided to have another one as she would need the energy today to tackle the Pedro issue and tell him his attitude had upset her. But just as she got up from the little table, Sarah came back out.

'Look, I'm sorry, I shouldn't have said some of those things. It's just ... I'm worried about you. I don't want you to go back to Alexander. You're worth a lot more than he deserves and I don't want you to get hurt again.'

'Thank you. So much of what you've said is right and I'm beginning to think I should never have come here to Tenerife. I know Mum thought she was doing the right thing suggesting it so we could rest and clear our heads, but I should have stayed home and faced up to my problems.'

'No, Sarah, we needed this break, and it was perfect timing as it meant you were able to run the bakery so Iballa could have her operation. I know that – for both of us – it's been a few steps forward and then a few back, but I'm glad we came here. Now, today is a good day and I'm feeling confident so I'm off to have it out with Pedro as I've done nothing wrong.'

'I'm very happy the old Debbie is slowly coming back. I'm also hoping some of the fighting spirit rubs off on me.'

'It will. Now, give me a hug and wish me luck.'

'You don't need any luck.'

****

As Debbie reached the edge of Tillandsia she took a quick look in one of the shop windows to check her appearance. She was glad to see she looked ok but the most important thing was that her head was in the right place. She felt ready to take on the world ... well, perhaps not the world, but at least Pedro. She glanced across the street to Bentor's restaurant where staff were laying the tables and placing cushions on the outside chairs. She also noticed work vans and men in the new cocktail bar. The work was obviously underway.

As she approached the door there was no sign of Pedro, but she did spot the waitress she'd met previously, Patrice.

'Hello, hi! I was wondering if Pedro might be around to have a quick word with?' Debbie asked.

'No, I'm sorry, it's his day off today. Bentor is next door if you wanted to speak to him instead? I think the builders would like it as he's only getting under their feet. You know what he's like, he wants everything to happen right away, no patience. By the way, have you decided if you'll be coming to work with us? Pedro mentioned Bentor had offered you a job at the new cocktail bar.'

'No, sorry, I'm going back to England in a few weeks.'

'Oh, that's a shame. Perhaps you'll change your mind once you see the refurbishment Bentor has planned. Speaking of the boss, here he comes now.'

'Debbie! This is a nice surprise. Have you come to look at what's happening with my new place?'

'No, I've actually come to have a quick word with Pedro, but Patrice tells me it's his day off.'

'Before you go, would you have time to come next door and have a look at the work that's been done? I'm asking as a friend, not as an ex-boss, I promise. No pressure.'

Debbie had to admit she was a bit intrigued so after saying goodbye to Patrice she followed Bentor next door.

'What a transformation!' she said with a gasp as she stepped inside. 'I love the bar, it's very glitzy and glamorous.'

'Most places have feature walls so I thought I'd do the opposite and keep all the walls, tables, chairs, and sofas in soft, muted colours, and make the bar the showpiece, with a gold leaf effect.'

'It has the "wow factor", as they say. So I presume that's where the opening to the restaurant will be?' she asked, pointing to the plastic sheet along the far wall.

'Yes.'

'I'm really impressed, Bentor, and so happy for you. I'd best get on now though, and get out of your way.'

Just as Debbie turned to leave, Pedro walked in. Her heart sank. He would undoubtedly put two and two together and make five, and that would make the situation even worse. Before she could say hello, he brushed past her, completely ignoring her.

'I just popped in to give you the wine order for the restaurant,' he said to Bentor. 'Once I have your go ahead, I'll place the order.'

'Thank you, Pedro. I'm sure it will be fine but I'll

look at it today so it's ready for you to phone through tomorrow. I was just showing Debbie—'

'Right, I'll be off then,' he said, cutting Bentor off.

Debbie could scream. How rude of him to not even acknowledge her! But her visit was meant to give her the chance to clear the air with Pedro, and so she would have to get through to him, one way or another.

'Have you got a couple of minutes to have a chat?' she asked.

He ignored her and carried on walking towards the door but one of the tradesmen was coming in with some wood, so he had to pause and stand to one side. This was Debbie's opportunity.

'Pedro, I came here today to clear the air with you because I want us to be friends again. You weren't here so Bentor asked me to come and take a look at the work that has been done on the bar, and he's my friend, so I agreed. And another thing, I'm not accepting the job because I'll be heading back to England to work. The fact that you aren't being offered it has nothing to do with me so you need to grow up. I'm sorry, Bentor, for causing a scene. It wasn't my intention and I wish you all the best with your new project. Goodbye.'

She could feel her blood boiling and she was so annoyed with herself for going off like that with all those builders in the room. This day hadn't turned out at all like she thought it would and she needed a drink, even though it was only just mid-day.

A few minutes later she was down on the coastal path heading back towards Kalanchoe. She decided she would stop at the beach restaurant she'd been to a few times now and in addition to a large glass of wine, she'd also order a big bowl of cheesy chips.

Her phone beeped and taking it out of her bag she saw that it was a text from Bentor asking if she was ok. She decided she would reply once she got to the restaurant and calmed down. As she approached the restaurant she was glad to see that there were lots of empty tables. Before she grabbed one, she placed her order.

'Hi, could I have half a carafe of house white wine, and a bowl of cheesy chips. Oh, and some bread, please.'

She sat at a table in the shade, took out her phone, and texted Bentor, saying she was ok and apologising again for causing a scene. She also reiterated how much she really loved the work he'd had done. The wine arrived and the waitress said the chips would be a few minutes but Debbie was in no rush.

Her phone beeped again with another text from Bentor.

I've told Pedro that what you said, he deserved. And I've told him again that the offer of the job was my doing, and nothing to do with you.

She put her phone back in her bag without answering. As far as she was concerned, the matter was over. The first glass of wine went down nicely and she told herself to relax and forget what had just happened. The chips arrived with the bread she'd asked for and some mayonnaise. She elected to make a chip sandwich and she really didn't care who saw her do it.

****

Three quarters of an hour later every scrap of food had been eaten. She was feeling full but also very satisfied. Another half a carafe of wine had been ordered and she was just about to text Sarah to see what she was up to when she noticed someone walking towards her.

It was Pedro.

'Can I join you?' he asked a bit sheepishly.

'Yes. What would you like to drink?'

'A beer, please, but I can go up and order it. No, it's ok, the waitress is coming over.'

As Pedro ordered the drink, Debbie tried to compose herself. Should she apologise for shouting? No, Pedro was the one who should apologise for being rude. Perhaps it was best if she didn't say anything? No, she had to talk about something.

'I'm really impressed with the new space. The actual bar itself is stunning, and it will work so well with the restaurant—'

'I'm sorry,' Pedro interrupted. 'I've been a real idiot and I have no excuse for my behaviour.'

'I'm sorry, too. I shouldn't have gone off on you like that, showing you up in front of everyone. That was a horrible thing to do.'

'No, I deserved it. I've been so stupid and to be honest it wasn't about you being offered the job; it was more about Bentor not thinking I could do it.'

'Shall we draw a line under it and forget any of it ever happened? I only have another few weeks here and it would be great to be friends again, like we were before.'

'Thank you, I would like that. But there's just one more thing I need to say, which is that I would be happy if you took the job ... because it would mean we would be working together again.'

'That's a nice thing to say but my life's back in England, though doing what and where I'm not quite sure of yet.'

'Sorry, I'm confused. You haven't got a job to go back to?'

'No job, no home, no anything. It will be a fresh start.'

'So, if that's the case, why not stay here? You have a home in Kalanchoe, and you could have a job at Bentor's, and you love Tenerife. Surely that's a no brainer, isn't it?'

'I don't know myself, but there's one thing that is very tempting here on the island, and that would be being here with you.'

Chapter 26

'Good morning, Mum. You ok?' Debbie asked.

'I just feel a bit useless sat here, not doing anything. Iballa insisted that I take the day off as I haven't taken a break since she came back from the hospital. At least she compromised by letting Sarah help her instead.'

'I think it's good for you to take a break. You've worked so hard helping her, and not just that, you've also spring cleaned her and Ancor's house from top to bottom!'

'Perhaps you're right. Come on, I'll make us a drink and then we can have a good chat. There are a few things I want to talk to you about, one being your sister.'

Debbie smiled to herself. She knew her mum inside out. The conversation might start with Sarah, but it certainly wouldn't end there. She would soon move on to Debbie.

'Where Sarah's concerned, I've made my thoughts clear to her. I've said she has thrown herself into everything so she doesn't have to face up to her future, and this business with Ergual and reopening the café is just something else to put off making any plans.'

'I agree, but the only way it will reopen is on your uncle's say.'

'But why is Ancor like that?'

'He just always has been. He's the kind of person who must be in control. The issue is that Ergual has opinions, and if you're dealing with Ancor, opinions aren't allowed. If your father, God love him, were here now, he would and could tell you so many stories...'

'I can't remember Dad ever saying anything bad about Uncle. They always got on so well together, and there were never any arguments or cross words between them ... well, not that I can remember ever seeing, anyway.'

'I'm afraid there were strong words before you were born, and that's why we moved to the UK to live. Your dad would have loved nothing more than to stay here, working at the bakery, but for that to happen things would have had to change and expand – moving with the times – for them both to make a good living out of it. But no, Ancor was having none of it and your grandfather took his side. The whole thing was so sad and upsetting at the time.'

'Oh dear, I knew nothing of this. Dad never showed any signs of bitterness and I always thought he was excited to move to the UK to be with you and your family.'

'He was. Once the decision to leave Kalanchoe was made he never looked back. With your dad, everything was about the future, whereas for your uncle, it's always been the complete opposite. He loves to live in the past.'

Debbie could see that this chat was beginning to upset her mum and although she had a hundred more questions to ask, she knew the conversation needed to move away from any more mentions of her dad, so she explained what had happened yesterday morning with Pedro.

'I'm glad to hear you've made up and that the future's looking brighter. Perhaps it even includes a new job?' her mum suggested tentatively.

'You still think I should take the job then?'

'My thoughts don't come into it, darling. You have to decide for yourself and I'll be so happy for you, whatever choice you make. The real Debbie is back, which is all that matters. As for your future, you could live with me and see what opportunities come up in the UK, or you could take the opportunity that's on the table here in Tenerife. I'm looking forward to hearing what you decide to do, and for now, I'm off for a shower and then a lazy day with my book in the sunshine.'

Her mum thought she was back to her old confident self, but if she was, surely decisions about her future would come as easy as ABC? Debbie was still pondering that question when her mum returned after her shower.

'I'm all ready for my feet up with a book day, but I think we might have a major problem ahead.'

'What's that, Mum? What's happened now?'

'Nothing yet, darling, but do you have any plans for today?'

'No, I thought I would stay here with you and keep you company.'

'I was right, major problem. We both love that corner seat! Do we toss a coin to see who gets it?' Gina winked and Debbie released a breath she hadn't realised she'd been holding.

'It's not an issue as it's your special place. It always has been, and of course it always will be, every time you come here. And on the subject of you coming to Tenerife, I think it's about time you explained why you've made every excuse in the world not to come here since Dad died. I'm going to nip out to get something for lunch and some groceries, but I expect an answer when I return.'

****

On her way through the square, Debbie spotted Ergual walking towards her. A couple of weeks ago, when she had just arrived here, she would have turned around to avoid him, but not today. She could handle whatever he had to say, and with all this business of him and Sarah getting along together, perhaps he would be nice to her as well.

'Hi, Ergual, are you ok? How's your mum doing?'

'She's getting better every day. It's been a big help having Aunt Gina here as Mum actually listens to her and does as she's told.'

'Yes, my mum can certainly be bossy when she wants to! Sarah told me about the café; it sounds exciting.'

'It did sound exciting ... but my dad's put a stop to it.'

'Why? It would bring in a good income and it would be great to see the space in use again.'

'He said I can open it, but only if I don't change anything.'

'But Sarah said you were only adding some plants to give it a freshen up, not doing any kind of structural alterations to the space.'

'Yes, that was the plan, but he's refusing to have any plants in there. He is so stubborn and won't listen to anyone.' He said his goodbyes then, and she watched him walk away.

Poor Ergual. Debbie actually felt sorry for him – something that had never happened before. She was also glad she'd bumped into him before going into the bakery and mentioning the café and sticking her foot in it. Continuing on to the fruit and veg shop, she spotted her sister.

'Hi, Sarah, you ok?'

'Yes, thanks. Iballa fancied some grapes and oranges, so I nipped out quickly. She's a lot more mobile now than she was when she first got back, and apart from housework she's more than capable of doing everything else herself.'

'That's great she's making progress. I've just bumped into Ergual; he wasn't very happy.'

'I know. Uncle Ancor is so stubborn, and to be

honest, he's getting worse. The couple of weeks he was away everything ran smoothly – no hiccups, nothing – but this week he's apparently taken two orders over the phone and forgotten to write them down, and then when he remembered, he got both wrong. Cutting a long story short, the customers weren't happy when the orders were delivered and he blamed Ruben for the mistake. And Ruben being Ruben, he just took the blame. I just wish he would realise how much easier his life would be if he had a little more give and take in things.'

****

'Hi, Mum, I'm back! Uncle has sent us a treat: two villa pies just out of the oven.'

'Oh lovely, thank you.'

'I'll make us a drink to go with them.'

'Sounds good. I'm ready with my answers to all your questions by the way. You can feel free to fire away.'

'I'm not here to interrogate you. I'm just finding a few things hard to get my head around.'

'The main one being why I've not been to Kalanchoe since your dad died? Well, it's quite simple. It's because I blame your uncle for your father's death. If we hadn't had to move back to England, where your dad worked so hard with all that traveling and physical labour, he would still be alive. Yes, he would have had to work longer hours here at the bakery, but the pace of life would have been slower, the warm climate and fresh air good for him. I truly believe that his early death was all down to a stubborn Ancor, and that's why I've avoided coming here – because I know I'll end up telling him that, and the last thing we need is a family fall out.'

'Oh, Mum, are you sure? Why have you never talked to Sarah and me about this? You've kept this bottled up for the last five years?'

'Yes, he knew that if he stayed he and Ancor would have fallen out forever, and so he left. There is nothing you can say to convince me otherwise.'

Chapter 27

The apartment door closed behind Gina as she left to help Iballa, and within seconds both Debbie and Sarah were up and out of their rooms. When Gina had gone to bed last night Debbie had explained to Sarah all about why their mum hadn't visited and both of them now felt relief that they knew the truth, but also sadness.

'You couldn't sleep either?' Sarah asked. 'The thing that I keep thinking about is the fact that Dad was happy in England. He wasn't bitter or anything, like ... there was never any comment about wanting to be here.'

'I agree. Of course Mum is devastated that Dad died, that's very natural given her life has been forever changed, but I worry she's just looking for someone to blame and she's decided on Ancor. The fact of the matter is that Dad could have stayed here if he wanted to as he didn't need to keep working in the family business. He could have walked into any place on the island and been offered a job.'

'I've been thinking along similar lines. Don't you think it's possible that his real reason for moving to England was simply because Mum's family were all there and he wanted her to be near them and be happy?'

'It absolutely could be. I assume that's crossed Mum's mind as well but she has to take her sadness and grief out on someone, and she's chosen Ancor. All we can do is support her through her grieving process, and I'm hopeful that because she's now here on the island, next time it won't be so hard for her to come back.'

'If you were living and working here she would

be more than happy to return for holidays. In fact, you never know, she might end up moving here full-time. There's nothing keeping her in England after all... Or am I jumping to conclusions? Have you decided yet if you want to take Bentor up on his job offer?'

'Yes, the more I think about the job, the more appealing it's becoming. I think that's because I went in and saw what Bentor is creating. I can picture it open in the evenings, with all the customers and the atmosphere.'

'But can you picture yourself working there?'

'I think I can, but I can also picture myself with Pedro, and that's the problem. Being in a relationship with him and working together as well will never work. But enough of that. Did you call Alexander back and find out what he wanted?'

'No, but I was tempted. Instead I texted and asked what he wanted, and he didn't reply, which has really annoyed me. For one, I wanted to know what the problem was, and two, well ... I don't have a two, just the fact that it was nice to be needed, I suppose. Have you any plans for today?'

'No, not really. I said I might pop over and spend a couple of hours with Pedro between his two shifts but I'm not sure. What I need to be doing is making my mind up. Is my life here in Tenerife or in England? Oh, that's my phone. No, it must be yours,' she said, having checked her mobile.

Sarah looked at her phone, read a text, and quickly answered it.

'Talk of the devil; that was Alexander asking if we could meet up. Apparently he'll be near mum's house in the next few days.'

'What have you said?'

'I told him I'm not there, I'm on holiday here with Mum and not sure how long we're staying. I think that should shut him up. Now, my plan today

197

is a little cunning and manipulative. It could go one of two ways, but it's worth a try.'

'Tell me more, I'm intrigued.'

'No, I need to think it through a little more. I'm off to get ready and I'll see you back here tonight with either good news or bad news.'

****

Sarah was on a mission and the first stop on her adventure was the bakery. Today was a big delivery day and Ancor would have to do three trips. It was the last one that she was interested in, and her timing had to be spot on.

Approaching the bakery, she saw that the delivery van was there so she went around the back to chat with her mum and Iballa until it left.

'Hi, Iballa, how are you today? I expect you're being looked after a lot better than yesterday,' she joked.

'Your mum is far bossier than you. I can't move without her wanting to know where I'm going!' Iballa said with a huff. 'She's so strict but I really couldn't have coped without her – or you, come to that. Ancor and I are just so thankful that you were here to run the bakery.'

'Like I've told Uncle, it was Ruben – and of course Ergual – who did the hard work. I just stood behind the counter and served.'

'You are very kind. I know Ruben could run the baking side with his eyes closed, but you know Ancor, he doesn't think anyone can do anything better than him. If he just let Ruben get on with everything without interfering he would be fine, but no, he has to butt in every five minutes checking what he's doing. Look, there he goes now, off out doing deliveries. He is too proud to ask Ergual to go; he thinks he is Superman. Shall we have a drink? I could nip in and make us a coffee without your mum

198

seeing me.'

'No, Aunt, I just popped in for a quick hello as I was passing. I think I might visit the bakery now and get a small cheese pie.'

'Will the small cheese pie be the only thing you're going in there for, Sarah? Or might there be a certain baker that you want to see, who is all alone now that Ancor's out doing deliveries? From what I can gather from some of my customers who visited while I was in hospital, you and that baker were getting on *very* well together.'

Sarah laughed. 'I don't think you should be listening to idle gossip.'

'Why not? What else have I to do? Your mum won't let me lift a finger! But joking aside, you could do a lot worse than Ruben as a boyfriend. He's the type of man that would treat you like a princess and what woman wouldn't like that?'

'I think you've been reading too many romance novels. In real life there's no such thing as a happy ever after.'

'Now that's where you're wrong, Sarah.'

Sarah could feel herself blushing as she walked away. There was no denying that her aunt was right, she *was* looking forward to seeing Ruben, but she had to remember that she was on a mission and that was her priority today.

****

'Hello, Ruben, how are you?'

'Hi, Sarah, you've just missed your uncle. He's gone out with the deliveries.'

'I know, that's why I've come in now to see you. I need a favour.'

Ruben went all shy and now he was the one blushing.

'I know the delivery up to the little village of Priviaata in the hills is today, and I just wanted to check if it will be one of the last deliveries Ancor makes.'

'Yes, it will, and he should be back in about an hour to collect it. Is there a problem?'

'No, I just fancied a ride up there with him, that's all. You say he'll be back in an hour? I'll have a walk around to kill time and come back when I see the van return.'

'If you'd like, you could stay here and chat. There won't be that many customers now all the orders have been collected... But only if you want to, of course. Don't think you have to.'

'I'd like that. I've missed our chats since I've stopped coming here. To be honest, I've missed the bakery and the customers as well. Everything, really.'

'Yes, since Ancor came back it's been a bit stressful. I thought because we had both done a good job, with no mistakes, that he would let me just get on with things. But to be honest, it's the complete opposite. It's odd.'

'No, unfortunately it's not that odd. That's just how he is and the more I hear and see, the more annoyed I get. Also, I feel sorry for Ergual, something I *never* thought would happen.'

'I know they had a falling out about the café, but I don't really know any of the details, apart from Ancor saying something about people thinking he runs things incorrectly and wanting to change everything.'

'That is complete rubbish. I don't want to talk about my family anymore so tell me, what have you been up to, Ruben?'

'Nothing. Work and that's it. But I was hoping to catch you as I have a question. Do you fancy going back up to Alejandro's restaurant for another meal one night?'

'I would love to. You choose the evening. I've

nothing planned whatsoever.'

'Shall we say the day after tomorrow?'

'Perfect! That's a date then... Oh, sorry, I didn't mean a date as in a *date*, I just meant ... well... I'm making things worse, aren't I? I'll stop now. I'm looking forward to it.'

'Me, too. Now I best go and finish cleaning before Ancor comes back.'

'Oh yes, don't let me stop you. I'll go sit in the square and wait for Ancor to return. Shall we say seven o'clock for our evening out?'

'Yes. I'll pick you up at your apartment, but I would sooner use the word "date", rather than "evening out".'

They both smiled and Sarah turned around without replying. She liked the word 'date' as well.

She walked over to a bench in the square that was in the shade but close enough to see when Ancor returned to pick up the next delivery. When he did, she headed over to speak to him.

'Off with a delivery?' she asked innocently.

'Sarah, hello! Yes, last of the day. I'm off to Priviaata with this lot.'

'Do you fancy some company? I'm a little lost now that I'm not working in the bakery so thought it might be nice if we could chat. And if you don't drive too fast, I'll treat you to an ice cream.'

'That will be lovely. Hop in the van. I've just got to fetch the last box and we'll be on our way.'

The first part of her plan had worked. Now she needed to fill the ride with conversation, but it couldn't involve Ergual or the bakery. Once Ancor had loaded the last box and they were on their way, she spent fifteen minutes filling him in on all that had been happening with her sister.

'Do you think Debbie will take the job? I think she would be brilliant at it,' Ancor said approvingly.

'I hope so.'

Before Sarah knew it, they had arrived at the village and pulled up outside the shop. Now it was time for the next part of her plan. First, she helped Ancor with the boxes, and then she suggested, 'How about a cold drink and that ice cream I promised you, here in the garden? We're in no hurry as Ruben will have closed up for the day.'

'Yes, why not. But it's my treat as you've done enough for us already. Do you know, I've never actually stayed to have a bite here before.'

This was it the final part of Sarah's plan, and also the most difficult. She had to convince Ancor that Ergual's idea – well, hers, actually – was the way forward for his business. Now to find a table where he could take it all in and see the effect the plants had on the space, and more importantly, the money that was going into the till from all the happy customers.

'There's a table over in the corner. It's very busy here. Surprising, as it's not like it's a tourist town.'

'Yes, and to think that this once was just a bit of waste land next to the shop. Look at it now! I'm having a small beer and an ice cream. How about you, Sarah?'

'The same, I think.'

A young girl came over and took the order as they settled in. Sarah could see Ancor was taking everything in. A couple of locals acknowledged him and he said hello back, then laughed to himself as they wandered away. It was something Sarah didn't see very often. Something had obviously made him giggle!

'What's so funny?'

'Before we even make it back to Kalanchoe the gossip will be that I was sat here with a young woman. I wonder how long before it gets back to Iballa? Of course she'll find it hilarious.'

They both laughed at the image of Iballa hearing

the 'news'.

The drinks and ice creams arrived, and they sat in happy silence as Sarah tried to figure out how to steer the conversation around to the bakery café.

'This makes a nice change, doesn't it? Especially for you, as you never stop, you're always on the go,' Sarah observed.

'Yes, and sat in here, amongst the plants, you could be anywhere really. It's lovely but...'

'But what, Uncle?'

'Plants... Yes, plants! It all makes sense now. Ergual ... the café ... this is where he must have got the idea from... Judging by the look on your face, you know exactly what I'm on about. Is that why we're here, Sarah?'

'Please don't be cross. I admit that yes, I did sort of plan this. I just thought it would be nice for you to see what's possible. I'm sorry, I shouldn't have tried to trick you. And please don't blame Ergual; he knows nothing about this.'

'I'm shocked you would do this for Ergual when he has been nothing but snappy and nasty to you and Debbie since you arrived back in Tenerife.'

'Oh, he's not too bad, just a bit headstrong, and when you were away on Gran Canaria he was very helpful.'

'Headstrong. That runs in the family...' Ancor said, looking a bit sheepish.

'You just have a lot to think and worry about with the bakery, Uncle. It's only natural that you'd be protective of that.'

'Worry is the word, Sarah. From the moment I left school I knew the bakery would be my responsibility until the day I died, and not just to provide for my family, but for the whole of Kalanchoe. They rely on the bakery; if it wasn't there, how would they cope, especially the elderly? I know people think I'm a stickler for things and everything has to be done a certain way, but I don't know any differently. I just think that if things have worked – and worked well – since my grandfather started the business, why mess with that? This belief has caused friction with people around me – it was Ancor's way and nothing was going to change that – and I know I've upset people along the way, and that wasn't right.'

This was a very different side to her uncle and Sarah could see he was getting upset. She felt bad.

'I don't think you need to focus on that. The past is the past. You need to think of the future instead. Ergual wants to help and he needs you to help him achieve his potential. Why not let him give things a go in the café? What's the worst that could happen? He needs something in his life to focus on. He's not a kid anymore, he's a man, and if you do this together it could bring you so much closer. I don't want to speak out of turn, but I think he wants the same relationship with you as you have with Ruben. He wants that same mutual respect.'

Ancor looked as though he was shrinking into his chair, the upright man crumbling. She worried she had gone too far and said too much, not just overstepped the line but raced way past it, but there was no going back now she had put her cards on the table.

'Thank you for bringing me in here to chat. I needed it and although I'm upset, I'm also happy. Before we go, there's something else I need to say. I know your mum thinks I drove your dad away to England, but I didn't. Ultimately it was what he needed to do, because he could never have stayed here in the shadow of his dad and grandfather and me. He was his own person and his life in England was far happier than it would have been if he had stayed here.'

Chapter 28

Debbie was ten minutes from Tillandsia. She was meeting Pedro for a coffee before he started work as he'd said he needed to chat to her about something very important. She'd guessed it was probably about staying here in Tenerife, and she had an answer for him, though he wouldn't be happy. She was going back to the UK and she would live with her mum until she had sorted out a job.

'Morning, Pedro, what was so important that I had to meet you so early?'

'Before I explain I need you to promise me that you won't interrupt or walk away.'

'I promise.'

'Are we good friends?' Pedro asked.

'Yes, we are, but I'm not sure where this is going,' Debbie answered, a bit confused.

'Good. Now, as you know, sometimes a friend can see things a lot clearer than the other person does, and so it's their responsibility to help their friend out.'

'You have completely lost me.'

'I've done something that I feel is the right thing to do.'

Pedro looked nervous and it was clear that he was taking this conversation very seriously.

'I've made you an appointment with Bentor for you to talk about the job offer. Debbie, the cards are in your hands. Ok, Bentor is a good friend of yours, but you need to get the best deal you can, as your main objective is to start saving money for your future. It's not just about the hourly pay, it's all the other bits you need to consider, like getting meals provided on shifts – that would save you a fortune on food – and you need to discuss if the job is five nights a week or six. If it's five, you need to negotiate doing an extra one for overtime payments.'

As promised, she had sat silently listening, but she realised he had now finished.

'But Pedro … *you* want the job.'

'No, this is a chance for you to get back on your feet. It's the new start you're looking for, giving you a brighter future.'

'But why?'

'That's quite simple. You're my best friend and I want you to be happy, and this job will make you happy. Now, you have twenty minutes before your appointment, so I suggest you take this notebook I've got for you and read the page of questions suggesting what you need to be asking. I'll see you after the interview. Remember, Debbie, Bentor needs you a lot more than you need him. Use that to your advantage.'

With that, he was gone. She was gobsmacked. How and what had just happened? To think, he had gone to all this trouble for her…

****

Twenty minutes later she had read the list of questions she had to ask, and she was stood outside the restaurant, ready to go in.

Right, here goes. Five, four, three, two, one… I'm through the door.

'Hello, Bentor.'

'Hi, Debbie, can I get you a drink?'

'No, thanks, I'm ok.'

'Well then, shall we get down to business? Quite a lot has been done next door since you last saw it. I really think you'll be impressed.'

Debbie followed him into the bar area and to

her surprise there weren't many workmen in there, just a couple of painters.

'It really has come on. The bar is standing out even more now the walls have been painted and it looks great.'

'Thank you. Yes, it's almost ready for artwork and mirrors, which I really can't wait for.'

'It's going to look so chic and will definitely blend well into the restaurant next door.'

'So that's the niceties over with. Shall we get down to business?'

Debbie nodded and they each took a seat at the bar.

'Before we start, I know you will have given this so much thought – it's not a spur of the moment thing – and that's good as I want us to be on the same page from day one. I suggest that you tell me what you want out of the job, and then I'll explain what I need from you, and we can find the best way forward. What do you think?'

Debbie was a little shocked. Bentor was clearly under the impression that she had asked to see him when really this was all Pedro's doing. He had set them both up, but in the kindest way possible.

'Yes, that sounds fine with me. But why don't you start first, Bentor? Tell me your vision and what you expect to see here in the evenings... Why are you laughing at me?'

'Sorry, it just feels as though you're interviewing me when it should be the other way around! But that's not a problem. Now, you remember how when you and Pedro worked for me in the club we had our bonus system, which was based around how many people you brought in, and how much they drank? Well, I thought something similar might work here, and we could split the bonus between you and the cocktail barman.'

'Have you employed a cocktail barman yet?'

'No but that's only because I've been waiting for you to accept the job so we could interview the candidates together. There was no point in me doing it by myself as I need someone that you can build a good relationship with as you'll have to work as a close-knit team.'

'So how did you know I would accept the job? My intentions were to go back and work in the UK.'

'Because the job has your name written all over it ... and now you're laughing?'

'Because that's what my sister and Mum said, almost verbatim! So, let's get down to the nitty gritty. Let me get my notebook and you can tell me what I'm worth in euros.'

****

Over the next couple of hours they covered everything there was to cover about the new bar and how it would operate.

'So, we've covered everything apart from the most important thing,' Bentor said as they were finishing up.

'Oh yes, of course, when do I start?'

'Oh, two things then. I think it will be in a couple of weeks, as long as we can get a barman that we like by then. And I don't want a big opening. I want the cocktail bar to just slip in slowly so we can deal with the teething troubles before we start promoting it. No, the important thing I was referring to is the problem of Pedro. What are we going to do about him? With you running the cocktail bar you'll sort of be one of his bosses.'

'There's no problem there, Bentor. If anything, I think Pedro will be very supportive.'

'I like your confidence, but somehow I'm not so sure. Please let me know if you run into any issues. The only other thing to say is that having you on board is such a relief. I just know you'll work as if it's your own business and that having this to focus on will help you to heal and move past the last few years. Now, was there anything else?'

'No, that's it from me,' Debbie said happily.

'Then I'll be off. I have a very interesting meeting to attend with my accountant. Actually, it's likely to be more of a telling-off as I've gone over budget with the refurbishment. Wish me luck!'

'Good luck!' she said with a laugh as Bentor bounded off.

Looking at the time she saw she had about an hour before Pedro would finish work. It would give her time to have a quick look around a few of the clothes shops in the area for a little inspiration for what she would wear for the new job. The fact that she was allowed to choose for herself made her smile. It would never have happened if she was still with Steven, and it showed how far she'd come.

Right, she needed practical clothes, not formal but not too casual, and she had to look the part of a manager but also blend in with the surroundings. She went through a few shops before she found something she liked and was looking over her options when all of a sudden her phone rang. It was Pedro.

'Oh no, am I late? Sorry! I'll be right with you. I just got carried away in the shops and time has run away with me.'

'No problem. Shall I walk towards you and we can find something to eat?'

'Yes, that would be nice. Actually, why don't we meet at our favourite pizza restaurant? I'll head that way now.'

'Great, give me two minutes and I'll be there.'

****

They arrived at the pizzeria at the same time and quickly placed their order without looking at the menu. There was no need as they both always had the same thing.

'How did it all go with Bentor? He was so excited when he popped back into the restaurant after your meeting. I hope you got a good deal from him, but saying that, you probably could have named your price.'

'I'm more than happy with the benefits he offered and so now it's full steam ahead. The bar is taking shape and I love the design. Once the two buildings become one it will flow brilliantly. We just need to find a good mixologist.'

'Sorry? What or who is that?'

'A mixologist is someone who makes bespoke cocktails, and we need a really good one as he or she will be what helps to draw the punters in. To be honest, they will be the person who makes or breaks the bar. Oh good, here come the pizzas. I'm so hungry!'

She eagerly tucked into her pizza but Pedro sat silently, leaving his untouched.

'Are you ok, Pedro? You've gone all quiet. I expect having a mixologist won't affect the restaurant part at all. If anything, it will make things easier as the wait staff won't need to be pouring the drinks or opening the wine anymore. It will all be dispensed from the cocktail bar.'

'I thought he would choose one of the staff who already worked there to do the job, but it all sounds a bit specialist to me.'

'Oh, yes, it is. The best mixologists are a bit theatrical and flamboyant. They make the drink mixing over the top and a bit of a show for the patrons.'

'It seems a waste of time to me as it's the food that people come for, not to be entertained by someone making drinks with paper umbrellas.'

'You need to remember that the cocktail bar is the next step in Bentor's plan to take the business a step forward, and the reason he's able to be hyper focused on it is because he's so happy with how the restaurant is being run. You and Patrice are a great team and he doesn't have to worry because he knows it's in very good hands.'

'Yes, but we were also a good team, and we still could be if I was working in the bar.'

'But that would mean the restaurant wouldn't run as well. Bentor needs us both to play to our strengths.'

'I suppose you're right.'

'Have I said thank you yet, for doing this for me? I needed the push. Even though my sister and mum kept telling me I could do it, I still didn't believe I actually could until you gave me the nudge I needed. You really are a good friend, and I'll always be so grateful for what you've done.'

'You don't have to thank me. I'm just sorry that it means I'll have to sacrifice the one thing I really want.'

'I don't understand.'

'You once told me that we could never be in a relationship if we were working together, and now we'll be working together again.'

'I'm sorry but you and I both know it would be too complicated.'

'That's where you're wrong. It would work. I would make sure of that because you're the most important thing in my life.'

Debbie didn't know what to say.

Chapter 29

Sarah had spent the afternoon in the apartment by herself planning what she was going to wear this evening on her night out with Ruben, as she wanted to put a bit of effort into it. Actually, if she was really honest, a lot of effort. She wanted it to be the perfect evening with no talk of the bakery or Kalanchoe, a complete switch off for them both. She had just made a cup of tea and was going out onto the balcony with her book when her phone rang. She saw it was Ancor. Hopefully nothing was wrong.

'Hi, Uncle Ancor, is everything ok?'

'Yes, thank you. I just wondered if I could ask a favour of you.'

'Of course, anything.'

'Would you be free to come down to the bakery tomorrow afternoon, say just after two, when it starts to get quiet? I need to have a chat with you.'

'Yes, that's no problem.'

Coming off the phone she hoped the chat would be about Ergual opening the café, but she dared not think that because she would be so disappointed if it wasn't. But what else could it be? Something to do with her mum? Her brain was working overtime, and she knew she had to switch off from those thoughts, so she focused on her night out with Ruben. Of course, the other thing on her mind was Alexander. She hadn't heard back from him so perhaps he had finally taken the hint and it was over for good. Yes, she was turning a corner, but though turning a corner was one thing, looking to the future was another ... and something she was still avoiding. Not like Debbie, who had made a decision – an exciting one – and grasped it with both hands. She was pleased for her, and happy to see her sister looking forward to the future. She had come a long way.

'Hi, Sarah, I'm back.'

'Hello, Mum, how was your day? Come sit on the balcony. I'll make you a cup of tea.'

'Thank you, darling, I'll just go and change first. Give me two minutes.'

Checking the time Sarah worked out she had an hour before she had to start to get ready for her night out.

Tea made and accompanied by the biscuit tin, she went back onto the balcony.

'Oh, thank you, but no biscuits for me. I've been snacking on them all day at Iballa's. Are you all set for tonight? I did briefly see Ruben today as I had to nip around to the bakery to pick up some things for your aunt and Ancor was busy serving. I asked Ruben if he was looking forward to his night out and he blushed and smiled. Eventually he said "yes, very much so". He's a nice lad. Your dad always said so as well.'

'He is, and he's so different once he's away from the bakery; he chats and the shyness goes. I'm beginning to realise more and more that it's all down to Ancor, whereas I always thought it was Ergual. And talking of Ancor, he phoned me and asked if I could pop down to the bakery tomorrow for a chat. I'm hoping it has something to do with the café.'

'That's interesting. I think you're right because as I left to head back today I saw him in the café courtyard chatting to an older chap. By the way, Iballa has decided she doesn't need me to go and help her every day as she's managing to dress herself and do most things, although she has agreed for me to still go and help with her cleaning a couple of days a week.'

'So you're officially on holiday! We need to plan things – beach days, shopping trips, and of course meals out – and hopefully Debbie will be able to join us before she starts working at the bar.'

'That would be nice. Now tell me, what are you wearing tonight for your date?'

'It's not a date, we're just going out for a meal.'

'Either way, I'm so pleased for you, Sarah. You did have me worried for a time there!'

'Even though I'm no further on with sorting everything out than I was the day I arrived? At this point the only thing I'm sort of sure of is that I'll move back in with you, and please don't think I'm taking that for granted. I'm very thankful I'm able to do that.'

'Of course, darling, that's not a problem. Like your father and I said to you both when you moved out, it will always be your home and your rooms are always there for you. But would you not be tempted to look for something here in Tenerife? You speak Spanish, the apartment is here, and now you're dating Ruben... Could Tenerife perhaps be a fresh start for you?'

'I think you're getting a bit ahead of yourself. I'm just going out for the evening with Ruben; I'm not in a relationship with him! And on that note, I'm off to get ready.'

Sarah smiled to herself at how her mum never missed an opportunity to say exactly what she was thinking. But no, Tenerife wasn't on her life plan. Ok, it has been good to come here for a break, but as for living here... For a start, she couldn't do what Debbie was doing; working in the catering industry and dealing with people wasn't her thing. But saying that, the few weeks in the bakery serving customers were fun, very laid back and not at all stressful. But no, she was best sitting in an office and organising things, that was what she was cut out for, and once back in England that's what she would be doing.

'Oh, darling, you look lovely! I've not seen that dress before; it's gorgeous,' her mum exclaimed as Sarah emerged from her bedroom.

'Thank you. I've never worn it because it was for something Alexander and I were going to go to, but then everything happened, and I didn't get the chance to wear it. I'm going to have a glass of wine as I have half an hour before I need to meet Ruben. Would you like one?'

'That would be lovely. Was that a knock at the door? Perhaps your date is early. We both know how keen he is.'

'Very funny, Mum.'

As Sarah walked to the door, she had butterflies in her stomach. Clearly Ruben wasn't the only one that was keen. Before opening the door, she quickly straightened her dress and took a deep breath.

'Hello, Sarah.'

Her jaw nearly dropped when she saw who was standing in her doorway.

'Alexander! What are you doing here and why?'

The butterflies in her stomach turned to a sick feeling. She couldn't speak. Come to that, she couldn't even think!

'Aren't you going to invite me in? I've come all this way to see you.'

On autopilot, she stood to one side so he could enter.

'Who's at the door?' her mum called, coming around the corner and stopping short. 'Alexander. What are you doing here?' she said, echoing Sarah's question.

'Hello, Gina, I've come to see Sarah. I was trying to figure out the last time I was here. Didn't Sarah and I come over for a surprise on your birthday? That must have been four or five years ago now.'

'Yes, that's right. Why don't you take a seat out

on the balcony? Sarah and I won't be a minute.'

'Mum, what do I do?' Sarah whispered in panic as soon as Alexander was outside.

'You will do what you were going to do. You'll go on your date with Ruben and I'll sort Alexander. He shouldn't be here and he's not welcome. Would you like me to ask him to leave? As far as I'm concerned, he can get the next plane back to England.'

'No, Mum, it's ok. I'll talk to him but first I need to tell Ruben I can't go out tonight.'

'Why can't you? You've been so looking forward to tonight and so has Ruben. Please don't let Alexander spoil your evening.'

'I have to. I need to talk to him and find out why he's here and ... I want to hear what he has to say.'

'I can tell you exactly what he's going to tell you. He'll say he's sorry, that it was a mistake, a spur of the moment thing, and if you'll only forgive him, it will never happen again... It's all utter rubbish. It's your choice, but I have no interest in listening to Alexander's pitiful excuses so I'm going to my room.'

'I'm sure it's not like that at all.'

'And I'm sure it is. He has come to grovel and win you back because he needs someone to run his business while he is out on the road chatting up other women.'

With that Gina went off to her room. Sarah picked up her phone to text Ruben, but she knew he deserved more than that, so she went into the bathroom where she could phone him without being overheard.

'Hi, Ruben, it's Sarah.'

'What good timing. I've just pulled up outside the apartment.'

'I'm so sorry but I can't make it tonight. We have a family emergency.'

'Oh dear. Is there anything I can help with? No one is ill, I hope.'

'No, we've had someone turn up unexpectedly and it needs sorting. I'm so sorry but I need to go now. I'll call you tomorrow, ok?'

'Of course—' Ruben began but Sarah had already ended the call.

Right, she needed to pull herself together. She wanted answers as to why he was here.

'Sorry, I just had to make a call,' she said as she went through to the balcony. 'Can I get you a drink?'

'That would be nice. A beer, please. I did wonder if you would even let me in, but I kept telling myself you were always so thoughtful, kind, and understanding. Slamming a door in my face was never your thing.'

Without answering she went to the fridge and fetched him a beer. Her hands shook as she poured it into the glass. He was right; going off on one wasn't her thing. So, she would sit quietly and listen to what he had to say before doing or saying anything. She handed him the glass and then sat on one of the other chairs.

'Is your mum not joining us? I guess she's not that happy I'm here.'

'No, she just has things to be getting on with.'

'Is that why you're all dressed up? Were you off somewhere?'

'Yes, but only a family thing. It's not important.'

Why was she lying? She had done nothing that she had to make an excuse for.

'So, Alexander, why are you here?'

'I just felt I needed to explain. We've had quite a few weeks apart to give us some breathing space, and it goes without saying how sorry I am, but like I said at the time, it was a spur of the moment thing, and it meant nothing. That woman was only after one thing, and it wasn't me – she wanted free greeting cards so she flirted and came on to me to save herself the money. So now that's out of the way,

I thought we could talk about how we can move forward.'

Sarah heard the apartment door open and realised she'd entirely forgotten about Debbie.

'Mum, I'm back! Did Sarah get away ok? Did she look nice... Sarah, you're still here? Oh no, why is *he* here?'

'Alexander has come to Tenerife to talk over a few things.'

'Oh, *has* he? Well, it's not happening here because he isn't welcome in this apartment. I suggest you tell him to leave because if it's left to me, it won't be done politely,' she said, as if Alexander couldn't hear her perfectly.

'It's not like that. I've flown over to sort things out with Sarah.'

'I think it's exactly like that. My sister ran your business brilliantly for you while you drove around the country chatting up every card and greeting shop owner you could. If my sister is stupid enough to even consider listening to anything you have to say, that's her choice. But it's not happening here in our family home. Now get out before I throw you out.'

Chapter 30

Sarah wasn't looking forward to leaving her room. She knew she'd have to eventually, but after Debbie had thrown Alexander out the apartment last night she had fled to the security it provided, only creeping out to get a drink and make a sandwich after her mum and sister had both gone to bed. It was all very much like being a teenager, and a little stupid really. No, it was ridiculous. She wasn't a teenager, she was an adult in control of her own life! She needed to leave the room and face the music.

'Morning, Mum,' she ventured quietly.

'Good morning, darling. It's another lovely sunny day.'

It was clear that as far as her mum was concerned, last night's episode was over and done with, and she was going to carry on as if it was just a normal day. It wouldn't be the same story with Debbie when she got up though. Oh no, there would be lots of questions. Hopefully she would at least be a bit calmer now.

As she poured herself a coffee and made some toast she flicked through her phone. There were no new texts from Alexander but there was one from Ergual saying his dad wanted to talk to him in the café this afternoon. As Ancor had mentioned she would be there as well Ergual wondered if she thought Ancor might be coming around to the idea of having the plants in the café. Her phone rang before she had time to answer, and she saw it was Alexander.

'Hi, how are you today?'

'I'm fine, thank you. I've just had a big breakfast in the hotel and I was wondering when we can meet up. Obviously not at your apartment as your sister has made it more than clear I'm not welcome there.'

'It would be good to talk but I have somewhere to be this afternoon – a family thing at the bakery. I could meet you afterwards if that fits with your plans?'

'Perfect. We can have dinner and make a night of it.'

'I'll text you later and let you know when I've finished with my uncle and cousin.'

'Yes, do that. I'll only be at the hotel pool.'

'Ok.'

As Sarah ended the call she could hear her sister moving around in her room. It was time to prepare for the worst. She wouldn't argue back, she would just be calm and say what she had to say in a clear manner.

'You have perfect timing, Debbie, the kettle just boiled,' Gina said.

'Great! Mum said you have an interesting day planned today, Sarah.'

'Sorry?'

'She said you're meeting Uncle Ancor down at the bakery.'

'Oh, yes, and I've had a text from Ergual to say he'll be there as well. I think after our outing Uncle Ancor might have come around to the idea of Ergual filling the café with plants, but we'll have to see. You look very smart today. Are you off to meet Pedro?'

'No, I'm meeting Bentor to go through all the applicants for the bartender job. We hope to start interviewing them in the next few days.'

'That's great news. What are you planning for today, Mum?'

'I thought I would pop over to Iballa's for a bit, just to make sure she's ok, but apart from that, nothing really. Shall I cook us something nice to eat tonight?'

'I think I'm going out, Mum, sorry,' Sarah said.

'Oh, you've rescheduled your meal with Ruben? How exciting.'

'No, I ... have other plans. If no one else needs the bathroom I think I'll have a quick shower.'

As Sarah got up to leave, she could see Debbie and her mum exchanging a look. It was clear they knew she would be meeting Alexander, but thankfully neither of them brought it up. They were going to let her sort it out herself, for which she was grateful.

****

'Hi, Uncle, I'm a bit early.'

'Hello, Sarah. You look very nice. Are you off somewhere?'

'I might as well tell you as you will inevitably find out. Alexander turned up yesterday, and we're meeting later to have a chat.'

'So that explains it.'

'Sorry?'

'Ruben was so excited to be going out with you last night and then this morning his chin was on the ground and he was even quieter than normal. When I asked him if he had a nice evening, he said you cancelled as there was a family issue and I was wondering what that was. The nerve of that man, turning up here in Tenerife after what he did to you. Well, at least you've had the last laugh.'

'I don't know what you mean,' Sarah said, perplexed.

'Well, he spent all that money on flights and a hotel only to get the kick up the backside he deserves. Have I said the wrong thing?' he asked, seeing her expression. 'Oh... You haven't told him to get lost, have you? Look, I know it's none of my business, but if your dad was around he would certainly have had something to say, and I know Alexander would be on the first flight off the island.'

Sarah suddenly realised Ruben was stood in the doorway. Had he heard the conversation? She was about to go and speak to him but Ergual came through the door just then.

'Great! You're both here. Shall we go into the café?' Ancor said, all the seriousness of the moment before forgotten. 'Ruben, can you keep an eye on the shop? We won't be very long.'

Sarah smiled at Ruben but he looked the other way. He had definitely heard the conversation and now knew she had cancelled a night with him to be with Alexander. But just like her mum and sister, he didn't understand the circumstances. There was nothing she could do about it for now so she followed Ancor into the café, quickly looking at Ergual and showing him her crossed fingers.

'Now, where do we start? At the beginning is probably best, so talk me through the thoughts you both have about this space.'

Sarah could see Ergual was nervous, and that she might be needed to take the lead, so she got the ball rolling.

'Well, Uncle, what we both thought – and please don't take this the wrong way – was that the café needs freshening up. One way to do this would be to do something similar to the space you and I saw the other day, with big pots of plants employed to break the place up and mask some of the areas that need to be overhauled. This would allow us to refresh the space without changing any of the original features that were here when our great-granddad started the business.'

'And that's what you think as well?' he asked Ergual.

'Yes. The plants wouldn't necessarily be cheap, but we wouldn't be doing any damage to the building, which I know is a major concern of yours.'

'I have to admit that I was impressed with what the owner of that place has done with that horrible piece of ground. It's magnificent. It has also made me stop and think about this place, and see it in a new light. Now let's cut to the chase. How do you see the future of this place?'

'What do you mean?' Ergual asked, shooting a concerned glance at Sarah.

Sarah could see Ergual was confused, but she wasn't. That trip with her uncle had obviously had a significant impact and she was beginning to see that this meeting wasn't about plants at all.

'Say, for example, that I had nothing to do with the café, that it was entirely yours and you had some money to spend on it. What would you do with that cash? Where would you start?'

The smile on Ergual's face was something Sarah had never seen before, and she was happy to stand back and let him have his moment because she knew the enthusiasm would shine out of him.

For the next half an hour Ergual walked them through the premises, talking about each part in great detail, from knocking down the wall to make the kitchen area so much smaller, to a little bit of levelling off the floor needed, to having the walls redone to see if there was exposed brickwork hiding behind the plaster. He had put so much thought into it. Ok, a few of the things he mentioned had originally been Sarah's ideas, but he had run with them and thought them through in new ways. She was so impressed. She was also impressed with her uncle, who was taking it all in and listening without interrupting.

'And Sarah, what are your thoughts on what Ergual has had to say?' he asked at last.

'I think it's exciting. It's very ambitious, yes, and will require a huge commitment – of both money

223

and time – so the two of you will have your hands full, but the final result will absolutely be worth it. And it should go without saying that if there's anything I can do to help, I'm more than willing.'

'Actually, there is something you could do,' Ancor said. 'Would you be able to do a few hours in the bakery shop some days so we can get the ball rolling? I'm also hoping it might bring a smile back to Ruben's face if you're there.'

She didn't know what to say. Of course she didn't have a problem with helping, but cheering Ruben up? Well … she couldn't see that happening as she had cancelled on him and didn't have a good excuse for doing so.

'I'd be happy to. Just let me know what days and what times work best. For now, I think I'll let you both get on with the planning. I can't wait for the work to get started!'

What an outcome! Sarah was over the moon and couldn't wait to tell her mum. First, though, she needed to call Alexander to see where he wanted to meet up.

She called but there was no answer, and it was half an hour before he called back.

'Hi, sorry, I was in the pool playing water volleyball.'

'I've finished with my uncle and am ready to meet up.'

'What? Now? I was just about to join in with a few more pool games and I'm sort of committed to them for the rest of the day.'

Sarah could hardly hear what he was saying with all the loud music and shouting in the background.

'Ok. Text me a place and time we can meet up later and I'll be there. Can you hear me? I said text me… I'll let you go as I can hear a woman shouting your name,' she said sharply before hanging up.

Why, oh why, was she even meeting up with him? Her excitement after the great meeting about the café had now fizzled and she was frustrated because she couldn't talk to anyone about it as she knew they would simply tell her to get rid of Alexander once and for all. Of course that's what her head was also telling her to do, but her heart wasn't so certain. There was just so much history between them, and a safety in returning to what she already knew so well.

Rather than go back to the apartment she decided to kill time with a walk. She knew most hotel pools closed at six in the evening, so she would only have a few hours to fill, and if she headed towards Alexander's hotel, she would be near when he phoned—

Her phone beeped and she breathed a sigh of relief. He had obviously had second thoughts and was ready to meet now. But looking at the screen she saw it was Ergual instead, asking if she was free for a chat. She rang him.

'Congratulations!' she said as soon as he answered. 'I'm so excited for you!'

'Thank you, and thank you so much for taking Dad up to the village to see the space. If it wasn't for that, I'm sure none of this would be happening.'

'No problem at all. He just needed to be pointed in the right direction. I'm really looking forward to seeing everything start to happen.'

'That's actually what I'm calling about. Would you be able to meet me at the café when the builder comes to look at the work he has to do? I know my dad has agreed to everything in theory, but I'm worried about him changing his mind and I don't want him and the builder outnumbering me and leading us to end up with something completely different to what we had planned.'

'I'd be happy to help. Just let me know when

and I can fit my schedule around you.'

'Thank you, Sarah. Hope you have a nice rest of your day!'

Coming off the phone Sarah couldn't believe the difference in her cousin. The use of 'please' and 'thank you', the lack of aggression in his voice – he was a completely different Ergual, and that was a good thing.

Now to the task at hand for today: how was she going to approach her meeting with Alexander? The thought made her smile as she sounded just like the old Sarah. Before she knew it she would be getting a pen and paper out and making a list.

Heading along the coastal path towards Alexander's hotel she decided to stop for a drink at one of the beach bars. Taking a seat in the shade under an umbrella she ordered a gin and tonic and a bowl of cheesy chips. The drink was to steady her nerves, and the chips, well ... they would stop her stomach rumbling. Now it was just a waiting game until he called.

****

One gin led to three and before Sarah knew it, it was getting late. She was just about to call Alexander when he texted to say he could meet her somewhere in half an hour. Instead of texting back, she called him.

'I'll meet you at your hotel and we can have a drink and a chat in the bar.'

'No, not here, let's go somewhere else. You choose.'

'Ok,' she said, confused at his vehemence. 'How about the hotel next to yours, the one with the big boat in the middle of the front flower bed? I can be there in five minutes. I'll see you there.'

As she walked over to the hotel two questions

circled in her mind: Why had he panicked when she mentioned going to his hotel? And had he been having a good time with someone he didn't want her to know about? All of a sudden she could hear her mum's voice in her head saying that if he cheated once, he would do it again.

This was a bad idea. She should never have let him into the apartment, let alone agreed to talk things over. Before she could leave, though, Alexander appeared.

'You look lovely. Shall we go in? Are you sure this place is ok for you?'

'Thank you and yes, this is perfect.'

Alexander led the way through the hotel to the bar and they took a seat at one of the tables outside. Sarah knew she should have ordered a soft drink rather than another one with alcohol, but it was too late now.

'How were the pool games?' she asked.

'Oh, it was fine. You know how it is when you're by yourself, it's always difficult to say no when people invite you to do things.'

'No, I don't know. Now why are you here in Tenerife? Or to put it another way, what do you want from me?'

'I missed you and wanted to see you and to find out what I can do to put things right between us. How can we get back to how we were before my mistake? The business needs you. I'm struggling with being on the road all week and having to spend the weekends doing the paperwork and invoicing. The filing is also out of control. I don't think either of us is happy and as I see it, there's an easy way to fix that. Come home with me, Sarah.'

The gin had really kicked in and all of a sudden she felt strong and in control.

'I can imagine the business is in a right mess and I'll admit I do miss it. We started it from nothing and look how successful it's become.'

'So we can get back to normal after you've come back to England?'

'Yes and no. The only way I would come back to work is if I get to be the one on the road, selling the cards, getting new customers, and looking after the clients we already have. You can run the office.'

'But ... but it won't work like that. I need to be the one on the road. My customers like to see me,' he said, almost whining.

'And look where that got you. That's the deal so you can take it or leave it. Thank you for the drink and there's no need to get up. I can find my own way out. Goodbye.'

Chapter 31

It was interview day and Debbie was heading over to the new bar to meet Bentor. They had five cocktail barmen to interview and she already knew from the CVs Bentor had emailed her which one she liked best.

'Good morning, Bentor. Oh my goodness, it's really taking shape now, isn't it? There can't be much more to do.'

'It's certainly getting there, and I'm really pleased. Not long now until we can get the furniture in and then we'll really notice a difference. Are you ready for today? Have you looked over the CVs?'

'Yes but what's on a CV is one thing, chatting to them will be completely different.'

'For me the main thing is that they have to fit in and gel with the other staff, especially you. As we have an hour before the first candidate arrives, do you fancy a coffee next door?'

'Sounds great,' she said as they stepped into the restaurant. 'Which order are the interviews in? Also, I find it strange that one of them is flying in for this. He must be keen!'

'Yes, that's Estefan. I know he's very good as I've seen him in action entertaining the customers with his cocktail making. I know you would get on well with him and I can see you being a good team, so my only concern is that he could be a bit over the top and not really suited to the restaurant, but we will see. Here you go, one coffee.'

'Thank you.'

'I cannot wait for it all to finally be opened between the two units,' he said as they made their way back outside and across to the bar. 'When the connecting doorway is finished and unveiled, that's when the final vision will really take shape. I know it's going to look spectacular.'

Bentor had made sure there were no workmen on site today so there wouldn't be any interruptions, and he had given plenty of time between each of the interviews so there was no overlapping and they would be able to discuss each one after they had left. Debbie was feeling a little nervous; she had only been in this situation once before and that was when she and Steven had interviewed staff for the nail salon. Not that she'd really been needed for that given that she wasn't allowed to speak or ask questions, and he'd decided who they hired entirely on his own. She was glad to know that on this occasion Bentor would appreciate her feedback. She got her notebook out and turned to the page where she had jotted down a few notes about the first candidate when she'd read through his CV. She was ready.

The first lad was early – and she used the word 'lad' literally as he looked about twelve or thirteen, even though he was actually in his twenties – and so quiet it took everything Bentor had to coax him into answering their questions. Although he had been working in a very prestigious hotel on the island, it was clear from his answers that he'd never come into contact with the customers, only the waiting staff. He was definitely a 'no' for the job.

'Hopefully the next one will be better,' Bentor said after the lad had left. 'He speaks multiple languages and he's been doing the job for about ten years.'

'Yes, he's the one I'm putting my money on, I think. That looks like him at the door now.'

Bentor got up and went to see the candidate in and Debbie couldn't help but think that he didn't really look the part. But then, he wasn't here to look good, just to entertain and serve the customers.

'Acton, this is Debbie, who will be running the cocktail bar. Please take a seat.'

'Hi, Acton, thank you for coming to see us today. Your CV is very impressive.'

'Thank you.'

For the next half an hour they chatted about Acton's work history and what he loved and didn't like about the previous jobs he'd held. He was ticking all the boxes with Debbie and she could tell he would be methodical, reliable, and perfect for what they needed. She also felt she could work well with him, although she got the impression Bentor wasn't keen, which was confirmed once they had thanked him for coming and he'd left.

'Ok, he could do the job with his eyes closed, but I don't think he's the right one, do you, Debbie?'

'I think he could be, but he's only the second person we've spoken to. We have three more to go today and if none of them suit, we'll just keep looking.'

The next two were definitely both a 'no' though – one had clearly lied on his CV as he had no knowledge about cocktails, and the other made it clear that he thought he was right and everyone else was wrong – so that just left the chap who was flying over for the interview.

'We have about an hour and a half before Estefan gets here so do you fancy a little fresh air?' Bentor asked. 'We could walk down to the sea front and have a drink or a snack, if you like.'

'Ok, that would be nice.'

They walked in silence, both going over the last few hours in their heads. Debbie did think Acton could do a great job, but as Bentor wasn't keen they might need to continue their search. Considering he had invited this Estefan chap for the interview, he must really want him for the role. But what if she didn't? Finding someone they both liked sounded easy on paper, but in reality, it seemed as though it was going to be a lot more difficult.

'I'm having a club sandwich, what do you fancy?' Bentor asked as they settled into a table.

'I'll have the same, please.'

They both ordered a Coke to go with it.

'So how are you enjoying your first day of work?' Bentor asked.

'It's been good so far. Whoever would have thought I'd be here though.'

'Oh, I knew the minute you told me you weren't currently working that I could persuade you. There was never any doubt in my mind. And I'm so glad to have you onboard. My life will be so much easier with you here.'

'That's very kind of you to say.'

With that the food arrived and the conversation turned back to the interviews.

'Tell me more about this Estefan chap. You obviously think very highly of him, so why not just give him the job? Why go through all we've been through today?'

'Because I'm not a hundred per cent sure he's the right person. He'll be great with the customers – I'm sure he'll have them eating out of his hands – and he definitely looks and talks the part, but – and it's a bit of a big "but" – I don't know that he and the rest of the staff will gel.'

'What makes you say that?'

'Because I suspect he'll think he's better than them, and will struggle to conceal that.'

'Oh dear. Are you sure it's a good idea to consider him then?'

'We have to – his skills are really something and he would bring a lot to the experience for customers.'

'So what are you going to do about his attitude?'

'Nothing. I'm leaving that up to you. Not in a horrible way,' he rushed to add. 'I just mean that I've no doubt that you'll be able to handle him and bring him in line.'

'You're scaring me now, Bentor. I'm not sure I want to meet this Estefan,' she said, slightly alarmed.

'You'll be fine. And if we do take him on, after a couple days of working with you he'll fall in line. Mark my words; you'll kick him into shape.'

'I'm glad we had that sandwich as it sounds like I'll need the energy to conquer this Estefan!' she joked. 'I think we need to be getting going now though. We don't want to keep him waiting.'

As they got near to the restaurant Debbie could see a chap stood chatting to Patrice. She knew it must be Estefan because he looked the part – tall, immaculately dressed, and very handsome. She smiled to herself, thinking how good he would look in the new space. It was as if the cocktail bar had been designed around him.

'What are you laughing at?' Bentor asked.

'Nothing really, just a few thoughts going around in my head. Why don't I go through to the new unit to get set up while you go and fetch Mr Fabulous.'

'Mr Fabulous?'

'Well, he's not yet told us that he's fabulous, but I'm sure he will within a few minutes.'

One thing she was sure of was that this interview would be nothing like the others. She placed some bottles of water on the table and grabbed her notebook out to have another quick read through of Estefan's CV.

'Please come in, Estefan. I'd like to introduce you to Debbie.'

'Hi, nice to meet you, Debbie. The space is gorgeous, Bentor, I love what you've done with the place. The bar is so shiny and it really will show me off to the customers.'

Debbie suspected that every night with Estefan behind the bar would be 'showtime' to him. She loved his confidence, but it was a fine line between confident and cocky...

'Now, Estefan, I know a bit about you and have seen you in action, but Debbie hasn't, so could you tell us both a bit about yourself and your work history?' Bentor began.

'There's so much to say so it's hard to know where to start. I'm one of the top mixologists on the island of Lanzarote, I've won multiple awards for my work, and people travel miles to see me perform. That's it, really, in a nutshell.'

Bentor talked a bit about the semantics of the job – how the shifts would work, how the restaurant would funnel patrons into and out of the bar, the type of clientele they normally served – but Debbie could tell Estefan wasn't really listening, probably because it was nothing about him. They chatted for half an hour or so, covering general information, important things to note, and learning a bit more about Estefan. Debbie realised from Bentor's demeanour that he was most likely going to offer Estefan the job regardless of what she thought, but she had to acknowledge that he was suitable, and the customers would love him.

'So, have you anything to ask Debbie or myself, Estefan?' Bentor concluded.

'When is the bar opening? I'll need to give a few weeks' notice.'

Debbie's suspicions were confirmed; he was taking it for granted that he would be offered the job.

'We think in a few weeks.'

'Oh, that will be fine, and it will give me time to find somewhere to live. I think that's it, really. I'm happy with the hours and wage – and of course I'll be making tips, which will be a bonus – and I assume the staff are up to scratch for a high-end cocktail bar? I don't want to be let down by them.'

'Yes, the staff have worked with me for many years, and they know exactly what I expect from them. There's no need to worry about that. But in here it will mainly just be you and Debbie working together.'

'That's good as it means we can build up a rapport. And once you know and understand what I expect of you, we should hopefully work well together,' Estefan said brazenly.

Debbie couldn't believe the nerve of him. Before she could go in all guns blazing, however, Bentor said, 'Estefan, I just need to talk over a few things with Debbie. Would you excuse us for a minute or two? Debbie, shall we step outside?'

Debbie followed Bentor out. She knew what was coming: he would try to persuade her that Estefan was the one for the job. If she was honest with herself and looked at the situation as if she were a customer, he was right. Estefan was a showman and that was what the job needed. But that attitude...

'You don't like him one bit, do you?' Bentor asked. 'I know he's a bit full of himself, but I think a lot of that is just bluster because he really wants the job and is trying to appear confident. He just needs to be shown who is boss and I know you can do that very easily. At the end of the day he answers to you, and if he wants the job he'll have to play by the rules and do what you say.'

'It's your business, Bentor, and I know from experience that you're always right with your gut instincts, so let's go back and put him out of his misery and tell him he's got the job.'

'Thank you, Debbie, and I think you should be the one to tell him.'

They walked back inside.

'Sorry to keep you waiting, Estefan. Bentor and I have talked it over and we think you're just what the cocktail bar needs to make it a success. There's just one little thing to clear up first. I am your boss, and *you* will be working *for me*, not the other way around. Now, are you sure you don't have any more questions? No? Ok then, if you'll excuse me, I need to pop next door to have a word with someone.'

Debbie took glee in the shocked look on Estefan's face as she waltzed out of the cocktail bar.

Chapter 32

The following morning both Gina and Sarah were in hysterics listening to Debbie telling them about Estefan's interview. They couldn't wait to meet him.

'So, what happened after you laid down the law and came back from the restaurant?'

'He was gone. Apparently before he could even say anything Bentor made it clear to him that what I'd said was true. I'm the boss and what I say goes.'

'That's good. At least you both know where you stand so you're starting off on the same page. It's so lovely to see you back on your game, Debbie, but as your mother I never had any doubts you wouldn't be. Now, Sarah, dare I ask what's happening with Alexander? And the million-dollar question: Does it involve you?'

Sarah had been waiting for this because if it hadn't come from her mum, it would have come from Debbie. She knew they didn't mean it in a horrible way, it was just that they really cared for her.

'As you know, we went for a drink. It wasn't the nicest of evenings. There was no kneeling down and begging me to come back, though I do believe he is genuinely sorry for what he's done. But I'll be honest with you, I did say I would help with the greeting card business ... but only on my terms, which would mean us switching roles so that I would be the rep and he would be office-based.'

'I bet that went down well,' Debbie said with one eyebrow raised.

'I don't know how it went down because I didn't wait for an answer before leaving, and I've not heard from him since.'

'Darling, thank you for being so honest with us. You could easily have lied or skipped around the question.'

'I agree,' Debbie said supportively. 'You have to do what's right for you. The last thing Mum and I would want is for you to take our advice and then regret something for the rest of your life. We love you and we're here for you. And on that note, what have we all planned for today? I have nothing. Do you have to go over to Iballa's, Mum?'

'No, not until tomorrow. How about you, Sarah?'

'I have an appointment with Ergual at the café. One of Ancor's builder friends is coming to discuss the refurb and Ergual asked me if I would be there to provide support. It should only take an hour or so, but they aren't sure what time the man is going to be there so it's a bit of a waiting game. I think that one of our phones is ringing...' She trailed off, stepping inside to see whose phone it was. 'Oh, it's mine,' she said, picking it up, 'and it's the call I've been waiting for.' She stared at the screen in indecision.

'Darling, why don't you take the call in the bedroom and talk to Alexander in private?'

'No, Mum, I've nothing to hide... Hi, Alexander.'

'For a minute, I didn't think you were going to pick up.'

'We were on the balcony and my phone was inside.'

'I was wondering if you'd like to meet for dinner tonight so we can talk over the practicalities of your suggestion. I could come over to Kalanchoe if that's easier for you?'

'Yes, it's fine for us to meet tonight, but I'll come to you and we'll eat in your hotel.'

'Oh no, the food's not that good. What say we meet in between?'

'Fine. How about Tillandsia? I know a lovely restaurant there. I have things to sort out with my uncle today and I'm not quite sure what time that will be done, so shall we say eight-fifteen?'

'That works for me. See you then.'

'See you then,' she echoed, hanging up. 'Mum, Debbie, I know what you're going to say – that I should just tell him to get lost. But if I did that without giving him the chance to speak I would always wonder "what if".'

'We support you completely,' Debbie said kindly. 'Now, another drink for either of you?'

'Not for me, thanks. I think I'll have a shower as I want to be ready for when Ergual calls to let me know the time of the builder's visit.'

While Sarah went to get ready, Debbie made two fresh coffees for herself and her mum. She couldn't wait to hear Gina's thoughts on that phone call.

'There you go, Mum. So, what did you make of all that?'

'Did you hear the panic in his voice when Sarah suggested meeting at his hotel? If I remember correctly, she mentioned earlier that when she met him last night for a drink, he wanted to go somewhere other than where he's staying. That seems very suspicious to me. Do you think he's hiding something?'

'Definitely.'

'It makes me suspect that Alexander is here for two reasons – to sort out his business, which is obviously in a mess without Sarah, and to have a fun holiday that doesn't involve your sister. But I have to say, Sarah is a lot cleverer than him, and I feel the outcome will be ok. Everything here in Tenerife is sorted.'

There was a long silence and although Debbie agreed that her sister's problem would soon be sorted – because she knew Sarah, and even though she might be doubting herself, Debbie would never doubt her – her mum's issues with Ancor definitely weren't, and this was an opportunity to mention them.

'But everything isn't sorted, Mum, because you still blame Ancor for Dad's decision to move to England. Until you clear the air with him, you will still be unhappy being here.'

'You two look like you're putting the world to rights,' Sarah said as she came back into the room, interrupting the conversation and giving Gina a reprieve from having to answer. 'Ergual just called me to see if I would go and look at a restaurant in Playa Del Duque with him before we meet the builder. He thinks it has the type of look he should create – the way they've done the tables, chairs, that type of thing – so do you mind if I nip off now?'

'No, of course not, darling. Good luck with the café this afternoon and with Alexander this evening. I know you will handle it perfectly.'

'Thank you, Mum, I promise you I won't be stupid.'

****

'Hi, Ergual. So, Del Duque. This sounds very interesting and I'm intrigued.'

'Thank you, but it might be a complete waste of time. I just thought it would be helpful to get your thoughts to see if it could work or not in Dad's café.'

'You've got that wrong, Ergual. You have to start thinking of it as *your* business, not your dad's.'

'I think you're jumping the gun there. It's one thing for Dad to agree to the renovation, but for him to actually hand it over to me is another thing entirely. And we both know what he's like, he still could change his mind about everything.'

240

'Don't think like that! Anyway he's not going to change his mind, and together we'll convince him your ideas to remodel the café are the right ones. I'll be honest with you though, I'm a little concerned his builder friend will find the image you want to create a little scary ... well, different. Something he's not used to doing, I mean. But enough of those doubts. We both need to be positive and focus on how exciting this is!'

****

Four hours later they had both drunk multiple drinks in half a dozen cafés and restaurants. They had started with the one Ergual wanted to show Sarah, but as they were there, they took the chance to tour others as well, and they were both on the same page. They knew what they liked and disliked, and they agreed that the look had to be plain and simple, nothing ornate or fancy. The brief for the reno would be fresh, clean, and minimal, which was a mixture of a few things they had seen.

'Thank you so much, Sarah. I really couldn't have done this without you. Now, we know what type of tables and chairs we need, but the crockery... I think that could be a sticking point with Dad as he won't necessarily understand why we can't use the old stuff.'

'Yes, I was thinking that too, but perhaps that conversation should be saved for another day. Small steps are the way forward with your dad, I think. That said, today will be the mountain we have to climb with him and the builder because you just know the chap is going to be older and love the traditional look. But if we stick together and make things clear there will be no grey areas.'

'But what if we've gone through all this, with the look and the fixtures and fittings, and Dad is having

241

none of it? I'll be so disappointed.'

'Come on, Ergual, we need to be positive! It may be time to go into the lion's den, but we're ready for him, and we'll present a united front.'

They drove back to Kalanchoe in silence, both very nervous, and Sarah kept thinking about Ancor. He didn't like change and this project wouldn't be cheap. There were so many obstacles they'd likely have to overcome. She also just knew the builder would be an old school friend who would think their ideas were rubbish and unachievable, but what she was worried about the most was Ergual. After all these years he finally had something to focus on, that he was excited about, and he was becoming a nicer person. The last thing she wanted was him to go back to the old Ergual.

'Right, here we are, Sarah. Are you ready? It's make or break time.'

'Yes, come on, let's do it.'

There was a builder's van parked outside the bakery and they could see the café lights were on.

'Hi, you two, how has your research trip gone?' Ancor asked as they stepped inside.

'Fine, thank you, Dad, it's definitely given us a few ideas.'

'That's good. My friend is in the café looking around. I'll just get Ruben to come through and cover the counter while we have our meeting. Oh by the way, Sarah, Iballa asked me to try and persuade you to come to dinner tonight. Your mum and sister are coming but apparently you have a business meeting with that Alexander. Couldn't you put him off until tomorrow?'

Of course Ruben had just walked into the shop and heard what Ancor said. This was so awkward! At least her uncle had said it was a meeting and not a date.

'Sorry, Uncle, but I can't. I really need to go

through some paperwork with Alexander and it can't wait. Now, are we ready to meet the builder?'

Sarah could see Ruben looked so sad and she really felt dreadful. She gave him a little smile before following Ancor and Ergual next door into the café. The first thing she noticed was exactly what she had expected – the builder was on the older side. Not that she had anything against old people, of course, but it did mean he would likely take a lot of convincing when it came to their modern ideas.

'Sarah, Ergual, let me introduce you to my good friend Angelo. We go back many years – far too many to remember – and he is one of the most respected craftsmen on the island.'

'You are very kind, Ancor. That means a lot coming from the best baker on the island.'

Ergual and Sarah gritted their teeth and smiled. It was clear that Angelo and Ancor were in lockstep, so this wasn't going to be an easy ride by any means.

'Now, Ergual, your dad tells me that you're taking over running the café but first a little refurb is needed. That's very exciting and also not before time, for both you and the café. I always thought one day I would drive by and the place would have collapsed as nothing had ever been done to it. It's great that it's finally going to get the love it deserves.'

'Thank you, that's what my cousin Sarah and I were thinking. Now-'

'Oh, I'm going to stop you right there as we need to wait until my son Pero and grandson Nico get here. They're the ones who are going to be doing the work, so they'll want to hear all your thoughts first-hand.'

'So, it's not you who will be doing the reno, Angelo?' Ergual asked, confused.

'What, at my age? No, I've not done manual work for years. Why should I when I have family that can do it for me? I'm just there to count the money and that's what your dad should be doing as well. I've been telling him that for years. Oh, here they come now.'

Sarah breathed a huge size of relief. Perhaps things would be a lot easier than they'd thought!

After all the introductions were over she stood back and let Ergual explain his vision for the café. She was ready to jump in at any point with support if needed, but it was clear Ergual didn't need it. Ancor didn't say a lot – to her great surprise! – but it was clear that he was taking everything in.

All the chatting between Pero and Ergual took about three quarters of an hour, and everything was very positive. They agreed that the wall between the kitchen and the café needed to come down and the walls needed to be skimmed, both of which wouldn't be a problem, Pero reassured them, as it was all very straightforward.

'So, Ergual, that's all fine,' Pero said as they wrapped up. 'But now the shop. What's your vision for that?'

They all exchanged confused glances. What did Pero mean?

Ancor was the first to speak.

'Sorry, Pero, I don't follow you. It's just the café we're renovating. We aren't changing the shop.'

'Oh, I just thought that you would want to make the entrance between the café and the bakery bigger as the shop is huge and from what I can see you have so much wasted space. It would be good to combine the two as I'm sure you would get at least four or five more tables in. You could add nice new shelves to display the bread and a new counter to help it all to flow together. That way the person serving in the shop would be able to give a hand with the café without having to walk all the way around outside.'

'That does sound wonderful, Pero, but my dad doesn't want to change the shop or the bakery part of the building.'

'Just a minute, Ergual, let's hear what Pero has to say. You never know, it might be just the right idea.'

Sarah was flabbergasted. Was this actually her uncle saying this? She wanted to laugh. To think it was only a short time ago that he had come back from Gran Canaria and moved everything back that she had spent hours reorganising. It made her realise that she wasn't needed here to support her cousin; he was more than capable of dealing with all of this by himself. She took a step back and smiled, feeling happy with how far they had all come.

'I need to be off, but it looks like you've all got a firm grip on this. It was lovely to hear how it's all going to come together, and I look forward to seeing the results.'

As she left the bakery and started to walk out of Kalanchoe towards the coastal path she felt thrilled with how everything was coming together, and took a moment to acknowledge that a lot of this wouldn't have happened if it wasn't for her. It wasn't being prideful, just honest. The other thing that crossed her mind was the fact that her dad would have been very proud of her.

Now that the café was moving forward in safe hands, it was time to face the problem of Alexander, and this time there would be no sitting back and watching everything pan out in front of her. No, her future was firmly in her own hands, and seeing how Ergual had stepped into a position of authority, she was ready to do the same. She got her phone out of her bag to text Alexander that she was free and on her way, but decided at the last second to call instead.

'Hi, Alexander, I'm on my way to Tillandsia and

I shouldn't be more than three quarters of an hour.'

'But I thought we were meeting later for a meal, not during the day.'

'Yes, but there's been a change of plan. I assume that's ok?'

'Not really. I'm sort of busy at the moment.'

That was it. Sarah had had enough.

'Ok, then I'll help you out. I'll come to your hotel for our chat. It won't take long to go through everything. Oh, but of course that's no good as you don't want me there, do you? So let's meet at the hotel next door to yours, the one where we had the drink. I'll see you there at three o'clock.'

With that she cut off the call. She knew he wouldn't cancel because at the end of the day, he needed her. He couldn't run the business without her.

She was almost at the hotel next to his, but she was early. How should she work this? Should she keep him waiting or be early to establish the upper hand? Knowing he could be late, as was his habit, she decided she would go into the hotel to sit and have a drink on the terrace while she waited. Her phone rang once she was settled at a table and as she went to grab it from her bag, she assumed it was Alexander calling with an excuse for why he would be late. She was pleasantly surprised to find it was Ergual instead.

'I hope I'm not disturbing you? I just wanted to thank you for your support today. It really helped.'

'I don't think it did. You were brilliant all on your own! And as for your dad... What was all that about? I was shocked at how calm he was while we were discussing all the changes.'

'I think it was all down to your chat with him. He's come to realise that change isn't a bad thing after all. I'll let you go now but I have to say how grateful I am that you came to Tenerife when you did. You've helped to change my life and I'll always be grateful.'

'You don't need to be thankful, Ergual, you were the one who did the heavy lifting. I was just the one who got you going. I'm so glad you're happy.'

'Talking of happy, there's someone here who isn't happy at all. He was so happy when you were working with him, but now he always has such a long face. What have you done to upset him?'

Sarah knew he meant Ruben and she didn't need the telling off because she felt bad enough already about that.

'Don't worry. I'm about to do something about that.'

Putting her phone back in her bag she headed into the hotel and ordered herself a glass of wine. Now all she had to do was wait for Alexander to arrive. She flicked through her phone and fired off a quick text to Debbie to say that there had been a change of plans and she wouldn't be having dinner with Alexander after all.

****

'Hi, Sarah, can I get you a drink?' Alexander asked when he arrived a while later.

'No, I'm fine, I've just had one.'

Sarah could see he looked nervous as he went to the bar to get a pint of lager. Once back she waited for him to speak first as she wanted him to start the conversation. She was interested to hear what he had to say.

'Are your mum and sister ok? Are they having a nice holiday?'

'They are, thank you.'

'And are you having a nice holiday?'

'Well, it's not really been a holiday for me as I've been helping out at the bakery. And now I'm here to

247

put things right with you. We really need to get back on track.'

'Yes definitely,' he agreed.

'I've been having second thoughts about what I said yesterday.'

'I'm very glad to hear you say that because it would never have worked, you out on the road visiting the shops and me at home doing all the admin. The customers love seeing me and I can always charm them into buying more stock. Now that's sorted and we've cleared the air, we can get back to normal.'

'You misunderstand me, Alexander. I've changed my mind about the business altogether. It was stupid of me to help you out once I had left you – that was a big mistake – but thankfully I've come to my senses before it's too late. You see, Alexander, since you cheated on me my life has been a mess, and I'll be honest with you, I've not wanted to face up to my future. Instead I've filled my days with all sorts of things to avoid thinking about my next steps. But today something clicked for me. All the things I've been involved with – the drama with the bakery, my sister's indecision about her future, and my mother's hesitance around returning to Tenerife – have sorted themselves, and walking here I realised that *you* are the last thing I need to fix before I can move on with my life. So, all I have to say is that I don't want anything to do with you anymore. I'm done with the business, and I'm done with you. For good.'

Before Alexander could respond a young woman appeared across the other side of the terrace and started to call his name, weaving through the tables towards where they were sitting.

'So, Alex, you've come to this hotel to avoid me, have you? Am I too much for you to handle? We did party pretty hard last night but from what I can remember it was fun. I was hoping the fun would have continued this morning, but you had gone by the time I woke up. Oh, sorry, you must be Alex's sister. It's Sarah, right? I must apologise as I'm the one to blame for his not being able to spend more time with you. I'll let you two chat for now, but Sarah you *must* come and party with us tonight at our hotel! Your brother is so much fun, but then I suppose I shouldn't be saying things like that to his sister as it's a bit embarrassing, isn't it?' She laughed uproariously as Sarah stared at Alexander, stony faced.

With that the girl left and Sarah wasn't hanging around either. She found she didn't need an explanation or an excuse from Alexander. He was now well and truly forgotten and out of her life forever.

'It's not just a goodbye from me, Alexander, it's also a huge good riddance.'

Chapter 33

Two weeks later

'Good morning, Mum. Did you sleep well?'

'Yes, thank you, Sarah, but it's always hard waking up to a sad day.'

'I don't understand. What's wrong?'

'Our holiday is over. After being happy holiday makers for the last two weeks you're now off to sort out café things with Ergual, and Debbie is off to prepare the new cocktail bar for its grand opening. I'm so glad we had such a nice time these past couple of weeks and it's hard to know it's now at an end. With the trips around the island and the lovely meals out – though I know I've eaten too much – I've really felt the benefit of the break.'

'I feel the same. It's done me good to unplug and relax,' Debbie added as she joined them.

'You look very smart,' Sarah said to her sister.

'Thank you. I thought I needed to make an effort as Estefan arrives for his first day of work today. He has a week to set up the bar the way he wants it, but the place is already looking lovely with all the furniture in and the paintings on the walls. Just a few days and the partition between the premises comes down.'

'Do you think it's done you good to have time away from all the organising with Bentor, and of course, Pedro?'

'Yes, I've really enjoyed the time the three of us have spent together. We have had fun, haven't we?' she said, smiling fondly. 'And as for Pedro... The few times I've seen him, when I've popped into the restaurant, he's been friendly, but I think he might change today.'

'Why do you say that?'

'Because he'll see me with Mr Fabulous Estefan.'

'Oh dear, but I'm sure you can handle things, darling, and it will all be fine. So Sarah, what have you and Ergual planned?'

'We're off to a catering supplier to look at crockery and coffee machines. Not quite as much fun as your day is likely to be, Debbie. I can't wait to meet this new barman.'

'Oh, he's not just a barman, no, he's a *mixologist*.' She overemphasised the word, making her mum and sister laugh. 'And on that note, I best be off. I have a lot to learn about cocktails! Have a good day, both of you.'

'Good luck, Debbie, and don't go drinking too many of those cocktails.' Gina chuckled.

Although she had given her mum and Sarah the impression that she was confident about the new job, secretly Debbie was nervous. For one, she only had the most basic of cocktail knowledge, something that was playing on her mind because she was Estefan's boss and it was worrying that he knew more than her. For another, she was worried about Pedro. Her coming back to the island had really messed him up and that was never her intention. She needed to be more like Sarah, in control and unafraid. She was so proud of her sister for sending Alexander away. She knew it would have been so easy for Sarah to fall back into a relationship with him, but no, she had worked out by herself how much better off she was without him. Debbie knew that once her sister was back in the UK she would find a great job and start flying high again, and with her plan to live with their mum, the two would be able to be there for one another.

She took a moment to brace herself as she walked to work. Breathing deeply, she felt her heartbeat calm and the focus set in. She was ready for the day.

Looking at the restaurant as she approached, she saw that there were no lights on and she was the first one there. Good job she had a key! She was looking forward to walking around the restaurant to get a better feel for the place. Once the partition between the two units came down and it was one big space she would need to feel comfortable moving between the two areas so she looked like she was part of the team right from the off, and not a newbie.

The first job of the day was to switch the coffee machine on. She also wanted to spend some time looking at the menu as she needed to know it inside and out. As she walked around she noticed one of the workmen going into the bar next door. Once one of the restaurant staff arrived she would head in there. As she made her coffee the door behind her opened. It was one of the chefs whom she had met the other week, after she'd agreed to take the job.

'Hi, Debbie, oh you're a star to get the coffee machine up and running. This is a real treat as normally I'm the first in and I have to set it up myself. You can stay,' he joked. 'Are you excited about your new job? Bentor hasn't stopped talking about you; he's very excited you're joining the team.'

'Good morning, Sammy. I can't promise I'll have a coffee waiting for you every day but I'm happy I could do it for you today. And yes, I'm really looking forward to the new job. I just want it all to start already, for the place to be one unit and the bar to open. The build-up is a little nerve-racking.'

'Oh, you'll be fine, and the good thing is you've worked with Bentor before, so you know how he works.'

'Yes, and I've also worked with Pedro, so that's an advantage as well.'

Talk of the devil, Pedro was the next one to arrive. She knew she had to start off as she meant to carry on, so she would kill him with kindness. She turned to Pedro as Sammy took his coffee and headed off into the kitchen.

'Good morning, Pedro, can I get you a coffee?'

'Yes, please. I won't be a minute, I just need to put my bag out the back.'

His tone of voice was friendly, and he seemed quite happy. So far, so good. Now to put her plan of action into place as she had a good hour or so until Estefan was due to arrive. She made Pedro his coffee and got a copy of the menu.

'There you go. One coffee, just as you like it. If you have a moment, I was hoping you might teach me the daily routine. You know, what gets done when ... and how? Also I could really use your help with the menu so I know what I should be pushing, and which are the most popular dishes. Basically, I need to learn everything!' she joked.

He looked a little taken back and he was probably a bit suspicious about her motives but the fact was that these were all things she needed to know, regardless of their situation. She had to learn the routine from someone, so why not him?

'Ok, where do I start?' he finally replied. 'From what I gather from Bentor, the cocktail bar will only be open during the evenings and the daytime trade will carry on as normal. As that's the case, it makes sense to start here in the restaurant. The first job of the day is to wipe all the tables down and then get them laid out for service. At that point, one member of staff would usually prepare the bar as well, but Bentor has said that this new chap will have all that done the night before. Once the tables are done, we check the bookings for the day and answer any phone message. We then let the kitchen know how busy the lunch shift is likely to be, based on the number of bookings, and find out what dishes we should highlight, and which aren't available that day, all that type of thing. There's a folder in the back office with more in-depth details of the dishes on the menu – like the specific ingredients – which you can study if you'd like, but the more orders you take, the quicker it will sink in. That's basically it in terms of prep.'

Debbie couldn't help but notice that the conversation felt very official, and not at all like two friends chatting, and she wondered if asking Pedro for help had been the wrong thing to do. Did it make him resentful that he knew more than her about how things operated? Did he think he should be the one doing her job?

'I'm really happy you're working here,' Pedro suddenly said, 'and I know we'll be a good team with you in the bar and me running the restaurant. I know things have been a bit uncertain between us lately, but I want you to know that I meant what I said the other week, and I still stand by it. I care about you, and just like I know you'll do a brilliant job in this role, I also know you'll eventually realise that you feel the same about me and we'll be together. And because I'm so sure, I'm willing to wait as long as it takes.'

Before he could say any more the front door opened and in walked one of the chefs and a waitress. That was a blessing as it meant she could hold off responding to Pedro's declaration. She said good morning and once the introductions were over and they'd headed towards the kitchen and staff room, respectively, Pedro was still stood there, waiting for her response. But she didn't want to carry on the conversation. This wasn't the time or place, and she needed to figure out how she truly felt before responding. Pedro deserved that.

'Right, I best head next door and get ready for

Estefan's arrival. Thank you for running through all that for me, Pedro. It's been a huge help, although I'm sure I'll have lots more questions over the next few days.'

'Yes, you wouldn't want to keep Estefan waiting, would you. I've looked at some of the videos he posted of himself online. He's more of a performer than a barman and seems kind of full of himself. It's clear he thinks he's a celebrity so I'm not sure why he'd want to come here to work. Surely he'd prefer to be on a stage in Las Vegas, throwing his cocktail shakers in the air.'

With that he turned around and walked into the kitchen. He was obviously ruffled but Debbie wasn't going to make any comment. It was his problem, not hers. Though there had been one thing Pedro had said that she agreed with. Why was Estefan coming to work in this little place when he could quite easily be having a better time working in one of the big top hotels or abroad?

She pondered this as she exited the restaurant and headed next door to the bar.

The door and the windows of the cocktail bar were still covered with paper so it was impossible to see the inside until actually going in, and every time she opened that door Debbie was excited anew. There was very little left to do to prep the bar, and today's job was to put all the alcohol away. It would be an opportunity to get to know Estefan a lot better but there was a chance that it could be a little awkward given that the last conversation she'd had with him, she'd been very forcefully telling him she was the boss. They needed to work together to make this place a success so moving forward she was determined to be a team player.

****

255

For the next half an hour she pottered, moving tables and chairs just a few inches this way and that, turning the sofas a little bit, and standing behind the bar to make sure there was a straight view across the whole of the unit. She also spent time looking in the mirrors to see which tables were in view from where. It was so important to see when their customers' glasses were emptying, and another sale could be made. She was miles away, focused on the task and making calculations in her head, when all of a sudden she heard her name being called.

'Good morning, Debbie, I didn't mean to startle you,' Estefan said, smiling.

'Oh, that's ok. Welcome to your first day of work! Have you settled into your new place here in Tenerife ok?'

'Yes, I've had a few days to get my bearings and now I'm excited to be starting work. The place is looking lovely, so fresh and new.'

'Yes, both Bentor and I are really pleased with how it's come along. Once we add the finishing touches and get the bar fully stocked it will be perfect. I can't wait to see it finished! I thought today we could unbox all the spirits and mixers so that you can lay them out the way you want behind the bar. I'll fully admit that I don't currently know a big amount about cocktails beyond the names and what I've read in the last few weeks about the ways they're mixed, so I'll be asking dozens of questions. I want you to teach me everything you know.'

'That's fine, I enjoy doing that. Where do you want to start?'

'I don't know. I want you to look at me as your assistant today. I'm happy to fetch and carry for you so we can get everything in place and just the way you need to be as efficient as possible while you're working. I don't know how long it will take but we've got plenty of time so there's no rush. By the way, the new cocktail menus have arrived. They're in a box on the side, just there,' she said, pointing to it, 'so why don't you pull them out and see what's on offer as it might impact where you place things. While you do that, I'll nip next door to the restaurant and fetch us each a coffee.'

'That would be nice, thanks.'

Sarah turned to walk out but when Estefan spoke, she halted and turned back towards him.

'Don't you want to know how I like my coffee?'

'I already know. I remember when you came for your interview you took it strong and black with one spoon of sugar.'

'Spot on. I'm impressed. I obviously made an impression on you,' he joked. 'I'm really looking forward to working with you and getting to know you a lot better.'

Sarah didn't reply but she could feel herself blushing. Was he flirting with her? She would have to be careful she didn't do the same with him.

****

'I think we've done,' Estefan said several hours later. 'Of course there will be lots of tweaking once we actually open the bottles, as the ones we don't use a lot will be moved to the side and others nearer to the centre, but we can sort that out as we go. To be honest, I'm feeling a little nervous. I've never worked at a brand-new place before; all my jobs have been at existing bars where there were already ways of doing things in place. The freedom to make it my own is nice, but I feel like there's a lot of pressure on me to succeed.'

'Not just you, Estefan. This is a whole new game for me as well. Ok, the smiling and greeting customers and taking orders from them I'll be fine with, but if and when they start asking specific questions about the cocktails, I'll be out of my depth completely.'

'Well, the good thing is we have one another and we'll either sink together or fly together.'

'Let's hope there's strength in numbers!' Debbie said with a laugh. 'I think we'll be ok though. The bar looks fabulous with all the colours from the bottles and you've really balanced everything out beautifully. I know Bentor will be so happy.'

'Did I hear my name?' Bentor asked as he walked through the door.

'Yes, you did, but I promise it was in a good way. I was just saying to Estefan what a great job he's made of the bar. It really sings, don't you think?'

'Absolutely. I just knew he was the perfect man for the job. And you're the perfect woman for the job as well. I'm sure you'll be a great team.'

Sarah felt uncomfortable with Bentor's praise and wanted the topic of conversation to change. Thankfully he'd clearly picked up on that.

'Now, we need a plan of action. First of all, have you introduced Estefan to all the staff?' he asked Debbie.

'Actually, no. Sorry, we just sort of got stuck in and haven't stopped.'

'That's not a problem. Why don't I arrange a little get-together so everyone can meet our dynamic cocktail bar duo? I'll message everyone on the staff group chat and get the chefs to cook up some pizza. We can gather here in the bar as it would be good for them all to see it now we're nearly ready to get going. How about tomorrow night? We could close the restaurant a little early and do it around nine-thirty or ten.'

'That's a good idea. That way Estefan and I can mix with the staff in a social way before we're all actually working together.'

'Right, that's sent,' Bentor said as he put his

phone back in his pocket. 'Now show me around. What you've created here looks great, Estefan. I'm so glad we kept the walls and the furniture simple as it makes the bar area really pop. I know I said I was going to open without the razzmatazz, all very quiet, but do you know what? I think we need to go full-out and have a big opening. What do you think?'

'That's fine by me, but when? Do you have a date in mind?' Debbie asked.

'No, I think we need to look in the diary and choose a day when we've got some big business names booked in. Or do we find a quiet booking night and invite special guests? I'm not sure... Would you do me a favour and nip next door to get the diary, Debbie? We can take a look through and see what makes the most sense and then pick a night.'

'Ok, I won't be a minute.'

Debbie had been looking forward to a quiet opening with very little fuss, but now she was facing a big event that was sure to be busy. Not exactly what she needed on the first night, when she still wouldn't have a clue about what she was doing.

'Hi, Pedro, Bentor's sent me in to get the diary. I suggest if anyone phones to book while I have it you should just take their numbers and call them back.'

'Will do. Here it is,' he said, handing it over. 'How are things going in there? I got the message about the party. It'll be good for everyone to get the chance to mix, and for Bentor to explain all the changes.'

'I think you're right. I'd best be getting back. Oh, before I go, there was one thing I wanted to mention. Now that Bentor has decided to close on Mondays, I thought perhaps we could have a night out, like the old days. What do you think?'

Pedro smiled but didn't say anything. Was that because he'd already said everything he needed to when he made it clear that he wanted more than a friendship with her?

'Ok, thank you for the diary. I'll be as quick as I can with it.'

'There's no rush. I'd love to hang out on a Monday, by the way, but perhaps you could come and have a look at my little house rather than us going out? I could cook us something nice, if you'd like?'

The straight line that Debbie had drawn in her head separating her work life from her private life was now getting a little wobbly. But perhaps that could be a good thing?

She smiled warmly at Pedro and left without answering his question. It wouldn't hurt to keep him on his toes, she thought wryly...

Chapter 34

Sarah nearly jumped out of her skin when her phone rang and before she had time to fumble in her bag for it the ringing stopped. Before looking at the missed call she had a swig of water from her bottle. She didn't know how long she had been sitting on the bench halfway between Kalanchoe and La Caleta, just watching the waves coming in and the little fishing boats. It was all so soothing, a real restful morning, which was just what was needed after the hectic day yesterday choosing china, cutlery, and furniture with Ergual.

Seeing the missed call was from her mum, she called her right back.

'Sorry I couldn't get to it quick enough.'

'That's ok, darling, it's just a quick call to tell you Iballa has invited us around to dinner tonight. I've called Debbie but she can't make it as she has things to go over with Bentor. Are you ok to join? I know Ergual will be there and there will be lots of chat about the café and the bakery, which is likely not what you really need after the busy day you had yesterday.'

'No, it will be fine. What time do we need to be there?'

'Not until half seven or eight o'clock.'

'Ok, I'll be back by six-thirty at the latest so I'll see you then. Oh, before I go, I was going to stop at the supermarket like we discussed but I won't bother now if we don't need to cook. Is that ok?'

'Of course. I can always go tomorrow if need be.'

'Great. Bye for now.'

She put her phone back in her bag and took another gulp of water before looking at the time.

Could she be bothered to walk into Caleta? She could always just turn around and walk slowly back to the apartment, but no, she was in the mood to carry on and it would clear her head. She also just really enjoyed this particular walk around the headland with the cool sea breeze.

Once in the town she headed to one of the little restaurants looking out over the harbour. It was lunch time, and she fancied a white wine and a tuna salad, something a little different than what she usually had. The town was very quiet so it meant there wouldn't be a rush for tables and she could probably sit and take her time. She had brought her notepad because she wanted to look at office agencies back in the UK on her phone and jot down the contact information for any that looked promising. She had been a temp before and knew exactly what the jobs consisted of, so it would be a good place to start as it wouldn't need to be full-time, allowing her time to get settled into a routine with her mum.

The salad was lovely and once she had eaten it, she ordered another wine. While she was eating she'd made a list of the best agencies to apply to, all of which dealt with basic clerical work. That was more than fine for her as it would be nothing truly taxing.

'Hi, excuse me, it's Sarah, isn't it?'

'Oh, hello, Bentor! You must be getting excited for the opening of your new cocktail bar? But saying that, you might not need to be as my sister has enough excitement for both of you. It won't be long now.'

'How lucky am I that timing was on my side? With Debbie coming back to Tenerife and accepting the job so much pressure has been taken off of me. I also think this job is just what she needs, for so many reasons.'

'Yes, both my mum and I are over the moon for her.'

'So how about you? Are you staying, or going back to the UK?'

'Back to England. There isn't anything here in Tenerife for me to do.'

'Weren't you working in the family bakery?'

'Yes, but that was just while my aunt went and had an operation. I held the fort for them. I enjoyed it, but now my uncle's back and my cousin Ergual is reopening the café. It's all being modernised.'

'Ergual working? That is a first! Sorry, that's your cousin I'm talking about. I wish him well.'

'You don't need to apologise. It's a big shock for the family as well, but something tells me he will be just fine. I've actually really enjoyed helping him and supporting him, the same as I have with Debbie. We both arrived here a little battered and bruised but we've had a great time together sorting things out. I know I'll look back in years to come and appreciate our time here all together.'

'I'm so glad for you. Now, talking of your sister, I best get over to the restaurant before she gives me the sack. I expect she'll also appreciate the backup as she's most likely stuck in the middle of Pedro and Estefan, the new bartender.'

'Oh, I know who he is. I think within a couple of days so will the whole of Tenerife! Debbie's shown me some of his videos and he's very lively – the complete opposite of Pedro.'

'I think both are out to win your sister over and the sooner they realise neither of them will, the better.'

'I don't know Bentor, I think you're wrong there. Pedro is the one who will win my sister's heart. She doesn't know that quite yet but it's just a matter of time, you'll see. When she was working here for you before she was different. She's learned a lot of lessons since then and she just needs to be reassured that Pedro won't hurt her or take advantage. All he will do is love her and look after her.'

'I hope they figure it out soon because they're both such special people. I need to be going but it was nice seeing you again, Sarah. You must come to the restaurant again before you head back to the UK.'

'I will, thank you.'

As Bentor left Sarah thought how lovely it was for Debbie to have a good boss who appreciated her. She knew her sister would succeed with the new job as she was perfectly cut out for it. But what was Sarah cut out for? Turning her notepad over she started a list of jobs she would love to fly at, jobs she would really love doing.

She found herself thinking back to the day she'd left school and done a similar exercise, writing down every possible job she could think of with a rating out of five next to it. She started writing all the jobs she'd ever had, assigning them stars. She finished her wine at the same time as she finished the list and she was shocked at the results – no, she was upset. Of all the jobs only one had received five stars, and that was the one job she would never have thought it would be.

'Can I get you anything else? Another wine?' the waiter offered.

'Oh no, just the bill, please. I need to be going.'

As she left the restaurant she felt in a panic and uneasy, all over a stupid list that didn't really mean anything. As if writing jobs down could show her the way she had to go.

Come on, Sarah, pull yourself together and make your way back to Kalanchoe.

****

As Sarah got to the apartment door she knew she needed to snap out of the way she was feeling and paint a smile on for her mum.

'Hi, darling, you're earlier than I thought you'd be. Have you had a good day? Can I get you anything?'

'No, I'm fine, thanks. I just need to use the bathroom; I won't be a minute.'

Looking in the bathroom mirror she saw she was flushed and visibly upset. Her mum would see something was up. She shouldn't have made that stupid list. It meant nothing and she was determined to forget it.

'I'm going to have a quick shower,' she called through the door. 'I won't be long so once I'm ready shall we have a glass of wine before we go over to Ancor's?'

'That would be nice. I'll have it poured by the time you come out.'

****

The twenty minutes in the bathroom helped her to calm down and think through how stupid she had been getting upset over a silly list. One thing was for sure, that wouldn't happen again. From tomorrow she would do the sensible thing and register with half a dozen employment agencies.

'That's better. I was so hot and sticky as there wasn't a breeze while I was walking back from Caleta. By the way, I had a chat with Bentor. He's so excited Debbie is working for him again.'

'Yes, I expect he is. What brilliant timing it was that she came here just as he was planning to open the new cocktail bar. Just like how you were here at just the right moment to be able to step in at the bakery so Ancor and Iballa could go away for her surgery. Everything has worked out perfectly.'

Sarah didn't want to talk about the bakery. She needed to focus on going home to the UK. Yes, she was thinking straight now.

'Mum, have you given any thought as to how long you're going to stay here in Tenerife? I was thinking tomorrow I would knuckle down and register with some employment agencies and see what they have to offer. That way I can start making my plans to go back home. But you don't need to come at the same time as me, of course.'

'Oh, darling, surely you can't go until the café is open. You have to be here to see how it all turns out after you've worked so hard getting it all together. You can't miss that.'

'That's ok. I can see photos; I don't need to be here.'

'I'm confused. Ancor mentioned that you would possibly be helping out when it first opened, and I got the impression from him that you were excited about it all.'

'Of course, I'm happy for Ergual, but with it all being connected Ancor will be able to float between the café and the shop. They won't need me around. Anyway, by the time it all gets done Iballa will be back working. Right, shall we have another wine before we get going?'

Sarah could tell by the look on her mum's face that she wasn't convinced and that she'd likely dig deeper at a later date, but for now the subject was thankfully closed.

****

Once they finished the wine, they headed over to Iballa's. It was a very warm evening, nice enough that they would be able to sit outside in the courtyard.

'Here they are! Ancor, Gina and Sarah are here,'

Iballa called over her shoulder into the house. 'Come in and take a seat. What can we get you to drink?'

Sarah felt uncomfortable and that was before they'd even sat down. Why oh why was she so screwed up? This was nonsense! Before she could reply Ergual had appeared with Ancor and she was momentarily distracted. She had never seen father and son like this before and it was lovely to see them so at peace with one another. It was how things always should have been.

'Hi, Sarah, I'm glad you're here. Dad and I have something to show you and we'd like your opinion, please.'

'Before the three of you go running off into the bakery you can pour Gina and me a nice glass of wine,' Iballa instructed.

'Ok, Mum, here you go, and we won't be long,' Ergual promised.

Sarah followed her cousin and uncle next door and as they walked through the back of the bakery, she noticed some of all the old stands from the shop had been moved into the kitchen. She knew the wall was coming down to add more tables but she hadn't realised that the racking where the bread and orders were kept was also being replaced.

'Are you ready for the surprise? Ta da!' Ergual said, ushering Sarah ahead of him into the shop space. 'Look what happened when we were out looking at equipment yesterday. The whole shop's been gutted and they've started putting new pieces in!'

Sarah couldn't believe it. The shop counter was new and had been moved to the side of the space with lovely new racking that would be so easy to access. There would be no more bending down and stretching up for Iballa as everything was now easily to hand.

'And by moving the counter over here to its new

location, Dad's worked out another four tables will fit in. The café's going to be huge! Come through and see what the builders have done in the old part of the café.'

Sarah followed them through to what was now just an empty shell. The old kitchen had been ripped out, the dividing wall between the kitchen and café was down and the other walls had been plastered, ready for a coat of paint. It was unrecognisable.

'So, what do you think? Isn't it different and so big?'

'It is. The walls look great but what about the plan to see if there was exposed brick underneath?'

'We checked but unfortunately no luck there.'

'That's too bad, but the plaster looks really sharp so it's not a huge loss. You get a much stronger sense of the size of the space now that the wall is down. So what's the next step?'

'Getting paint on the walls. We're going to close for two days so everything can get done and finished a lot easier. We've probably stayed here too long so we'd best be getting back to Mum before she starts to get annoyed,' Ergual said.

'I was going to send a search party out for you three,' Iballa said when they returned to the house a moment later. 'I'm only joking. What do you think, Sarah? Can you believe how good it looks?'

'It's really nice, Iballa, and with the way the new counter is set up you'll find it so much easier to serve.'

'No, I won't.'

'Sorry? I really think you will.'

'You don't understand. I won't because I won't be there. I'm retiring – well, sort of. I'll do the odd day when and if I'm needed, but the day-to-day running of the businesses is all down to Ancor and Ergual now. Oh and Ruben. Can't forget Ruben!'

'Yes, Mum, the three of us and a new person.

We can't manage the shop and the café just between Dad and me, so we need someone who knows the business, gets on well with us, and, of course, it would help if they were a family member as well. Do you know of anyone who might fit the bill, Sarah?' Ergual asked, as everyone's eyes turned to her.

Chapter 35

Debbie couldn't believe the time when she woke up – it was nearly nine-thirty! She was going to have to start setting her alarm on her phone now that she was back to working regularly. She'd gotten home late last night as she and Bentor had gone for a meal after work and non-stop chatted about the new bar, and she was disappointed she hadn't had the chance to tell Sarah and their mum all about her exciting day setting up the bar. They'd probably both left for the day by now and she would be gone before they got back. But then she heard someone in the apartment.

'Hi, Mum, I've overslept,' she called from her bed.

'No, it's me,' Sarah replied, appearing in the doorway. 'Mum has gone out as she's helping Iballa clear out her spare bedroom today. Long story short, they're going to turn it into an office for Ancor and Ergual. No more having piles of paperwork all over the house.'

'Are you not meant to be over helping Ergual with his refurbishment?'

'That's another long story. Let's have a coffee while I explain. I also want to know how you got on with Estefan on his first day. Did you gel?'

'We got on great, thanks, and the bar looks amazing. The place just screams style and gorgeousness. Now tell me, how was your dinner over at Ancor and Iballa's?'

'It was fine ... sort of. The work on the bakery and café is already well underway and they're going to look fantastic when it's all done. You really won't recognise the place as the café part is at least double

270

the size now. Ergual and Ancor are both happy with how things are coming along, and I've never seen them get on so well together, which is so lovely to witness.'

'And the "sort of"? What do you mean by that? I sense there's some sort of problem...'

'No, not a problem as such. Iballa is retiring, although she says she'll do the odd day to help out when she's needed – and I personally think she won't be able to stay away. She'll probably pick her table in the café and spend her days there, catching up with neighbours as they come in and watching the world go by.'

'That will be good for her, and I can picture it now. So what is the "sort of"?'

'The "sort of" is Ergual and Ancor have offered me a job. They want me to be a part of it all, working in the shop and café.'

'How ridiculous. What made them think you'd want to do that? I know you enjoyed looking after the place while Ancor and Iballa were over in Gran Canaria, but to be there all the time and living in Tenerife... That's not you at all. For a start, it's just a job when you're after a career.'

Sarah didn't answer and suddenly it crossed Debbie's mind that she might have said the wrong thing. Did her sister actually want to take them up on the offer? Oh dear, she felt awful and now didn't know what to say. Thankfully, Sarah broke the silence.

'You're right. Well ... sort of. There are those two words again,' she said, laughing lightly. 'I went to Caleta yesterday and sat with my notepad and pen to make plans and work out which clerical office work agencies to contact back near Mum's. Well, one thing led to another – and you know how much I love a list – and I wrote down every job I've done in my whole life. Next to each one I marked them out of five stars and... Oh, I really wish this was a list I hadn't done. It was so stupid and now I can't get it out of my mind. And then going to Ancor and Iballa's last night and being offered a job... Well, it complicated everything and I don't know what to do going forward. You see, the only job I gave five stars to was working in the bakery for those few weeks.'

'Why do you think the list was stupid? I think you've done the right thing. In fact, perhaps that's what I should have done weeks ago as I wouldn't have needed to put off agreeing to work for Bentor for as long as I did. But let me get this straight. You loved working in the bakery, and now you've been offered your dream role at said bakery – with a co-worker whose very name makes you smile and giggle – so what is the issue? You would be brilliant. I hope you said yes!'

'What do you mean? What co-worker?'

'Come on, Sarah, you know exactly what I mean. Every time you mention Ruben's name your face lights up. He and the job make you happy and now you have the chance to have both. It's a dream scenario!'

'I wish it was that easy. My gut is telling me to work in the family business, but my head is telling me differently. It's saying it could end in a family fallout. Ancor, Ergual, and I all have our own opinions and think we know best... And that's before Iballa puts her two pennies' worth in! I think I need to go with my head and start to make plans to go back to the UK. My holiday here is over and it's time to dive right back into the real world. If you don't mind, I don't think I want to talk about it anymore. I'm going to have a quick shower and then spend some time on a real job list, not a fantasy one.'

'If you're sure? Please know I'm always here for you. The only reason I'm here and in one piece is because of you, and that is something I'll be forever thankful for and never forget.'

'Thank you. I really have enjoyed our time together here and if you take away and forget all the circumstances behind why we came here in the first place, it has been really lovely.'

Left alone, Debbie sat there thinking her sister was probably right. Three strong, opinionated individuals at the bakery would never work, which was such a shame as she would have loved to have her sister living on the island with her.

Debbie had two hours before she had to meet Estefan in Las Americas to sort out a work uniform for him – Bentor had decided he wanted him in a black shirt and trousers as that would fit in with the other restaurant staff in their black and white uniforms, all very formal and classy – so she'd use the time for a plate of toast and another coffee. She also wanted to have a look at the restaurant's social media accounts to see if Bentor had started to mention the cocktail bar. As she scrolled through, she saw there were a few mentions of a top cocktail barman coming to work there with more details to follow. The suspense was certainly building now. Hopefully she and Estefan would be up to the challenge.

'I've finished in the bathroom,' Sarah said as she came back into Debbie's room. 'I'm going out for a walk to clear my head and come up with a thousand reasons to tell Ancor why I won't be taking the job. Thanks for the chat; it really helped. What have you got planned for today?'

'Shopping. I'm off with Estefan to get him suited and booted for the new job, and then tonight Bentor is having a little informal drinks thing to introduce Estefan to all the staff.'

'Oh, good luck with that. I'm sure Pedro will have his eye on you all evening, counting how many times you chat to the new chap.'

'No, something tells me Pedro will be fine.'

****

'Morning! This is a first for me – shopping for a uniform. Normally the hotel takes your measurements and then in a couple of days they hand you a bag with the clothes in,' Estefan said once they met up.

'Well, we're just a small business so we have a bit more flexibility. Did Bentor explain to you what he'd like?' she asked.

Estefan nodded.

'Great. I have the restaurant credit card, so let's shop!'

'I'm sorry to be a pain, but do you think we could get a coffee first? I overslept and didn't have time for a caffeine fix before I left to meet you.'

'Yes, of course, no problem. I know a nice place that won't be too busy.'

Debbie led the way and coffee and pastries were soon ordered. She found she was feeling a little uncomfortable for some reason. Maybe because this wasn't a work situation but a social one? Estefan was looking at her and she knew she needed to speak but what should she say? She didn't want to pry into his private life, and she certainly didn't want him to ask her anything about why she had come to Tenerife. The waitress brought the food and drink and Debbie decided that's what she would focus on. She tucked in heartily.

'You haven't asked me the big question,' Estefan said suddenly.

'Sorry? I don't know what you mean.'

'The big question of why I've given up my exciting life in the hotels on Lanzarote and come to work in a little restaurant in Tenerife.'

'It hadn't crossed my mind and it wouldn't

because it's none of my business. As far as I'm concerned, your private life is your own and has nothing to do with your job.'

'I think it has crossed your mind, which isn't a problem as I'd actually really like to tell you. I think it might help our working relationship – and come to that our personal friendship. As we're going to be spending so much time working together, I'd like it if we were to grow close to one another.'

If Debbie hadn't been uncomfortable before she certainly was now with all this talk about friendships and relationships. It was making her nervous.

'Really, Estefan, you don't need to,' she said, trying to shut down this topic of conversation.

'I've been in a relationship with someone for just over five years,' he began, oblivious to her efforts. 'To me, it was perfect and all I ever wanted. I was the happiest I had ever been in my whole life, and I thought my partner felt the same … but I was wrong. You see, they had been cheating on me for quite a while. Of course I didn't know, and the so-called friends who *did* know hadn't told me, which made it worse. My partner also worked in the hotel so when I did find out, things got complicated. Cutting a long story short, that's why I'm here in Tenerife. One other little detail that might help and make you feel a little more comfortable about our working friendship situation is that my partner was my *male* manager. I'm gay. I hope it helps you to know I won't be chatting you up … or anyone else, come to that. I'm a little bit fragile at the moment, but I'm sure with time I'll recover, and I promise that once I get behind that bar and start throwing cocktails the performer will appear and the show will go on.'

'Thank you for telling me. You being gay or straight makes no difference to me as I always knew we could work well together, and being fragile is something I know a lot about, but that story is for another time. Now drink up. It's time to shop. Do you like shopping, Estefan?'

'Very funny. I'm gay – I was born to shop!'

****

Four hours later they'd acquired two pairs of very smart black trousers and five black shirts for Estefan, as well as three over the top diva outfits that just sparkled for Debbie. They were three items that she would never have looked at, let alone bought, if she had been by herself, but her shopping companion had encouraged her to push the boundaries, and ultimately the looks were just what she needed to be wearing in the cocktail bar.

'My feet are killing me and I'm running late as I should be at the restaurant by now for a meeting with Bentor. I'm off to get a taxi, Estefan, and I'll see you there later tonight. Thank you for today. I've really enjoyed spending time with you not as work colleagues but as friends.'

'Me, too. I really am looking forward to us working together. It's going to be so much fun,' he enthused.

****

Debbie was first to the restaurant as Bentor was also running late, and she headed into the bar to get the beer and wine ready for the little party tonight. At one point Bentor had thought they could get Estefan making cocktails but they'd soon realised that would defeat the point of the gathering, which was to give him a chance to get to know all the staff.

'Hi, Pedro,' she said as he joined her in the bar. 'Do you know if Bentor has put the drinks for tonight's get-together to one side?'

'Yes, I've brought it all around and placed it by the bar just there. There's just one box of beers to go but it's heavy so I'll carry it for you.'

'Thanks, that's kind of you.'

He headed off to collect the beers and she took a deep breath. She really did feel energised by this new opportunity she'd been given and she would do everything in her power to do the best job ever. She was day dreaming and it took her a minute to realise Pedro had returned and was talking to her.

'Sorry, I was miles away.'

'I just asked if you enjoyed your shopping in Los Americas with the new member of staff.'

'I did. It was nice to get to know Estefan a little better.'

Pedro nodded briefly and then turned and left. She got stuck into getting everything sorted and by the time Bentor arrived she had filled the main fridge with the beers and the wine, and put all the glasses on the bar so no one had to go behind it. The last thing she needed was for it to be messed up before the place had even opened.

'Sorry I'm late, Debbie, how did the uniform shopping go?'

'It was really fun. We had a laugh.'

'That's good. I thought it would be a good little bonding exercise for you both.'

'We've definitely bonded. I think – no, I know – that we'll work really well together. Everything is sorted for tonight. The drinks are ready and the chefs will bring the food through at nine forty-five. We just need to get through some paperwork before the get-together.'

****

It was nearly nine o'clock and they had achieved so

much. They'd mapped out who was going to be responsible for what, everything from the ordering to cleaning rotas. Debbie was hungry and tired and really wasn't in the mood to be sociable for the next few hours, but thankfully it was Bentor's gathering and she was just a guest like the rest of the staff, so there wasn't much for her to do. As the staff that were off duty started to arrive she swung into action handing out the beers and wines. Everyone was in a good mood and when Estefan turned up Bentor introduced him around. It wasn't long before the restaurant staff finished cleaning up and joined them, and the chefs came in carrying the pizzas.

Debbie wasn't in the mood to drink a lot – one glass of wine was enough for her – but she was starving and was one of the first to dive into the food. The atmosphere was lively, and Estefan was in fine form, a real showman. The customers were going to love him.

'I think we're on to a winner, Debbie. Everyone seems to be happy, but I haven't seen Pedro. Has he come through from the restaurant yet?' Bentor asked.

'No, I've not seen him. I'll nip next door and see what he's up to.'

She put her glass down and headed outside and across to the front door of the restaurant. She could see Pedro laying the tables for the next day and she had to knock on the door to get his attention as it was locked. He turned, and seeing it was her, he went to get the keys and opened the door.

'Bentor and I were wondering where you were.'

'I got stuck into getting everything sorted, ready for tomorrow. I also wanted to take the opportunity to be here by myself for a bit. It's nice, but it feels different... Actually I think it's me that's different. After talking with you and Bentor I realised I need to step up a gear and really take ownership of my role in this restaurant. I'm excited about all the new challenges and it's good the three of us are all back together again. We were a good team before but I know we're going to be even better now. Sorry, I'm waffling on. How is the party going? Is the new chap fitting in ok? He's very good looking and I suspect all the waitresses have made a special effort to impress him.'

'It's a shame they'll be disappointed then.'

'Why is that?'

'Because Estefan is gay. You'd have more chance with him than them, but saying that, I know that's not going to happen because you only have eyes for one person.'

'Oh yeah? And who might that be?'

'Me. Now kiss me,' she said boldly, suddenly realising it was exactly what she wanted.

He stared at her in stunned disbelief.

'You heard me, Pedro, I want you to kiss me, and I don't want you to stop for many years to come.'

Chapter 36

Sarah couldn't help but smile to herself. She had just read a text from Debbie that had been sent late last night saying: *won't be home tonight. staying at Pedro's xx*

She was so happy for her sister. Debbie's new life here in Tenerife had now really taken off with a fabulous job that she would no doubt excel in, and now a new fella who was sure to treat her like a princess. It was everything she deserved after the last few years.

Sarah was hopeful she'd have her own happy ending soon as today was the day she would be sorting her life out as well. She had made a real – and most importantly, achievable – list of four reputable employment agencies to register with.

'Good morning, darling, you look like you've already been very productive and the day has only just begun.'

'Hi, Mum. Yes, I'm registering for jobs. I thought to start with I would say I'm willing to drive around an hour from your house, and then if nothing in that radius comes up I'll tell them I'm willing to go a little further.'

'That sounds reasonable. Can I make you a drink? And have I missed your sister? Has she left already?'

'Yes and no. That doesn't really answer your question though, does it?' Sarah laughed. 'She didn't come home last night, but don't worry, she's ok. After the party at the restaurant she went and stayed the night at Pedro's.'

'At last! Should I be saying that as her mother? Why not. I'm so pleased for her. For one, she was at her happiest when she worked with Pedro and for another, they know each other so well already. It's not like she's jumping into the unknown. I also think that because of what she went through with Steven, she will appreciate Pedro a lot more than she might have if they'd gotten together in the past. Oh, I am so happy for them both.'

'So am I. She's gone full circle from where she was, hasn't she? Now sit down, Mum, I'll make us something to drink and you can tell me what you've got planned for the day.'

Waiting for the kettle to boil Sarah was still smiling. It was lovely to see how happy her mum was. To think that only a short while ago the very mention of coming to Tenerife was a huge problem to her. It had obviously not been easy getting to this point, but she seemed much more content these days, and very comfortable in Ancor and Iballa's company. It was just like the old days when they had all visited as a family.

'There you go.'

'Thanks, Sarah. I think I'll stay here today and read. It will be busy over at Ancor and Iballa's as it's today that all the electrics in the bakery and shop are being rewired, and I don't want to be in the way.'

'Yes, I had a text from Ergual asking me to pop over as he wants to ask my advice on plug sockets and wall lights. But first I'm going to send these emails off to the agencies. Is there any shopping we need?'

'No, I can't think of anything, but if I do, I'll nip out myself to get it. I should be getting a little exercise every day anyways. Now, I'll sit quietly here with my book so you can get on with your emails.'

****

Two hours later Sarah had done what she had to

with the emails and was on her way to the bakery. She had also brought her beach bag with her so that she could grab a few hours in the sun watching the boats go by and enjoying the lovely sea breeze. It would be just what she needed today after helping Ergual.

'Thanks for coming down,' her cousin said when she arrived.

'It's really taking shape now, isn't it?' she said, looking around in awe. 'Look how big it is! You'll get so many more tables in here and the shop is looking fabulous. I like how compacted it is, so instead of that sparse look it had before, it will always look like there's a lot of stock.'

'Exactly. Now, I've marked where I think the wall lights should go ... there, there and there,' he said, pointing. 'There are only a few, but I think that's plenty for the space. Also, do you think two sockets in the big area will be enough? I don't know what they'll be used for aside from perhaps plugging the hoover in.'

Sarah could see her cousin had thought it all through. The wall lights would be in the perfect places to illuminate the space and it was looking good. She couldn't wait to see it with the tables and chairs set up. The little kitchen area was also taking shape and just needed the new equipment to be put in place.

'It looks perfect to me. You didn't need me to come down and help because it's already all sorted.'

'Thank you, but the electrical things weren't the only reason I asked you to come down. I also wanted to speak to you about the job. Have you reconsidered about staying and working here? Before you say no, could I make a suggestion? Why not give it a try? Stay for a couple of months and see how you get on, and then if you aren't happy, you can go back to the UK. Mum and Dad would be so happy if you were here, and of course I would be over the moon to have you on the team. I don't think I can do it without you.'

'Of course, you can. You don't need me.'

'I do though. You know as well as I do how popular I am here on the island. No one has time for sarcastic, grumpy Ergual and I worry it will affect the business. What if it gets out that I'm taking over at the café and suddenly it's payback time for all the people I've been rude to, and they boycott us? If you were here with Dad it would be completely different because the locals love you both. You're a friendly, welcoming face, Sarah, and we need you. *I* need you.'

'I honestly don't think you need to worry, Ergual. Your past will be forgotten the moment everyone meets the new, happier you, and the café is bound to be popular as it will be new, and people are nosey. You'll have everyone coming in to see what you've done with the place because they've missed it not being open. Without the café, there's nowhere for them to go until the restaurants open at lunch time. I promise you're overthinking it all.'

'Ok, say you're right. Can you see my dad and me coping with the café and the shop by ourselves? Because I can't.'

'I agree that you'll need someone else, but that won't be a problem. You and your dad have lots of contacts here in Kalanchoe, and you'll probably have people asking if you have any jobs as soon as they hear about the grand reopening.'

'Yes, but I don't want anyone else. I want *you* to work here.'

'I'm sorry, Ergual, but I've made plans to go back to the UK. But until then, I'm here to help and support you and Ancor. I need to be going now but message me if you need help with anything else.'

As she walked away, she was torn. Of course she

was excited about the café, and every bit of the planning had given her a buzz, but the three of them – Sarah, Ancor, and Ergual – working together just wouldn't work.

She walked to the little supermarket for a bottle of water and some crisps to take with her to the beach and she noticed Ruben coming out of the shop as she approached. She hadn't really had anything to say to him since she'd cancelled their date to deal with Alexander, and she was a bit embarrassed. What must he think of her? Plucking up her courage she called out a hello, and was pleased when he stopped and turned towards her.

'It's all action stations over at the bakery, isn't it? Are you looking forward to the new shop and café?' she asked.

'Yes, it's looking good. None of it will really affect me though as the bakery part is staying the same. Ancor keeps saying what a big help you've been to them and I'm sure it's true as it's all happened very quickly. One minute Ancor's putting back everything you had moved to make life easier, and moaning about why people always felt the need to change things, and the next minute he's ripping the building apart. I'm not complaining though. I'm liking the new Ancor – he leaves me to get on with things without interfering every five minutes. The biggest shock though is the fact that Ergual is being pleasant to me, which is a nice change, but such a stark contrast to how things have been between us in the past. But like I said, it's all happening so suddenly. I guess I just need to do my best to keep up. Sorry, I didn't ask if you had a nice time when your friend came. How was it?'

'That's a long story as it wasn't a friend that turned up, but rather a problem. Thankfully it's a problem that I can now confidently say has been sorted. I mustn't keep you though. You have a rare afternoon off and you should make the most of it because you're going to be very busy once the bakery and the café are finished.'

'Yes, I'm off to the beach, which is something I don't get to do very often, and usually only on a Sunday when everywhere is very busy.'

'That's where I'm off to as well! Can I walk with you?'

'You can do more than that. If you'd like, you can spend the day with me on the beach ... but only if you want to, of course.'

'I'd like that, though I have to say I'm surprised you've asked me after the way I treated you on our night out, cancelling at the last minute like that.'

'That's behind us, especially if the reason for cancelling the date is now gone.'

'Gone for good, and I really am sorry. I was very disappointed to have to let you down and it upset me because I was so much looking forward to it.'

There wasn't a lot of conversation as they headed out of Kalanchoe towards the coastal path. Sarah was analysing everything in her head and to her surprise the butterflies that she'd had before the date they hadn't gone on had returned. She was so happy she had bumped into Ruben and she hoped he felt the same. She suspected he did because the look on his face could only be described as 'the cat that got the cream'.

Once at the beach they decided on sun loungers away from the main tourist bit and took a dip in the sea to cool down. Neither of them said more than the odd word here and there, but they both had huge smiles on their faces.

Back on the sun loungers the situation changed. Sarah wanted to explain what had happened when Alexander turned up, but she didn't want to go into all the detail. The main thing Ruben needed to know was that her ex was out of her life forever.

'Ancor was telling me all about your sister's new job. You must be pleased for her,' Ruben said.

'Yes, I am, and she will be brilliant at it.'

'And have you decided what you're going to do? Ancor also mentioned that he's trying to persuade you to stay here and work in the bakery. I suspect you would be so bored though.'

'I don't think I would get bored...' she said, trailing off as she thought about it. 'I'm going back to the UK though. I've submitted my CV to a few temp agencies so hopefully I can start working in some sort of office role soon.'

'I'm sure before you know it you'll be climbing the ladder and running the company.'

'What makes you say that?'

'Oh, I didn't mean it in a bad way. I just meant that you're driven – you've always given me the impression that you're someone who succeeds at whatever they set their mind to. It's a good thing.'

'I think you're driven too. Look at how you run the bakery; that's not an easy job. A lot of planning goes into what you do and it's a real skill.'

'That's kind of you to say but it only comes from working there for so many years.'

'Given that you've been there for so long, how do you think Ergual will fit into the business? I get the impression he's very keen and excited about the whole thing.'

'Yes, and I really hope it all works out. My one concern is how he'll cope with the café and the shop on his own. I think Ancor wants to cut back on the hours he does as he keeps talking about the shop up in Priviaata where he delivers bread, saying that the owner has quite a lot of staff working for him so he can be sort of semi-retired. And then there's his friend the builder who organises the work while his son and grandson do the actual physical labour. After all these years of non-stop working six days a week he's finally realising there's more to life than just work.'

'That's good for him, I think, and I'm sure Ergual will be fine once he gets into a routine.'

But Sarah wasn't entirely convinced that she was right. Ergual might throw himself fully into the café, but what about the shop? That part of the business had never seemed to interest him much.

'You've gone all quiet, Sarah, are you ok?'

'Sorry, my head has been so full of all the bakery and café things lately, and it needs a break. Let's talk about something other than my family. Let's talk about you, Ruben. All I know about you is that you like to go to Alejandro's restaurant for an evening meal. What else happens in your world? What hobbies do you have?'

'I don't have time for hobbies because when I'm not working for your uncle, I'm helping my dad to do up an old barn on our land. It's not big like you might imagine a traditional barn, but it's a good size and we're converting it into a two-bedroom house. No, it's just got a ground floor, no upstairs, so I guess it's technically a bungalow. Once it's done, I'm going to move in. It will be nice to have my own place and after all these years living with my parents I'll finally be by myself.'

'That's wonderful.'

'I'm happy about how it's coming along. You'll have to come and have a look at our progress before you go back to England. I'd appreciate your advice.'

'I'd like that, but I really don't think I'm the right person to give advice. I know nothing about designing a house.'

'You helped design the café with Ergual. Surely it must be a similar thing?'

'Maybe,' she offered.

'Did you do design work in your previous job?' he asked.

There was another silence and Sarah felt uncomfortable. Explaining what she used to do would mean telling Ruben about Alexander. She knew she had said her problem with him was sorted, but she hadn't gone into detail, and now she felt she wanted to explain. But how to do so without Ruben feeling sorry for her?

'I want to explain about Alexander,' she began hesitantly. 'He's my ex and we had a greeting card business together, where he handled sales, and I did all of the administration. He cheated on me and I walked away from him and the business. When he came here to Tenerife I foolishly thought he was here to win me back, and I have to admit that I was flattered. Having been through such a period of uncertainty it was nice to feel wanted. That wasn't the case though. Cutting a long story short, he only wanted me back so I could run the business again and take all the pressure off him. Thankfully, it didn't take me long to figure out his game, and to discover that he was spending his time here in another woman's bed. Ultimately, I'm glad he came because it really did bring everything to a close for the two of us, and looking back now I can see that it wasn't Alexander that I missed, it was the greeting card business. It's sad in a way because it should have been the other way around.'

'You didn't need to explain, Sarah, it's not any of my business.'

'But I wanted to because I didn't feel good about standing you up, and I felt even worse knowing I missed out on what would have been a lovely evening.'

'That's easy to put right though. We can go up to Alejandro's any evening you like.'

'Really? That would be nice.'

'Sarah, if it's the business you miss, and not the ex-boyfriend, couldn't you just replace that business

288

with the bakery and stay here in Tenerife? Your sister's here, your mum has her apartment, and Ancor needs you. But more than that, *I* would like you to stay.'

'I don't know what to say, Ruben. I'd like to stay but you know my aunt, uncle, and cousin better than anyone. There would be so many strong opinions in the mix that in a matter of a few weeks we will all undoubtedly have fallen out and there would be no café or bakery left.'

'I think you're wrong. You and Ergual are getting on great together and once Ancor sees you organising everything, he'll stand back and let you work your magic. I'm sure of it.'

'I'm not sure. But I will say that if there is one thing that could tempt me to stay ... it would be you.'

Ruben smiled and Sarah grinned back at him.

Chapter 37

It had been three days since Sarah went to the beach with Ruben and tonight they were actually – finally! – going on their first official date. She was excited and she knew he was as well. These last few days she had spent a lot of time thinking about him, and also the bakery. Considering everything that had happened, she knew she needed to go with her head and not her heart, and so she'd followed up with the recruitment agencies. Her prospects were looking ok, not brilliant, but they were a start.

'Morning, Mum, did you sleep well?'

'I did, thank you. I think I heard Debbie come back last night rather than staying at Pedro's. I expect she will probably be a little on edge and nervous today as opening day has finally arrived for the cocktail bar, but I just know that once the first night is over everything will be fine and she will have the time of her life.'

'Mum, I've decided to stay until the café reopens at the end of next week and then I'll fly back to the UK. Have you decided what you want to do yet? There's no pressure whatsoever to come back with me if you'd like some more time here.'

'I really don't know, darling. In one way, I'd like to see the café reopen, but in another perhaps I don't.'

'Why do you say that?'

'Well, it's all new to Ergual and I really don't want to see him fall at the first hurdle. You know what the locals are like here in Kalanchoe, they'll all be there the first few days and I'm not sure if Ergual will be able to cope. It could become a little chaotic.'

'I was thinking the same and I wonder if I

should offer to serve in the shop on that first day so that Ancor will be able to give one hundred per cent to the café and be there to support Ergual— Oh, that sounds like Debbie getting up,' she said, interrupting herself.

'Good morning, darling. Tell us all about the cocktail bar, is it ready for the public tonight?' Gina asked Debbie.

'Yes, it is, and I have a big surprise for you both.'

'Oh, what's that, darling?'

'Bentor has invited you to the opening night and not just for cocktails but a meal as well! A table of five will be reserved for you two along with Iballa, Ancor, and Ergual.'

'Oh, I'm actually going out with Ruben tonight, and I can't cancel on him again. I'm so sorry, Debbie.'

'That's not a problem. It can easily be made a table for six.'

'But I'm not sure if that will be ok with Ruben.'

'Text Ruben to see what he thinks. I'm sure he'll be fine with it if you explain it's my fault,' Debbie suggested.

Sarah wasn't sure if it was the type of place Ruben would want to go, and did she really want their date to include her whole family? He and Ergual had been getting on better with one another at work, but socialising together after hours was a completely different thing.

'Go on, Sarah, text him. I'll give Iballa a call to tell her the good news. I know she won't say no,' Gina said.

'I'm actually going to the bakery this morning so I'll wait until I get there and ask him in person. It's a big day for the café as all the new tables and chairs are arriving. I'm looking forward to helping lay the place out. Right, I need a quick shower and then I'll be off,' Sarah said in farewell as she headed to her room.

'So, Mum, what's going to happen? Do you think Sarah will go back to the UK, or do you think the café will tempt her to stay?' Debbie asked as soon as her sister had left the room.

'I'm not sure. The café is a top attraction but my money is on Ruben being the deciding factor that leads her to stay, as he's an even bigger attraction.'

'If that's the case, and both Sarah and I end up living here, what will you do?'

'Being back here with you and Sarah has shown me that I've been carrying a lot of resentment and need to look at the past in a new light. I've changed, being here, and I've loved seeing both of you restart your lives, and being part of it all, so I think if you stay, I'll stay, too. And besides, why would I want to be in the UK when my grandchildren will be here on the island?'

'Excuse me but where did that comment come from? There's been no mention from me about having babies and I'm one hundred per cent sure Sarah hasn't mentioned it either.'

'I know, but if you think of it practically, you both seem to have found chaps that would do anything in the world to please you and make you happy. What better men to find your happily ever afters with? I'm doing some toast, would you like some?' Gina asked calmly, as if she hadn't just dropped a bombshell revelation on her daughter.

Debbie was flabbergasted. Where had that come from? But as her mum went to toast the bread she had to smile. Being honest, babies *had* crossed her mind once or twice while she had been pottering at Pedro's in recent days, but it wasn't something that was going to happen in the near future. For one thing, she couldn't imagine what Bentor would say if she told him she needed to go on maternity leave so soon after the bar had opened!

'I'm off now. I'll let you know what Ruben has to say and good luck for tonight, Debbie. I'm sure it's going to be brilliant and a total success.'

'There's something else you need to ask Ruben about – his feelings about babies. Mum has decided she wants us to produce grandchildren for her ASAP!'

'You what?' Sarah asked, her jaw dropping.

'You make fun but mark my words, give it a couple of years and I'll be on babysitting duty,' Gina said confidently.

The sisters were in fits of laughter as Sarah left the apartment to go down to the bakery, and as she walked a memory came to her. Within weeks of first going out with Alexander he had made it very clear that children didn't come into his life plan whatsoever. The thought made her stop dead in her tracks. How stupid she had been. He hadn't even discussed it with her, not considered her thoughts or feelings at all. Perhaps she and Debbie's lives hadn't been so different after all, both being told what to do by their other halves and both going along with it. She had been a complete fool and she was so glad that Alexander had been caught out. She had been given a second chance, a new beginning, and she had to grab it with both hands. Not because she might not get another opportunity, but because she had finally realised exactly what she wanted in life.

'Good morning, Ergual, big day today! I never thought I would be getting so excited about tables and chairs.'

'Exciting, yes, but also terrifying. It's almost time to reopen and I have no idea what people will make of what we've done to the place.'

'Oh come on, it's not like you to doubt yourself. Things are coming together nicely and it will all be fine, I promise you.'

'I wish I had your confidence, but in reality it

will just be Dad and me fumbling around, not knowing what we're really doing. We'll be the laughingstock of Kalanchoe, and I'll be the one that's brought the family business into ruin.'

'I refuse to stand here listening to this because that's not going to happen.'

'How can you be so sure it won't? Do you know something I don't?'

'It's called having faith. Right, I'm just going to nip in and see Ruben. I'll be back once the furniture arrives and I'm sure once it's all in place you'll feel better. In fact, I know you will.'

She took a deep breath as she walked through to the bakery. Where had that confidence and certainty come from? Had she found the old Sarah? No, this was a new Sarah, a Sarah with a life full of possibility in front of her, one that she was going to grab and enjoy.

'Hi, Uncle Ancor, are you and Iballa up to going to the new cocktail bar tonight?'

'Yes, and apparently it's going to cost me a lot of money.'

'Oh, no, Debbie said it's Bentor's treat.'

'The food and the drink might be free, but your aunt says we both need something new to wear. She's already had a taxi pick her up to take her into town to shop for outfits.'

'Oh dear, sorry about that! I think it will be a nice night though, and we can treat it as a sort of celebration for the café reopening as well.'

'Yes, but between you and me, Sarah, I'm a little bit worried about that. Ergual seems to be getting cold feet about the whole thing.'

'Don't worry about Ergual's cold feet. Once he's running around serving the customers his feet will be on fire! Joking aside, please stop worrying. Everything is going to be fine.'

'I wish I had your confidence, Sarah. Do you

know something I don't?'

'Actually, Uncle, I might do,' she said, a decision forming in her mind. 'Now, I just need to check something with Ruben before the furniture arrives.'

This time there was no deep breath before she greeted Ruben, just a huge smile and a stomach full of gorgeous butterflies.

'Hi, Ruben.'

'Hello, Sarah, is something wrong?'

'No, hopefully not, but I do have a little problem. You know my sister's new cocktail bar opens tonight? Well, she's surprised us with an invitation to come for dinner – the whole family – and I know we were meant to be going up to Alejandro's, but would you mind if we go there instead?'

'I don't think it's my type of place, but it's not a problem if you'd like to reschedule. You go off with your family and celebrate. We can go out another night.'

It wasn't the answer Sarah wanted to hear but she didn't know what to say to persuade Ruben to come with them. But maybe there was another way...

Before she could talk herself out of it, she walked towards him, placed her hands on the sides of his face, moved closer, and kissed him. This wasn't a little peck on the cheek, but rather a long, slow kiss on his lips.

Eventually she released him and stood back.

'I'll text you the time we're all going to meet to get the taxi. I'm really looking forward to the evening, and especially to being there with you,' she said confidently.

Sarah didn't wait for a reply. She turned and walked back into the shop and then through to the café where she could see a big lorry had just pulled up. Part of her future was in that lorry ... and the other part was in the bakery.

****

'Sorry I'm late,' Sarah called as she entered the apartment. 'Every job seemed to take twice as long as normal.'

'Come and tell me all about it. Did the tables and chairs arrive ok? More importantly, did they all fit into the space? I'll put the kettle on. Would you like tea or coffee?'

'Neither. I'll have a large gin, please.'

'Oh dear. Does that mean things didn't go as well as you had hoped? By the way, don't worry about being a bit late. Debbie called to say our table at the restaurant isn't booked until nine o'clock, so you have lots of time to get ready.'

'Great! That will give me time to work my way down the gin bottle. I'm only joking. The day has just been a little stressful. For some reason Ergual has lost all his confidence – and come to that, his enthusiasm – and it didn't help that Ancor nagged him.'

'I wondered how long it would be before Ancor took over. This is just what I feared. Did you manage to get the place looking nice despite the hiccups?'

'Oh yes, it looks gorgeous. The pictures are on the walls and the new crockery has been unpacked. Everything is ready to get going.'

'Everything apart from Ergual and Ancor, by the sounds of it. What will happen when they disagree? Will Iballa have to go in and take over? Because you know she will if things aren't working out between those two.'

'That's not going to happen, I can assure you. Now, about tonight, are you excited?'

'I certainly am. Will Ruben be coming with us?'

'Yep! I just need to text him the time. I thought

we could get two taxis from outside the bakery at ... should we say eight-fifteen?' Gina nodded. 'Great. I'll also call Iballa and let her know. That gin was lovely, thank you, I'm going to pour another and then I'm off to get ready.'

'Before you go, can I ask how you're so sure that everything at the café will be fine?'

'Just trust me, Mum.'

****

As Sarah and her mum walked down through the town to meet the others, she was excited for so many reasons. Ruben had texted to say he would be at the bakery for the taxi pick-up at eight-fifteen and she was relieved to know that the kiss hadn't scared him off. But deep down she had known it wouldn't.

'You ok, Mum?'

'I'm fine. And I don't need to ask how you are, do I? That permanent smile on your face says it all.'

'I don't know what you mean,' Sarah said innocently.

'Oh yes you do. Did you ever think the three of us could be this happy again after your dad passed? I certainly didn't. It's lovely and so special to me that we've all become so close again.'

'It is special, isn't it, and I know Dad would be so happy for us.'

Mother and daughter stopped walking and hugged tightly. There were tears in both their eyes – not sad ones, but happy ones.

When they got to the bakery they saw that the others were waiting for them, everyone all dressed up for the occasion. Sarah couldn't remember ever seeing her family looking so smart.

'Sorry we're late. Mum and I got chatting and, well ... you know how the time flies. Don't we all look so smart tonight. What do you think, Uncle?'

'I don't think that Tillandsia is ready for all this glamour coming from Kalanchoe. They won't know what's hit them when we walk in!'

'I just need to have a quick word with Ancor before the taxis get here,' Sarah's mum whispered before ushering Ancor aside. She watched as they talked briefly and then hugged. They were both wiping tears away as they came back to the group and she hoped it meant that her mum had finally put all those demons in her head to rest.

'Are you ok?' she asked quietly when Gina returned.

'Yes, thank you, darling. Ancor and I are both of the same opinion that your dad loved his family here in Tenerife but that he also loved his life in England, and that he lived his life the way he wanted and where he wanted.'

'I'm happy for you, Mum, very happy. Oh, here are the taxis. Are we ready?'

Everyone said yes although Sarah noticed Ruben looked a bit terrified. He was here though, and that was the main thing.

Now to get the show on the road! It was a night of celebration for so many reasons.

****

The taxis pulled up outside the cocktail bar and the place looked very busy. The tables outside were full and inside people were stood at the bar. Sarah spotted Debbie taking an order and she didn't need to have Estefan pointed out to her as he was in place behind the bar, laughing and joking with the customers. At one point she saw him throw a cocktail shaker in the air before twirling around and catching it.

In they all went and Bentor greeted them warmly.

'Come in! Come in! I'm so happy you've all been able to come,' he said as he ushered them to a table in the bar. 'Have a few drinks and take your time looking at the menu so you can soak up the terrific atmosphere in here.'

Debbie gave everyone at their table a big smile and a wave as she came over.

'So, what do you think?'

'It's amazing!' Sarah enthused and the rest of the table joined in, everyone saying how fantastic the cocktail bar looked.

'You all look at home here in your fabulous outfits. Shall I give you a few minutes to look at the cocktail menu? See what takes your fancy and I'll grab your order when I come back.'

As Debbie rushed off to help other customers Pedro ambled into the bar from the restaurant and came over to greet them. He gave Gina and Sarah each a cheek kiss and before anyone could speak Iballa chipped in with, 'Excuse me, young man, but where is mine? If you're going to be a part of this family, you need to look after the bossy old aunt ... because if you don't, she could be trouble!'

This caused a lot of laughter and helped everyone to relax. Debbie returned, and drinks were ordered, and the chat was all about Estefan entertaining the room. The only person who was a bit quiet was Gina, who was taking it all in with wide eyes, but Sarah knew her mum was in a happy place and that was the most important thing.

After a few cocktails they looked at the food menu and a lively conversation ensued about what everyone would be ordering.

From her position at the table Sarah could see through the opening from the bar into the restaurant where the waiting staff were clearing a couple of empty tables before they pushed them together. She suspected they were doing so to accommodate their party of six.

Bentor approached the group to let them know that their table was ready in the restaurant, saying, 'I think it will be easier and a lot quieter to take the food order at the table, if you would all care to follow me?'

They all got themselves together and headed through the restaurant, towards the merged tables Sarah had seen the staff preparing. But instead of the six chairs she expected, there were eight, which could only mean one thing.

She shot Bentor a questioning look.

'Two of my staff need to have a break now and I was wondering if you wouldn't mind their joining you. Come on, Debbie, Pedro, take a seat!'

The group smiled and laughed, happy to welcome Debbie and Pedro to the party.

'I am so very blessed to have had these two in my life because none of this would have ever been possible without all the hard work they've done for me over the years. I am a very lucky chap,' Bentor said warmly before departing to check on his other customers.

'Now, tell me, did I do the right thing nagging you to take the job?' Sarah asked Debbie playfully.

'Yes, you did. I'm very happy ... but also very hungry. So, come on, let's order! Once we have, I want to hear all about the café. What's been happening there today?'

****

The food was ordered and the conversation flowed, and by the time the empty plates were cleared away and the wine was topped up, everyone was as happy as could be.

'I think you're really going to enjoy working here,' Ancor said to Debbie. 'And it's so lovely having you living back in Tenerife.'

'Thank you, Uncle Ancor. There's still a lot to learn but I'm excited for the challenge. Sarah tells me things went well with the furniture today. Are you looking forward to the café reopening?'

Ancor paused before answering and Debbie wondered if she'd somehow said the wrong thing. Eventually Ergual spoke up.

'Yes, the furniture looks lovely and we're very happy, aren't we, Dad?'

'Oh yes, the place is looking smashing. I'm over the moon with it and we just have a few final things to sort ahead of the opening next week.'

'Speaking of those few final things...' Sarah interjected. 'I've been thinking about the practical side of things and I've decided that as there's no baking done on a Sunday, and it's Ruben's day off, that will be the day I'll take off as well. That way I can get stuck into helping Ruben with his barn. Because the sooner it's finished, the sooner I'll have somewhere to live.'

There was a prolonged silence as everyone at the table exchanged confused but hopeful glances, not knowing what to say. There was also not a dry eye in the house.

'Come on now, why the tears and the long faces? Don't you want me to stay here in Kalanchoe? After all, we have so much to look forward to now that we're all together again in Tenerife.'

THE END

Printed in Great Britain
by Amazon

36432018R00175